deleted

WINTER STALK

She yanked on the handle again, forgetting the door was locked.

David slowed the car; he didn't dare stop completely.

"Stop it," he said. "Everything's all right now. Look, the road's leveled out—"

"I'm getting out, David, let go—"

Crying, she opened the door. But David knew she wouldn't jump out, not with the baby in her arms, not at that speed. She seemed to be waiting for him to stop, but he couldn't, at least not until after he made the approaching curve.

Which he did.

Then he reached over farther, placing a firm grip on her shoulder, and as his eyes darted from Kate back to the windshield, he found himself staring—incredible as it was—at a figure just off to the left, below the road—a hunter with his bow drawn, aiming directly at the windshield of the car. *Aiming directly at him.*

"Mr Stowe has written a riveting, suspenseful novel, with believable characters who are very moving. The

WINTER STALK

James L. Stowe

Hamlyn Paperbacks

WINTER STALK
ISBN 0 600 20098 1

First published in Great Britain 1980 by Hamlyn Books
Hamlyn Paperbacks edition 1980
Copyright © 1979 by James L. Stowe

Hamlyn Paperbacks are published by
The Hamlyn Publishing Group Ltd,
Astronaut House,
Feltham,
Middlesex, England

(Paperback Division: Hamlyn Paperbacks,
Banda House, Cambridge Grove,
Hammersmith, London W6 0LE)

Printed and bound in Great Britain by
Cox & Wyman Ltd, Reading

This book is sold subject to the condition that it shall not, by way of trade or otherwise, be lent, re-sold, hired out, or otherwise circulated without the publisher's prior consent in any form of binding or cover other than that in which it is published and without a similar condition including this condition being imposed on the subsequent purchaser.

For my parents, Jesson and Bernice Stowe

Meeting a rival, [the buck deer] lowers his head and charges. The contestants come together with a resounding crash. Antlers locked and heads down, they tear up the ground with their hoofs, trample bushes, uproot small trees. Again and again they break their lock and lunge at each other.

Serious as these fights appear, few deer die from them. A losing stag often takes to the woods and the winner is usually content to let him go. If the loser battles on, his antlers may be broken—or he may be gored to death. Sometimes antlers become locked and the combatants face slow death together.

—*Wild Animals of North America*

From *The Albuquerque Journal*, August 22, 1978

FUGITIVES PERISH IN GASOLINE BLAZE

Senator's Daughter Among Dead

OROGRANDE N.M.—Barbara Melchor and three other members of an alleged drug-smuggling ring died today after a shoot-out with highway patrolmen at a service station in this small New Mexico town. During the exchange of gunfire, a gasoline pump, hit by a stray bullet, exploded into flames; the fire reportedly spread to an adjacent pump, which in turn exploded, consuming the entire station in a mass of billowing smoke and fire.

The battle began shortly after 12:34 P.M. MST when two highway patrolmen, having lunch in a diner across the street, spotted a yellow Datsun (reportedly stolen) making a U-turn in the middle of the main street and pulling into a Texaco station. The two men left the diner and began crossing the narrow street toward the station, where they were met by gunfire from the occupants of the car.

The shoot-out marks the end of the FBI's yearlong search for the daughter of Senator Richard Melchor, an undertaking which has been described as the longest, most frustrating in FBI history. Miss Melchor, who had not been seen since she fled her Washington home last October, reportedly contacted her father seconds before the first shots rang out.

"She wanted to come home," said Melchor, his eyes filling with tears as he talked to reporters shortly after the fire. "She knew there'd be problems, but I told her we would do all we could. She asked me if I would . . . well, then I could hear the popping over the line . . . it was too late . . ."

The three other victims have been identified by Albuquerque coroner Peter Zabriski as 30-year-old Russell "Natte" Collins, 26-year-old Pamela Chapman and 28-year-old Mark Van Pelt, Barbara's former lover, who was responsible, according to Senator Melchor, for his daughter's renunciation of her family last October and her subsequent involvement with drugs.

According to Officer Andrew Buckner, Miss Melchor was indeed using the public phone outside the station when the firing began. "Once they [the occupants of the car] spotted us," Buckner said, "they started screaming at her to get in the car. But then she started heading toward us, and that's when all of a sudden that other pump caught fire and the whole place went up. Jesus, it was all one big ball of fire." Arnold Potts, owner of the station, narrowly escaped injury by fleeing the scene shortly after the shooting began.

Fire trucks arrived some time afterward, but the blaze was not brought under control until shortly after 2:30.

Police have temporarily closed off the Melchor home and have declined to comment on the situation inside except to say that the Melchors are taking their daughter's death "very, very hard."

Earlier this month, Melchor gave some indication that he was thinking of resigning his Senate post, but as of last week he had not commented further on the possibility.

PART I

The Search

1

THE REAR tires skidded over the ice, fishtailing in slow motion as the car eased over the edge of the road to make the turn. David Meredith jerked his foot off the gas.

"Damn."

His wife, Kate, sitting beside him, said, "Shh. You'll wake him, David." She held the baby on her knees, rocking him gently back and forth.

The tires finally gripped the icy surface long enough to send the car onto the narrow mountain road above the cabin. David cursed again, silently. How long had it been since he'd decided to buy new tires? Six, seven months? Longer than that, because he remembered looking at a new set of steel-belted radials last spring. Top of the line, sixty-five bucks apiece, they would undoubtedly outlive the Malibu by three or four lifetimes. But he decided to settle for the sale-priced Shell polyglas, and even then he'd put off buying them, for no reason in particular except that other expenses kept cropping up: to wit, one infant boy, quite expensive. Quite priceless. So David figured the old tires could last for a while—and they had, in the city, on hot, weathered asphalt. They might even go another thousand under such conditions. But not in the snow.

The fierce weather had not let up since they'd arrived in Sierra Apache two days ago, and the forecast for tonight and the next three or four days looked grim. Winds from the north were expected to bring an icy blizzard to New Mexico and the neighboring states, and the damage wrought by such weather—not to mention the simple *inconvenience* the storm brought to travelers and vacationers—would be considerable. Jesus, David thought; if he had this much trouble maneuvering in light snow, what would he do in a blizzard?

—don't think about that, because by the time that sonofabitch hits, the three of us are going to be back safe and snug inside that cabin—

He straightened the wheel and directed the white Malibu down the road until the road intersected the main highway, and then turned onto the wider, snowplowed street.

He turned to Kate. Her slender build was hidden beneath the bulky thermal coat; her soft, pixielike features appeared drawn, the fair skin contrasting sharply with the dark brown, shoulder-length hair. "How is he?" he asked.

She placed her palm against the child's forehead. "I don't know. Worse, I'm afraid, he feels warmer." Gently she lifted back the layers of blue blanket that covered the tiny body and undid the first two buttons of the flannel pajamas. She took a deep breath and held a hand to her lips. "Oh, David—it looks worse . . ."

David looked down at his son.

—*his son*, the words came almost effortlessly now—

He had seen the small reddish discoloration on Brian's skin only briefly before leaving the cabin, and it was difficult to determine now, while trying to keep his concentration on the drive, whether the mark just below the child's collarbone had swollen in size. He turned his eyes back to the road just as a barreling semi roared past. The plows had managed to clear off most of the snow, but layers of ice ran along both shoulders, making it extremely difficult to maneuver in the far right lane. And from the look of the low-lying cloud bank in the north, it would be only a matter of hours before the snow began again.

Kate buttoned the pajamas and drew the blankets up high under the baby's chin. "Can you turn up the heater?"

He reached down and flipped up the fan. "What do you think it is?"

She brushed strands of shiny brown hair from her face and bent closer to the baby. She shook her head. "I don't know." Her voice was thin, uncertain. "I just hope to God this doctor knows what he's doing . . ."

He knew what was going through her mind. Christ, they almost hadn't found a doctor. If they'd been at home in El Paso, the situation would be different. They could call their pediatrician, or one of his associates. But Sierra Apache was over two hundred miles from the city, a winter resort area stretching along just at the base of the peaks, existing solely for the ski run and the lodge, which housed skiers and vacationers and served up the only reliable meal for miles around. Apart from the lodge and the ski run, the only thing left of Sierra Apache was the main highway that cut through its center, along whose borders were sprinkled a couple of cafés, gas stations, and rental cabins for those who stayed overnight. The nearest town was Ruidoso, sixty-five miles south.

"How much farther?" Kate asked.

"It can't be too far; we'll hit the junction pretty soon." The operator, whom David had called shortly after Kate had spotted the marks on Brian's chest, had seemed positive about her directions.

"There's only one doctor in town," she'd told him. "You wanna see Doc Bristol, that's who you wanna see."

"How do I get there?" David said.

"Just off your right heading toward the junction. Go *past* the junction, you know you've missed it."

"On the right. Yes, thank you—"

"Hey."

"Yes?"

"You tell Doc Bristol Amy says hi."

"Amy. Right."

They were heading now toward the junction, and so far no sign of the place.

"Maybe you passed it already," Kate said, her voice shaking.

"Couldn't have," he said. Firm. Positive.

He *had* to sound positive. Kate was sick with worry; he wasn't much better off himself. If they had stayed in town this weekend, they would be miles away from the frost and ice and the cutting wind. Hell, the blizzard could come and wipe out the entire resort of Sierra Apache and he wouldn't care.

Except that he *liked* the frost and the ice and the cutting wind. He loved—damnit—the snow.

When you come from a city like El Paso, surrounded by nothing but endless desert—miles and miles of scorching, sunbaked sand—you get to appreciate the soft, rolling layers of bright white. Besides, he had promised himself that this time he would take his first skiing lesson. Every time he mentioned going up to Sierra Apache, someone in the office would say, "Oh, you ski?" And every time he would answer, "Not really." And then, for some reason he had not yet been able to fathom, he always added, "well, just a little." He had, perhaps, the *look* of a skier—taut, sun-tanned skin, dark blond hair. But the resemblance ended there; his features were smooth, his eyes hazel, and the tan came not from spending hours on the slopes but from working in the courtyard of Berenson Engineering, tinkering with solar collectors.

Truth of the matter was, he'd never set *foot* on a ski slope, not a real one. A sporting-goods store downtown had a simulated slope for beginners to practice on—a continuous loop of white canvas, operated underneath by a motor which circulated the canvas at a speed designed to approximate the feeling of traveling down a slope—and David had been on that once, but never on the real thing. Perhaps he just felt guilty about admitting he drove all the way up to Sierra Apache for the express purpose of sitting by a huge fire, sipping brandy and smoking a long cigar and watching the snow fall quietly from a distance. After all, *everybody* skis these days, don't they? THINK SNOW, the bumper stickers read. SKI POLAND, SKI NEBRASKA, SKI THE BIG ONES, read the poster with the skier leaping off the nipple of a woman's breast.

And then Berenson had told him, three days ago, "Here, Meredith, take these." He handed David a set of keys. "You stay at my place while you're up there," he said. "No sense renting a cabin when you can have all the comforts of home for free." Then Berenson laughed and added, "You'll love the skiing, especially this time of year. Go crazy up there, I always do. Jesus—I've got some time off myself next month. We'll all go up, give each other some pointers on the slopes—what do you think?"

By then, of course, it was too late. He'd already told Berenson that he practiced the winter sport. And now the president of the firm, the most respected engineer and builder in the entire Southwest, was insisting that David Meredith use his cabin for the weekend with the assumption that he, David, would certainly take advantage of the "f-a-a-bulous" skiing conditions. What could he say to the man, his boss, his mentor?

"I'm sorry, I really don't ski," he could say. Sure. And then he could hear Berenson: "What? You don't *what?* But you're using my cabin. What else is there to *do* up in fucking Sierra Apache except ski, huh? Jesus, I can't believe my ears—you telling me that *you don't ski?*"

No—Berenson wasn't like that. Was he?

Anyway, it didn't matter, because by the time David returned to El Paso he would have had his first lesson or two, would have, if nothing else, a feel for the sport, a knowledge of the mechanics, the gear, the vocabulary, so if and when he and Kate found themselves spending the weekend with the Berensons and old Nick got him up there on Devil's Leap or whatever they called it, David could break every bone in his body secure in the knowledge that *he had tried*.

Well, that was what he had thought yesterday. Yesterday he was going to be the first one on the slopes. But now, even though he hadn't the remotest idea what was wrong with *his son*, and even though this country doctor would probably patch Brian up with iodine and tell Kate to give him plenty of liquids because all the kid had was a minor rash and temperature, David nevertheless found himself hating the thought of slithering down a training slope while half a dozen goggle-eyed pros watched him.

He turned to Kate. She was saying to the baby, "It's gonna be all right, gonna be all right."

She looked drained, exhausted from worry, and David felt the old pangs of fear piercing his stomach, shooting through his head, his whole body. Kate's trembling hand stroked Brian's tiny head. She glanced up at David, forcing a weak smile, perhaps to tell him, Well, as you can see, I'm still here, still hanging on, and I know what you're thinking, you're thinking I'm faking this, considering all that has gone on before, thinking I'm not, at this moment, really myself at all; that's what you're thinking, isn't it?

But then the look was gone and David realized there was nothing really there, only a perfunctory smile meant, at most, to appease. Brian was the focus of her thoughts and feelings now. . . .

Out the right window, an old shack belonging to a long-abandoned ski rental lay half-buried under a layer of snow. The road made a sharp curve around the edge of the mountain and they came upon a string of small cabins, a permanent NO VACANCY sign painted below the name of the complex. Up ahead David could see the junction sign, and he wondered if Kate hadn't been right, if he had indeed passed the office. He was about to pull off to the right and make a U-turn when he saw a small, rustic-looking house tucked away behind a string of cabins. In fact, he thought it *was* one of the cabins until he saw the sign hanging over the front porch.

"This must be it," he said, making the turn off the highway and onto the snow-covered gravel road leading up to the house.

"Thank God," Kate said. "He's burning up." She lifted the baby from her lap and held him tight against her chest, wrapping the blankets around the back and carefully securing them so that no part of the child would be exposed to the chilly air.

The tires slipped over icy patches in the road. David eased on the brakes carefully.

The hanging wooden plaque read simply, MARTIN BRISTOL, M.D. David brought the car up as close as he could to the porch, came to an uncertain stop, turned off the ignition.

The house was built in the same style as the series of cabins off to the right, but was much larger. To one side of the house stood a makeshift carport of pine logs and two-by-fours, housing an early-model Chevrolet.

David got out of the car, opened the door for Kate, and together they made their way across the icy slush bordering the walk and climbed the stone steps. There was no doorbell. He tried the screen door, but it was locked, so he rapped sharply on the wooden frame. A gust of wind whipped through the porch, piercing his body through the heavy leather jacket. Kate gripped the child tighter, her face raw behind her hooded jacket. Jesus, it was cold.

In a moment the door opened and an elderly, white-haired man peered out the screen. "Yes?"

"Dr. Bristol?" Kate asked.

"That's right." His voice faltered; they had probably awakened him from a deep sleep. David didn't know what kind of image Kate might have apprehensively drawn of the good Dr. Bristol, but he felt certain she was finding her worst fears realized.

(*I just hope this doctor knows what he's doing . . .*)

The face drew closer to the screen. "That sign blow down again? It's always blowin' down in this weather. Anyway, I don't think there's any vacancies."

"Vacancies?" Kate said. She turned and looked toward the cabins.

"Mmm," said Bristol. "This time a year they're all taken. My wife's up there now, in the office. You can go up and ask, but I'm sure they're all taken."

"Oh—no," Kate said. "Dr. Bristol, my name's Kate Meredith. This is my husband, David. We're not here about a cabin. Our baby's ill, and we were wondering if you could look at him?"

Bristol's eyes narrowed as he eyed the blue bundle in Kate's arms. "Wha— well, jimney crackers, you shoulda said so. Goodness me . . ." He unlocked the screen door, his eyes moving behind his glasses first to Kate, then to David, then to the baby. He gave a slight chuckle. "Looks like I can't even recognize business anymore unless it's a ski bum with a broken bone. Come in, come in, get the little fellow out of the cold. Must be twenty below out there."

Kate sighed thankfully and followed the old man inside, David behind her, closing the screen.

"My wife and I—we manage the cabins on the hill—that's why I thought . . . ah, guess I'm just gettin' too old. . . ."

David looked at Kate; her cheeks were white.

He led them through what evidently functioned as a waiting room. An oak partition separated the unoccupied receptionist's desk from a couple of torn leather chairs and a vinyl sofa. On the wall hung a handful of drab oil paintings of sunsets and valleys, and to the right of the partition, high on the wall, hung an assortment of rifles and shotguns, the spaces between them streaked with cobwebs.

"In here," he said.

They followed him through a doorway at the left and into a small examining room. "Lay the little fellow down there, will you? I'd better turn up the heat. A poor choice, this room—doesn't get the heat like the rest of the place. I s'ppose you heard there's a blizzard comin' in. All we need, huh, a blizzard?" He adjusted the thermostat on the opposite wall.

Kate laid Brian down on the single bed. The room was exceedingly small. The walls were paneled with oak or pine, bare save for a painting above the headboard and the thermostat on the other side. Near the bed, against the adjacent wall, was a white metal cabinet containing an assortment of glass jars filled with swabs, cotton, and wooden depressors; in one corner stood a gooseneck lamp with a soiled green shade. The cold air smelled faintly of alcohol.

Brian was crying now, wrestling back and forth beneath the blankets. The doctor went to the bed, lifted the retaining bars on either side, giving the bare bed the appearance of a crib. "Now, then," he said to himself, "what seems to be the trouble?" He began removing the blankets, studying Brian's face. He tested the baby's forehead with the back of his hand. He was a small-boned man with thinning white hair and moustache, wearing an incongruous pair of glasses with wide plastic rims that seemed to fit uncomfortably across his small nose.

"It was all so sudden," Kate said. "This morning he seemed all right—maybe crying more than usual. David and I—we're here from El Paso for the weekend—we were getting up this morning, and we heard him crying, and then the crying wouldn't stop. I noticed his face, it was bright red. And when I went to adjust the blankets I saw the spots."

"Spots?" Dr. Bristol looked up from behind the wide frames.

"Just below his neck."

Slowly, Bristol unbuttoned the front of the pajamas and bent closer to the bed, studying the small reddish marks above Brian's collarbone.

"Sure does have a fever," he said. He stared at the area on

the skin, then carefully, his long, aged fingers delicately searching over the baby's tender skin, examined the rest of the body along each side and, gently turning him over, across the back, buttocks, and legs. Brian continued wailing unmercifully, the red face growing more intense. Bristol then turned him on his back and again studied the inflamed area. He grumbled something under his breath, flipped on the gooseneck lamp nearby.

"I thought maybe it was a bite," Kate said nervously, "but it really doesn't look like a bite. Maybe a boil or a cut?"

She paused, waiting for a response, but Bristol didn't answer, just continued studying the patch of skin, running a weathered finger along the outer edge and feeling the flushed forehead and cheeks. Kate took a step back and stared at the floor, one hand nervously tracing a line across her lips. David wanted to say, *He's a child, Kate, kids are prone to all kinds of things, the doctor knows what he's doing, this sort of thing happens all the time*—but then quickly from somewhere in the back of his mind he could hear her saying just as assuredly, *No, he's old, he doesn't know . . .* And as David watched her he noticed more than ever the change that had taken place over the last couple of years, until the woman before him had seemed to literally split halves with the lively, dark-haired girl he'd married four years before. Her face usually possessed a light, almost white complexion, but always with a tinge of color that gave the skin a creamy glow; she was one of those people who never tanned, no matter how much sun they got, but in those first years there had always been *some* color. But not now. Now there was only a chalky pallor, the same pallor that had covered her face for two years and which had only recently been giving way to a speck of that glow which had existed before—had been giving way because finally the gods had seen fit to give them a break.

David didn't know why, he probably never would, because he had never really given thanks for many things and he certainly never prayed and he doubted very seriously if he was your loving-husband-great-provider type—but for whatever reason, the gods decided to give them Brian, and it was he who had slowly been returning to him the woman he used to know. Of course, it was also Brian who was at this moment destroying his mother with worry.

"Doctor?—" Kate began. She stepped toward the foot of the bed, her lower lip tightening every time Brian's screams rose to a high, painful level.

The doctor raised his head, pursed his lips thoughtfully, began buttoning the lower half of the pajamas, leaving the chest exposed. He adjusted the glasses on his nose and said, "You know, Mrs. . . ."

"—Meredith—"

"—Mrs. Meredith, I rarely get called on for anything more than the occasional delivery in the middle of the night, or a broken bone. And lots of them," he chuckled, "ski run gives me plenty of them—"

"But what is it, Doctor?" Kate asked impatiently. "What's wrong with him?"

The crying had momentarily subsided; Brian, his tiny arms held out before him, gazed up at the ceiling.

"One moment," Bristol said, moving toward the white metal cabinet on the other side of the room. "I want to put some of this on the infection."

"Then it *is* an infection?" David asked.

The doctor nodded, opening a drawer and withdrawing a small silver tube. He unscrewed the cap, squeezed out a small dot of white onto his index finger, and approached the bed. "This may control the swelling for a while, but you'll need to get him to the clinic."

Kate said, "You mean it's serious, a bad infection?"

Bristol looked up as he methodically rubbed a thin circle of white ointment over the skin. "A bad infection, yes. Serious? I can't say for sure." He reached for a tissue on a shelf nearby, blotted off the ointment residue, replaced the tube in the cabinet. "As I said, it's been quite some time since I've diagnosed anything more than a broken leg, but my guess is that the child has a severe strep or staph infection. I've applied an ointment of neomycin, which is really all I have here for this sort of thing."

Well, David thought, if nothing else, Kate can rest assured that the good Doc Bristol *seems* to know what he's doing.

"Tell me, Mrs. Meredith," he continued, "has the child ever had impetigo?"

Kate hesitated, glanced toward David. "I—I don't know. I mean . . . impetigo . . . I've heard of it, of course, but . . ."

"It's a superficial skin infection, commonly occurs in children, infants. Causes blisters or small boils, usually reddish with a white center. Ever seen anything like that on the boy?"

Kate was silent, thinking, the back of her forefinger pressed hard against her lips. She shook her head slowly. "I don't remember anything like that. He gets red—chafed—at times on his legs and arms—but don't all babies get that?"

Bristol smiled. "Of course—"

"Is that what he has? Impetigo?" David felt his fear assuming another form.

Bristol nodded. "I believe so. I saw many cases similar to this when I worked at the county hospital in Santa Fe years ago. It's called ecthyma."

"What causes it?" David asked.

"Well, I thought it might be a recurrence of an earlier infection. That's why I asked your wife—"

"You said—" David began, shooting a glance at Kate. Her eyes were fixed on his, and he knew the same question was going through their minds. "—you said this was an infection?"

"That's right."

"There's no question, then, is there, that it could be . . . hereditary?"

Bristol removed his glasses, held them up before the lamp, and then wiped them across the front of his shirt. He shook his head. "No. As I said, it's an infection; it could follow an insect bite or an accidental cut on the skin."

Kate sighed nervously.

David nodded slowly and said, "I must seem terribly ignorant about all this, but you see, well, the question came up because my wife and I just recently adopted the baby, and I didn't—"

"My dear Mr. Meredith," Bristol began, settling the large glasses on the tip of his nose, "you and your pretty wife here needn't worry about that. First and foremost is getting the lesions under control before they spread."

"Of course," David said, silently chastising himself for what must be the hundredth time today for using that word, hereditary. Jesus, he had to stop it, he would go crazy if he didn't. The word simply could not exist for him and Kate: Brian was "born" when he and Kate adopted him, and his past began with them—there *was* no other past, goddamnit.

Brian stirred in the bed, his small eyes blinking, closing almost involuntarily. His face still glowed a bright red.

"Dr. Bristol," Kate said, "you haven't said how serious this . . . ecthyma is."

Bristol managed a weak smile. "How serious is a common cold? In itself, not serious at all; but unattended it can weaken the defenses and lead to any number of complications. If this infection persists, it may weaken the child's defenses. The thing for you to do is get him to the clinic, where they have the facilities to make a positive diagnosis."

The clinic. They had driven by it on their way up yesterday, twenty miles outside of Ruidoso. If they left now they could make the drive in maybe an hour or so, depending on the weather. It might mean staying over in town tonight, but that was no problem.

"Well," he said, turning to Kate, "no sense wasting any time. It's a long drive."

Kate nodded quickly; her mind seemed to be elsewhere.

"I know you're both deeply concerned," continued Bristol, smiling, "but remember that this kind of thing is relatively common in infants—and, I might add, in old people. Knock on wood, huh?" He chuckled softly.

Kate smiled weakly, then began biting her lip nervously. Her hands would not be still. She went to the crib and began buttoning the pajamas.

Bristol went to her. "Here, let me do that. Poor thing, you need to calm yourself. The little fellow's going to be in good hands. That clinic is something else, a truly gorgeous place—the Apaches built it, you know." He completed the last button, lifted Brian, and placed him in his mother's arms. Then he went to the metal cabinet, took a pen from a stand nearby, jotted something down on a small pad. Then he took the tube of ointment from the drawer. "Here," he said, tearing off the sheet and handing it to David. "When you get to the clinic, ask for a Dr. Johnson. He's an old friend; we've both been around about as long." He smiled. "But don't let his age fool you. He's a capable man—and he can still beat me at handball. In fact, I'll give him a call after you leave, let him know you're coming."

"Oh, thank you, Doctor," said Kate. "We'd be most grateful."

"Don't mention it, my dear. And take this." He handed her the ointment. "It's all I have, but it should keep the swelling down until you get to the clinic."

He led them through the room, past the receptionist's alcove to the front door.

"Just keep him nice and warm, understood? He'll be running a spiky fever, of course—down until you think it's broken, then up again fast as fire. Most of the time, though, he'll spend sleeping. A blessing when you've got a fever."

Suddenly David stopped, turned to Bristol.

"I'm sorry, Doctor—what do we owe you?"

The old man smiled shrewdly, his eyes gleaming behind the spectacles. He placed an arm on David's shoulder, with the other opened the screen door.

"You just pay me when I set that leg of yours."

"Leg?" David asked.

"Uh-huh. The one you'll break on the slopes. You came to ski, didn't you?"

David forced a grin; Kate managed to say, "He'd better not break any bones."

Bristol chuckled. "He will, he will. They all do. How else could I survive out in the middle of nowhere?"

They laughed, thanked the doctor again, and made their way carefully down the snow-covered steps. A film of snow covered the windshield of the Malibu, and lightly falling flakes wet their faces as they walked to the car. The wind had picked up speed, chilling David's skin through the leather coat. Kate pulled the top of the blanket over Brian's bare head and clutched him tightly to her chest.

David turned the car around on the gravel road and drove to the edge of the main highway. As he pulled across the icy double-lane street, a tan LTD with two men inside nearly sideswiped them making the turn onto the gravel road. David swerved quickly to the right, checked for cars, then crossed the highway. Off to his left he saw the tan car stop at Bristol's place.

"Another broken leg," he said, nodding to his left.

Kate glanced out the window, shrugged, began to sway Brian slowly on her knees. Then she looked up suddenly. "Ruidoso's back the other way. You're not going back to the cabin, are you? We don't have time."

"Take it easy, hon. We've got to get gas or we won't make it anywhere."

Kate sagged back into the seat. "You will hurry, won't you?"

"It won't take ten minutes." Then he thought of something. "Jesus, I knew I'd forget."

"What?"

"The operator. She told me to tell the doctor hello."

Kate looked at him funny. "What?"

"The telephone operator. She said to tell Dr. Bristol that Amy says hi."

Kate smiled. That was good, it was the first time today,

and even though she was smiling at David as though he'd finally flipped out, she was still smiling, and now the smile was getting bigger.

"She really say that?"

"Sure, right before we left. Amy says hi."

Kate laughed.

"Why is that funny, my dear?" he said, trying to imitate Bristol but sounding now more like W. C. Fields. "I know everyone round these here parts. Treated Amy herself once for a chronic busy-signal, how 'bout that, and you think that's funny? Why, my dear, you don't know what pain is until your signal's busy all day long, now *that's* pain."

Kate laughed again, but when she took her hand away, the laugh, the smile, had slowly disappeared, and David felt disappointed, but there was no reason to be, not really, when you considered what she was going through. But the laugh was worth it; even though it hadn't lasted, it had brought a little color to her face. He reached over and put his hand under her hair, around the back of her neck, and squeezed gently. She tossed her head back farther against his hand and closed her eyes, rubbing her neck against him, and neither of them said anything for a while, not until Kate finally opened her eyes and looked down at Brian, a questioning look coming over her all at once.

"Still worried?" he asked softly.

She nodded solemnly. "A little."

A lot, he thought. "Try not to. Don't you trust the ol' doc?" This he said with his best Fess Parker twang.

But this time she couldn't manage the smile.

"I do. It's just that . . . I don't know. God, David, I don't *want* him to be sick. I want him well. Now. I don't like what the doctor said about . . . complications."

"What complications?"

"What the doctor said. He said—"

"I know what he said. But right now, what complications are there?"

Kate nodded resignedly.

"You see, you're worrying about something that hasn't

happened yet— and nothing's going to happen. Bristol said this sort of thing is common in kids."

She closed her eyes, nodded again. "I know, I know. It's just that we've . . . waited so long . . ."

A bright yellow rotating Shell sign appeared on the right. David turned off the road, drove into the station, and stopped the car at the Self-Serve side. The bell clanged in the office and a young man with long, dirty blond hair peeked out the open door, then disappeared inside, no doubt thankful he wouldn't have to go to work until after David had finished pumping the gas.

"Be right back," David said, and leaned over, kissed her lightly on the cheek.

He was watching the number of gallons click away on the pump when he heard the sound of an engine behind him, three or four yards away, and then a car door slamming—two doors—and the sound of approaching footsteps.

"Mr. Meredith? David Meredith?"

David craned his head back, maintaining his grip on the frozen handle of the nozzle. What the hell? he thought. Two men in suits were walking his way. He didn't recognize either of them, so how did they know his name? And what was this—stopping him in a filling station?

And then behind them he saw a tan LTD.

"Mr. Meredith?"

"Yes?" He shoved the nozzle deeper into the tank, held the handle tight, his fingers turning numb, and shifted his position on the concrete in order to face the approaching men.

The one in front was of medium height, and as he drew near, David could see that his suit under the overcoat had been custom-cut—a double-knit, three-piece affair. Probably mid-forties, his hair combed loosely back and receding on either side. His jaws worked steadily on a piece of chewing gum. The man standing just behind him appeared rather dumpy—shorter, about five-nine, of slighter build and with a head of bushy hair that was turning prematurely gray and which matched the color of his thick moustache.

The one chewing gum planted himself three feet before David and stared down at him through a pair of black pilot-style sunglasses. The guy must be a cop, or with the FBI, because only cops and agents could wear sunglasses like that.

"Mr. Meredith," he said again. "I'm terribly sorry to bother you like this. My name's Griggs. Laurence Griggs—with a u." He smiled dryly.

With a u, David registered the remark. Was that meant to identify or impress? It didn't do either. And how did he know David's name?

"I realize you don't know me, but I was wondering if we might have a little talk. It must seem rather awkward, I know, me coming up to you like this; but we haven't much time, and I wanted to catch you before you left for the clinic."

Jesus, David thought: no broken bone, he'd been dead wrong about that. But how did they know he and Kate would be at Bristol's, unless they'd been . . . following them? David swallowed hard. What could they possibly want? And what did he mean by *we haven't much time?*

"Talk?" David said nervously. "What about?" He suddenly dreaded the answer.

"Well, Mr. Meredith," the man said, smiling uncertainly, the faintest drawl in his voice, "it's somewhat of an important matter, you know, somewhat delicate, and I thought maybe, well, maybe we could follow you up to your place—"

"What?" He glanced at the pump. The wind continued to whip noisily around him. Eleven and three-quarters . . . twelve . . . twelve and a quarter . . . another two or three gallons and that would be it—

"*You* know, Mr. Meredith, where we'd have a little privacy, and could get out of the cold. I can assure you I won't take up any more of your time than is necessary."

Necessary? Christ—maybe the guy was just selling encyclopedias or something? (Only cops and agents and *Britannica* salesmen could wear sunglasses like that . . .)

"You selling something?" he asked hopefully.

The man laughed; his partner—for they must be partners—also smiled, as if on cue.

"No, Mr. Meredith, we're not selling anything. But we would like to make you a proposition that could benefit you financially."

Thirteen and three quarters . . . fourteen . . . fourteen and . . .

—click.

The nozzle handle snapped back in his hand. David gave it a last easy squeeze until the meter registered an even $9.00. He pulled the nozzle from the tank and replaced the gas cap. *Proposition?* David didn't know what the man meant by that, and he was growing uneasy for some reason. Whatever the proposition was, he didn't want to know; he had other, more important things to think about. He looked up, but couldn't see Kate over the trunk of the car. She must be frantic by now. He stood up, secured the nozzle on the side of the pump, and reached into his back pocket for his wallet.

"I'm sorry," he said, "but I'm in a bit of a hurry. Afraid we're not interested."

The young man with blond hair happened to be a kid. He hurried over from the office, looking curiously at the two men, shot a glance at David's rear license plate, then one at the pump.

"Afternoon," he said. "Nine dollars even."

David handed him the correct amount.

"Thank you," he said. He folded the money and walked back to the office, looking back once again at the LTD parked conspicuously away from the pumps, blocking the side entrance to the station.

There was a knocking on the side window of the Malibu. David could see Kate now, motioning wildly for him to get in, and through the window he could hear Brian crying.

The second man had moved away to the other side of the car.

"Sorry," David said. As he rounded the trunk of the car to

the driver's side he noticed the plastic bottle of window cleaner hanging on a post by the oil display, below it a paper-towel dispenser. *Damn*. He needed to clean the front windshield, but he knew if he took the time to do so he'd have to put up with this gum smacker for another two or three minutes, and by that time Kate would be in tears.

"Mr. Meredith, I've come a long way to talk to you. The least you can do is let me have a few minutes of your time—"

"I wish I could," David lied, getting into the car. "But we really are in a hurry. I've got a wife and a sick child inside, and I just don't have the time to give you."

"I see . . . I'm sorry . . . How *is* the child? . . . "

"Jesus," David said, slamming the door shut as the man began walking toward the driver's side. "Persistent sonofabitch."

"What was that all about?" Kate asked.

"Some crazy, who knows?" He started the ignition, released the safety brake, and put the car in gear.

Brian's cries filled the confines of the car, much more piercing than they had been in Bristol's examining room.

"Hurry, David," Kate said. "He's burning up."

In the side mirror, David saw the man approaching, his mouth opening and closing, shouting something through the window. He was almost at the door when David pulled the car out of the station. In the rearview mirror, David saw him standing silently by the pump, watching as the car maneuvered across the main highway.

Thank God, David thought. *That's* over with.

But a nagging doubt began to form in the back of his mind. . . .

The man watched the dirty white Malibu cross the double stripe in the center of the street and rumble steadily as it accelerated south through the meager afternoon traffic toward the junction.

He heard Kavanaugh's footsteps behind him.

"Not a very friendly fellow, huh, Larry?" Kavanaugh said.

Griggs reached up and pulled the stale piece of gum from

his mouth and tossed it to the ground. He shook his head, his eyes still following the car until it disappeared over a small rise.

He turned to Kavanaugh. "No, not at all."

Kavanaugh's feet stomped the concrete. "Jesus, it's cold. Why don't we just wait for 'em back in El Paso? We can head back now, wait for 'em at—"

"You know we can't do that, Sam. Time's running out as it is. We've got to be back Monday morning—terms of the agreement."

Kavanaugh shook his head slowly, gestured down the road. "Well, you just . . . you just gonna let 'em go?"

Griggs looked at him, surprised. "We're not being paid to let them go. . . ."

2

MICHAEL EASED the covers down over his legs gently, quietly.

His slender, sleek body lay still. He pulled away a curly length of dull black hair from his forehead, blinking away the sleep from his eyes and staring at the ceiling. The paneled walls in their varied shades of brown were fuzzy. He blinked again.

Rachel lay next to him in a deep sleep, her brown hair pushed from her forehead, her lips parted slightly, her breathing deep, monotonous. His left hand reached over, under the sheets, until it rested on the inside of her thigh. He stroked the flesh beneath the pink nylon, feeling himself aroused, wanting to bring his hand up to caress, awaken her. But he withdrew his hand and slowly sat up on the edge of the bed, the blur gone now from his eyes, his vision adjusting to the faint gray light outside the window.

He sat there for a long time, his hard, muscular body shivering in the coldness, remembering the weather forecast the night before and wondering if he should forget the buck for today.

Then he began to move, to get ready.

Half an hour later he was crossing the snow-covered ground toward the tiny wooden shed that stood on a small rise beyond the house. Patches of snow concealed the ancient splintery planks, giving the structure a rustic, almost toylike quality.

A moment later he was in the shed, standing before the case on the wall, withdrawing the arrows, inserting them in the mounted quiver on the bow. He was about to secure the last one when he stopped, regarded the green fletching. One finger brushed across the spine, stroking the delicate feathers. He held the shaft just below the broadhead between the thumb and index finger of his left hand; his eyes traveled up and down the aluminum shaft admiringly, finally stopping at the black-and-silver triangular tip. His thumb lightly traced the inner lines, barely moving along the edge of the razor; then his third finger met the top blade and with increasing pressure slid over the edge, leaving a barely detectable line of blood along the black steel edge, the remainder of the blood trickling steadily from the center of his middle finger. Numb, as if in a hypnotic state, he blotted the end of the finger on the sleeve of his thermal jacket. The material did not absorb the blood: when his hand came away there was a glistening red smear contrasting with the white thermal nylon. He held the finger in the light of the dim overhead bulb and squeezed his thumb into the finger just above the joint, causing blood to spill from the hairlike slit. Again he blotted the finger on the white jacket and watched the dark red smear increase in size. When the blood ceased to flow quickly, heavily from the wound, he took a bandage from the bottom of the case and dressed the finger.

Standing now in the open doorway, the bow strung over his shoulder, he breathed in the misty early-morning air. Far below the house, the side of the mountain dipped, leveled off just before the road, then dropped again until it met the forest floor far below. Pewter clouds gathered in the north, swirling slowly, gloomily, hinting of the storm to come. Even now Michael felt wisps of ice across his forehead below the wool cap.

The sky was still a faint gray across the expanse of forest; it would not begin to lighten for another thirty or forty minutes. He had made a good start this morning. And Rachel knew not to expect him until late this afternoon—unless by some chance his luck turned and he brought the deer back by noon, and he quickly dismissed that possibility. This buck was unbelievably cunning, and the thought that it might in fact be more clever than himself sent a surge of excitement through him. It was November, however, and the buck would have given up some of his caution because he was in rut. And although deer were naturally cunning, their senses of hearing and smell highly developed, this one exceeded all others he had ever hunted in its uncanny skill for playing the game. Some hunters would shudder at that word, "game"; certainly the stalking was much more than that for both the hunted and the hunter. Nevertheless, the game aspect prevailed, and appealed to Michael, who saw in the procedure a kind of mad courtship between himself and the creature—a courtship to be consummated, finally, in death. . . .

He closed the door quiey and stepped onto the damp earth, feeling the muscles in his legs constrict, awakening him, preparing him for the arduous trek ahead. Gazing out over the raw terrain, he could envision clearly his eventual victim. It would no doubt be moving now from its feeding area, perhaps stirring about more than usual because it, too, sensed the approaching storm. He imagined the erect, antlered head—tensed, still, listening—the glassy eyes darting back and forth, the coarse, hairy chest heaving, the slender but powerful legs poised in the snow and the rear hams rounding gently, leading gracefully to the delicate tassled tail. But the most expressive, provocative feature, the sight of which drew his breath away in awe, was the bony outgrowth of the two five-point antlers, jutting firmly, proudly above the noble head. Michael inhaled deeply, then let his breath out slowly, spasmodically. He would take that head. If not today, one day.

Cautiously, he stepped out over the frozen terrain, toward his prey. . . .

3

SNOWPLOWS HAD been working round the clock to clear the highway leading into Sierra Apache. Now, with only a few light flakes falling, most of the bulky yellow machines enjoyed a moment's respite before the next onslaught of ruthless wind and ice. Through the windshield, David saw the motionless monsters parked beside the road, waiting. The snowplows near Ruidoso were not dormant. He had switched on the radio a little while ago and caught an update on road conditions in the surrounding area. All roads into Ruidoso were temporarily closed; even with the plows working furiously, the ice was thought to be too dangerous in places. But David was concerned mainly with the road they were on now. All he wanted to do was make it to the clinic.

But although it had not yet begun to ice over, the road was wet, and David held the speedometer at an even twenty-five as he rounded the dangerous curve outside the junction. A few cars passed them on the road into Sierra Apache, but by this time, the middle of the long weekend, almost everyone had arrived at his cabin or at the lodge, and was at this moment either sailing down the slopes or huddled before a blazing fire drinking grogs and brandy. And that was fine with David; the fewer cars on the road the better. With conditions like this, it made him shudder to think of looking up and seeing a ten-ton semi tearing down upon them at fifty-five-plus miles per hour. Be realistic, he thought: David Meredith was an inexperienced driver when it came to foul weather. It rained maybe five times a year at home in El Paso, and if they were *lucky* it snowed once every other year. So the only time he ever really had the opportunity to get out in the snow and sleet and icy roads was when he drove the two hundred miles north every year. And when he did, his expertise as a driver quickly floundered in the ice and slush. Therefore he did not, like some people, take wet hairpin turns at sixty-five or seventy while steering the car with his index finger.

This was not to say, he tried to reassure himself, that he was, at twenty-eight, an overly cautious person, because he disliked that trait. He disliked it because overly cautious people tended after a while to manifest their caution in paranoia, in anticipating trouble before it actually happened. He was still berating himself for jumping to conclusions in Bristol's office—the very thing he'd warned Kate against.

There are no complications until those complications occur.

And they would not occur. . . .

So if he was not overly cautious or paranoid, he was, to put it simply, careful. Which was why he held the speedometer at twenty-five until he saw the highway straighten out before him, leading down deep into a valley between two peaks. The glistening road stretched as far as he could see until it met the top of a distant hill. He eased back in his seat, feeling more confident, his foot pressing steadily until the speedometer reached forty. Brian had finally returned to a deep sleep (Bristol was right: a blessing), and Kate wasn't far behind him; but he knew she couldn't sleep, she was just giving her eyes a much-needed rest.

For the next forty-five minutes the Malibu covered the miles almost effortlessly, until it descended the hill beyond the valley, where there remained along both shoulders of the road large chunks of ice and drifts of snow. He slowed the car down as he moved into the center, straddling the barely visible double yellow stripe. He passed one of the plows making its way grudgingly through the slushy mounds, and he knew that some luck was on their side, because the road they were on ran right past the clinic, and the plows had done a fairly good job of clearing the previous snow covering—and although most of the side roads leading off to farmhouses and pastures were still clear, some of them looked icy and dangerous.

Kate stirred, opened her eyes, shifted Brian carefully in her lap.

"You okay?" he said.

She nodded. "A little tired. How much farther?"

"Anytime now. We're about twenty miles from Ruidoso. We should hit the clinic any moment."

"Thank God."

Kate rested Brian's tiny head against the inside of her arm and delicately pulled aside the flannel pajamas. "Look, David." Her voice sounded at once disappointed and frightened."

The crusty red patches looked no better. David frowned. He didn't know what neomycin was or how it worked, but it hadn't effected any visible change in the infection. Of course, the doctor had said the ointment would control the swelling, not that it would clear it up. Still, shouldn't there be *some* noticeable change? And then, as David looked closer, he wondered if the red-and-white blotches didn't look worse. . . .

Reaching into her purse, Kate pulled out the small silver tube. Beneath the blue blanket a small hand or foot began searching outward; Brian's partially covered head turned slightly. David hoped it was just a reflex action. So far they had traveled in complete silence, and they would soon be arriving at the clinic: they could do without the helpless cries for a few more miles.

Kate unscrewed the cap and squeezed a dab of white cream onto her forefinger. Her fingers slowly spread the film over the red blisters in tender, rhythmic circles. The car bumped suddenly over a series of raised cracks in the road, and Kate looked up as David eased his foot off the gas. Her hand jerked up an inch or two from Brian's chest and remained fixed in the air until the road smoothed out. Then her fingers began again their gentle, soothing movements up and down.

But the restful silence was over. Brian's head turned to one side; his delicately curved mouth, once quietly parted in sleep, now drew back in painful distortion, revealing the soft pink undersides of lips and gums. The eyelids gripped shut, and then the weak but tortured staccato cries filled the car. David watched Kate's face grow even whiter; she began chewing her lower lip, her mouth twisting into a fearful grimace worse than the baby's. The cries inside the narrow confines of the car sounded louder, a hundred times more piercing than they had before, no doubt because now David needed to devote his entire concentration to the precarious road up ahead—

—It was making an acute angle around the outside of the mountain, and the snowdrifts blanketing the asphalt were only partially cut through by previous cars. He slowed down, almost pressed on the brake, but instead allowed the car to come to an all but complete stop, and then barely squeezed on the gas as the Malibu took the curve uncertainly.

Kate repeated to the child in soothing, reassuring tones, "Shhh, it's all right, it's all right—"

—Goddamnit, David thought, angry suddenly because of Kate's obliviousness to his own panic and to the precariousness of their condition.

"Shh," she repeated to the child. "It's all right."

And it was. The highway finally straightened out before them. The snow and ice appeared worse along the shoulders, but at least they'd have a level stretch of road and could now maintain a steady pace. And they hadn't much farther to go.

He glanced at Kate, feeling the guilt overcome him as it always did when he directed his anger toward her—toward them both. But Jesus, the driving was getting to him. Right now he didn't give a damn about the vacation or the skiing, he just wanted to get home, where it was hot and dry—he was learning very quickly to hate the goddamn snow. He reached down and turned up the heater: he couldn't get warm.

"It's all right," Kate continued. But Brian kept wailing, and as Kate tried everything, said everything she could think of to quiet the feverish child, David sensed something in her voice, a sudden nervousness—

—well, of *course* she's nervous, idiot. Her baby's sick, there's a blizzard coming in, our plans for a relaxed, leisurely weekend have been totally disrupted, ruined—how the hell do you expect her to feel?

But it was more than that. The barely detectable edge on her voice hinted at something more. There was fear, of course, but not fear for the road conditions, or even fear for their son's health, although the latter was no doubt foremost in her mind. No, the other kind of fear was all too familiar to David—the fear Kate had for herself. *Of* herself. Describing it like this made it all sound very melodramatic, he knew. But how else could he describe the same searching, hesitant tone he'd heard countless times in the past? And besides, wasn't that the way Dr. Kline had described Kate's behavior a year ago: fear of herself? In the four years they had been married, David had seen Kate go through more than her share of intense, traumatic periods. Periods when the doctors had told her that there was almost no hope at all of her ever having children, periods when even the chance for adoption had seemed impossible, and, of course, the time she'd lost the baby, the second time, and what happened afterward . . .

No. He wouldn't think about that, he had promised himself—

—but how could he ever stop?

"Of course, you must remember, Mr. Meredith, that your wife blames herself for what happened to the child. It's the inevitable 'if' *syndrome.* If *she had been more careful;* if *she hadn't attempted anything strenuous that day;* if *she'd left well enough alone;* if *she hadn't gotten up on that ladder and tried to do the job by herself;* if *she'd managed to brace herself before the fall,* if—"

—she hadn't wanted to please you—

—no—that wasn't Kline talking, not that last part, that was me; talk about blaming one's self, Christ!

"So you tend to blame yourself. But surely you cannot blame yourself for what happened the second time, the loss of the second child. And think of Kate. She must accept a truth about herself which threatens and frightens most of us; but not only must she accept it, she must learn to live with it. I'm not referring here to the loss of the child—that was tragic, indeed—but to your wife's actions afterward—"

—I don't want to hear this, David thought—

"—When I say that Kate fears herself, I do not mean that she fears for *herself, I think you know that. I mean that she isn't quite sure she can depend on the ability to make the right decision, that she may, as the young people say, 'blow it' at any moment. Consequently, Mr. Meredith—"*

—I don't want to hear you, I had to listen to this before, but not now, I don't want to—

"—your wife is afraid of what—"

—I DON'T WANT TO HEAR YOU!—

"—she might do—"

—NO!—

"—to herself—"

—but Kate is a strong woman, she—

"—on the contrary, Mr. Meredith, your wife suffers from severe depression. She's much, much better, of course, and you can be thankful for that. But the danger lies in—"

—no danger—

"—her own feelings about herself, and these feelings we must examine, probe, discover the cause, because if not . . . well, her situation will become not unlike the alcoholic's. Each day that she survives in a relatively happy, contented frame of mind will be a minor blessing. But also similar to the day-by-day plight of the alcoholic is the unquestionable fact that at any time she possesses the ability—the power, if you will—to—"

"An accident?"

The words seemed to float in the air, not really uttered by a human voice at all, but sounding from somewhere in the back of his mind, in a dream. Then he recognized the steady cries from the tiny bundle next to him, and Kate's voice saying, "Did we pass one down the road?"

He saw now what she was referring to—a flashing light in the distance, nearing, traveling fast. In a moment an ambulance passed them, its red and blue lights circling in opposite directions. Shortly after it, passed two more.

"Uh—I don't know," he said. "I don't remember seeing one. Maybe in town."

"In Sierra Apache? That's a long way, isn't it?"

"There's only one clinic—they must be coming from there."

Kate stroked the baby's head, rocked him gently in her lap. When Brian finally settled down, Kate eased back in the seat and once again closed her eyes. David rubbed his own eyes with one hand, then began massaging his temple. His head felt like a gourd filled with water, and the water was a constant maelstrom of thought, and he couldn't shut the damn thing off.

First there were those two guys back at the gas station. He hadn't been able to get them out of his mind. Something wasn't right; what the hell did they want so badly that they would follow him to the goddamn service station? He looked up once again in the rearview mirror, expecting at any second to see the tan LTD pop up over a rise in the road, but there was nothing. They must have known the baby was sick— or had they? They could have knocked on the door, and when Bristol answered, could have said, "We're looking for a guy named Meredith. Is he here? Has he *been* here? Do you know where we can find him?" And, because they certainly seemed to be in a hurry, when Bristol told them that the Merediths had just left, the two men might have left, too, without Bristol telling them anything more. Then again, there was the possibility that the tan Ford David had seen pulling into Bristol's place was a different one altogether, that maybe someone in *that* car really did have a broken bone or something and was going for treatment. After all, David hadn't gotten a good look at the two men inside. And maybe those two guys at the gas station really *were* salesmen of some kind, peddling *Brittannicas* or whatever. Doubtful, but maybe.

Enough. There was nothing he could do now about those two men; speculating didn't help any. All he wanted was for Brian to get well. And Kate. Jesus, he wanted her well. . . .

A gust of wind shook the car with a sound like that of someone battering the sides with a giant piece of cardboard. The snow-covered pines in the distance appeared motionless, speckling the terrain with tiny patches of green and white. David glanced at his watch, then out at the gathering clouds.

"The wind's picking up," he said, breaking the silence between them.

Kate nodded. "But it can't be much farther, can it?"

"It's just that it's getting late, and in this weather the drive back isn't going to be easy. I think we should stay over in Ruidoso tonight, if the roads are reopened. What do you think?"

"I . . . I don't know, David. I guess so, I just can't think. Let's see what the doctor says. . . ."

In answer, he reached over and gently squeezed her leg.

He hoped she didn't sense the worry, the anxiety he was experiencing. A few weeks ago he had tried to convince himself that things were on an upward swing, getting better all the time. Brian's arrival had created a marked improvement in Kate. But now this rash—or infection, or whatever it was—seemed to cause a setback, and what any other mother would treat as a normal, everyday occurrence *("this kind of thing is relatively common in infants")* Kate could not.

Because there had been too many setbacks in the past.

Twice before she had lost a child. The first time she had fallen from a ladder while installing a fluorescent light fixture—a gift she had bought him for his study, and which she had planned to surprise him with. He had not been there when it happened. But when he did get home he found her crouched on the carpet, against the wall outside the bathroom door. He ran to her.

"Kate?" he'd called. "Kate, what happened?" He knelt beside her, and asked again. "What's happened?"

But she couldn't speak. Her face was scarlet, the cheeks matted with strands of her hair and dried tears; both hands, balled into tight fists, clutched her face. She wouldn't answer his repeated questions, she just stared ahead, and then the thought occurred to David, and he glanced at the open bathroom door where the light was still on.

"Kate? Is it . . . is it . . . the baby—"

And that was when she gripped her eyes shut and collapsed on the rug.

That was the first time. The remembrance was painful, and David's eyes began to ache. He could feel the warmth from the car heater now. He blinked, focused his eyes on the stretch of road ahead, and wondered what was going through Kate's mind—what was she thinking about the infection on Brian's chest? And what did this illness mean to her in terms of all she had gone through the past two years?

It had nearly killed her at the time. Not the fall, but the loss. And a year later, Kate became pregnant again, but she miscarried after four months. This time Murchison had to prescribe some pills to calm her down. David didn't realize until the next morning how many Kate had taken. It was a Saturday, and he'd slept late. When he finally woke, he noticed the open amber bottle on her nightstand. He still wasn't sure what it was, but something had made him go over to her and touch her lightly on the shoulder. She didn't stir. He knelt, placed his hands on her shoulder, bent down and kissed her on the cheek. She didn't move. He nudged her gently, all the time eyeing the open bottle of pills.

Murchison said at the hospital later that it could have been an accident. "Those pills I gave her were extremely potent. An accidental overdose is quite possible."

It was after that when Kate began seeing Doctor Kline. David had gradually persuaded her, thinking it would be the best thing; but later she quit seeing him altogether.

"He doesn't believe me," Kate said. "He thinks I took those pills on purpose, I know he does."

And she never went back, insisting to this day that it was an accident. David wanted to believe her. And he would have if it hadn't been for what Murchison said when they were about to adopt Brian.

David felt the perspiration around his neck; it was odd how only a few minutes ago he could not seem to get warm, and now he was actually perspiring. The freezing wind tossed the snow about outside the car window, but inside, David was burning up. If it weren't for Kate and the baby, he'd turn off the heater. He looked over at his wife, wanting to say something, but was so lost in his own thoughts that he couldn't find the words. He was remembering the way Kate had looked in Murchison's office that afternoon, how her eyes lit up when Murchison broke the news— how different she had looked then, compared with how the worry and concern made her look now.

She had decided she could not try again to have a child.

"You realize," Murchison had told her, "that you are still physically able to carry another baby."

Kate shook her head. "I . . . can't. I just can't bear to lose it again . . ."

That was when they had decided to adopt. The doctor endorsed their request with the agency, but nothing happened for a long time.

Then one day the doctor called them into his office and said, "Are you still considering adoption?"

They both grew nervous with anticipation, and asked if the agency had something. But Murchison immediately quelled their hope when he shook his head and said, "As we discussed last time, the Child Welfare Bureau's procedure is long and exhaustive, and there is no guarantee. You may wait years and even then be turned down."

"Are you telling us," David had said, "that we should forget any chance—"

"No, I asked you here today to propose an alternative."

"Alternative?" Kate said.

"Yes. I'm sure you've heard of private adoption? In such cases the couple desiring a child arrange with the pregnant mother giving up a child, and when the baby is born it is turned over to the couple, the natural mother never seeing it."

They both nodded; they had heard of such arrangements.

"That's basically the situation I'm presenting you with now. Except that the child——a baby boy—has already been born."

It took a moment for it to sink in. "You mean," said David, "we simply adopt her baby?"

David could see Murchison now, rubbing his forehead and frowning. "Not exactly. You see, this type of arrangement cannot be classified as a formal adoption. That is, the Child Welfare Bureau won't be visiting your home from time to time, won't be monitoring the adaptation process." He sat back in his chair, folding his hands across his chest. "This is one of those situations which I have always believed must necessarily be left up to the physician's discretion. Of course, I realize this sudden option must come as something of a surprise, and if you want some time to—"

"No," Kate said quickly. Her large brown eyes flashed at David, at once questioning and pleading; then she turned to the doctor. "I mean, if there's a possibility we could have the child . . ." She looked again, the eyes begging for affirmation.

"What would we have to do?" David asked.

"The baby, as I said, has already been delivered, at the home of a woman I have dealt with in the past; a highly respectable, capable midwife. I'm sorry I cannot divulge any information whatever on the mother; in any case, she relinquished the child in the woman's care—is, in fact, no longer residing here. This woman, at my request, would sign the birth certificate with your names as the baby's natural parents. You would be, incontestably, the legal parents of the child. I propose this alternative to you because I believe you would make more than suitable parents for the child. It is the child's best interests, after all, which are paramount here."

Kate nodded. Her eyes were quick, alert. She stared at David for a long time, waiting for him to confirm her earlier answer, and he did. He told the doctor they accepted.

Murchison looked pleased. "There is one last thing," he said, rising. "You will have to answer questions, perhaps, concerning the adoption. I suggest you simply let people accept the assumption that your application at the agency finally came through, that this is a perfectly standard, legal adoption."

At the word "legal," David started. "This is . . . all right, isn't it? I mean, legal and all?"

Murchison's smile faded. He thought a moment and said, "Mr. Meredith, I would have preferred if you had asked me if this arrangement is ethical. In my mind there's a vast difference. I said before that what is paramount here is the child's best interests. In taking it upon myself to look out for those interests, I have placed a great deal of responsibility upon my evaluation of you and your wife. And as much as I place the child's welfare first, I must also consider your own. It's up to you, of course. I'm not forcing you to accept this—"

"—We know that," Kate interrupted, as if afraid the chance was slipping away.

"What I'm offering you," Murchison said, "is a chance to have a child now, not a year or more from now."

Kate put her arm around David. She watched him anxiously, afraid.

"I understand," David said at last. "When can we see our son?"

Kate hugged him.

Murchison smiled. "Tomorrow. Be here at ten o'clock."

Later, on the drive home, Kate said, "Why so quiet? Nervous about being a new father?" She smiled.

He returned the smile, put his arm around her. "A little."

"And excited?" she asked hopefully.

He laughed. "That too." And he *was* excited, no question about it, he wanted that baby more than anything else, and he told her so.

What he didn't tell her was that Murchison's words would not stop echoing in his mind: *As much as I place the child's welfare first, I must also consider your own*. Because there was something in those words, something in the doctor's motive for considering Kate and himself before another couple, the frightening suggestion that Murchison might have been entertaining the possibility that Kate's desire for a child was somehow more urgent than most women's, an altogether different case, and that as a doctor he was extenuating illegality with the conviction that a child at this point might inhibit a second onslaught of depression, a second attempt— Maybe Murchison himself wasn't entirely convinced the overdose was accidental. . . .

They had named the baby Brian Charles. And there was no question in either of their minds that he was the most beautiful child who had ever lived.

Only right now he was sick, David thought, steering the Malibu uneasily around a bend in the road, and he didn't look so beautiful. The blisters on his skin had spread.

Brian's illness had caused another setback. And as David looked over at Kate, the worried look on her face made him shiver with fear. . . .

4

A BLAST of wind shook the car, and David felt the rear tires falter on the cold, wet asphalt.

Goddamnit—he could almost see the bald rims sliding over the pavement, and he knew his anger to be directed more toward himself than at the slipping tires.

Steady. Nothing more than a little scare, you're almost there, just over the next rise and home free.

After that first blast there was another short gust, and then they passed for about a mile through a more or less steady breeze. He increased the speed of the windshield wipers, because the snow was coming down now in large flakes as they headed into the approaching storm. Behind him, he could barely make out the tops of the Sierra range, their white peaks piercing the clouds, blending with the hazy gray of the sky. The dormant snowplows he'd passed earlier were probably now grumbling into life as they prepared to clear the highway.

He glanced at Brian. His face had turned a deep crimson with the fever and the incessant crying.

"That must be it," Kate said.

Rounding an extremely sharp curve at the base of the mountain, they came upon an open stretch of road dipping down through another snow-covered valley: and at the point where the road curved before beginning its incline north, there was a blue rectangular building, half-hidden at the foot of the mountain.

The tension eased. At least they had reached the clinic.

As they neared the building, David saw that it wasn't really blue, but a dull green. The concrete walls peeked through giant patches of snow that covered the outside. He turned left across the highway and pulled into a small parking area. Two cars were parked up front near the entrance, their tops and sides obscured by mounds of snow.

Aside from a misty whirlwind of snow between the parked cars and the sides of the building, there were no signs of movement or activity. The only visible signboard was a legend across the top of the double glass doors at the front, made of large bronze letters, reading: LINCOLN COUNTY CLINIC.

Kate bundled up the baby, and they got out of the car and quickly crossed the ice-covered walkway to the front steps. The wind bit severely at David's cheeks and ears. Kate shivered silently until they reached the top step, and then David heard her say quietly, "Oh, my God."

He didn't feel the cold now. He looked at Kate as she stood frozen on the top step, staring at the entranceway. He hurried up the steps after her and saw what she was looking at, a white piece of paper taped to the outside of the double doors. Across the handles of the doors David saw a length of silver chain and a padlock.

Jesus, what the hell now?

Kate had pressed Brian closer to her and was fumbling with the top of his blanket.

The paper was a sheet of letterhead stationery. On it, hastily scrawled in green ball-point ink, were the words

> *Clinic closed until further notice due to major accident at Sierra Apache Ski Run—Lift breakdown. Several fatalities reported. All emergencies within next 24 hours referred to Ruidoso—Hondo Valley Hospital.*

"What are we going to do, David? My God, the baby. What can we do?"

David only half-heard her. He was thinking, Christ, how can they lock the whole damn place up?—

—then remembering, Jesus, the fucking roads into Ruidoso were closed, and what did they expect someone to do in this predicament? What happens now, for Chrissakes?

The wind tore through the entranceway; Kate pulled herself inside, against the corner by the doors. David brought up the back of his jacket collar as high as it would go. He turned and looked toward the parking lot, then out to the highway. Not a sound except for the building wind. Not a smell except for the raw, frigid air. No one. Nothing. They might as well be lost in the Arctic.

Except that they had a car. They were only twenty miles from Ruidoso; even in this weather, if they could make the hour-and-a-half drive from Sierra Apache to the clinic, they could certainly make it a measly twenty, thirty minutes more.

Except that the goddamn roads were *closed*, and remembering that made David shudder more than the cold did, because he was really starting to worry about Brian. He had been going along with the assumption that time was definitely on their side, and to hell with what Kate *thought*, he was going to put his faith in old Dr. Bristol because, damnit, the man seemed to know what he was talking about. And so they had done exactly what Bristol had told them to do, go to the clinic to see Dr. Johnson-don't-let-his-age-fool-you, and here they were, and here was where David's faith ran out, for no other reason than the fact that the ski lift had collapsed and any hope of following Bristol's reassuring instructions along with it, and—

"No one here."

The faint voice came from the far end of the porch, at the bottom of the steps. David turned and saw a figure staggering along the wall, through the deep drifts of snow. He looked like an Indian, probably one of the Mescalero Apache from the reservation. He clutched a long ice scraper in one hand. He stepped forward two or three feet and stopped. "No one here. All gone." He pointed to the sign on the door.

David descended the steps, the wind blasting his face as

he left the shelter of the porch, and crossed the length of the building, approaching the bent figure.

"I saw the sign," David said, shouting now above the wind. "Isn't there anybody inside?"

A dark, raw face peered out from behind the hood of a ragged parka. The eyes looked barely open, and as the Indian spoke, David detected, even in the frigid air, the stench of whiskey.

The Indian shook his head, again pointed to the front door. "All gone."

The man was undoubtedly a caretaker, someone to keep the entranceway cleared of snow and ice. He was also drunk. David thought it would be useless to continue, but said again, "Isn't there somebody in the back? A nurse or somebody? We've got a sick child—" He indicated Kate, standing on the front steps, huddled close to the building.

The old man turned slowly, looked toward her, then turned back and looked upward into David's face. His lips parted, broke into a slight smile, revealing aged, yellow teeth. If David was beginning to freeze in his leather coat, the old Indian must already be numb, his blood thinned from alcohol. But then again, perhaps in his drunkenness he felt nothing.

He steadied himself against the wall with the end of the ice scraper and looked at David curiously. "Medicine," he said. The smile grew, then faded, as if something had occurred to him. "Ruidoso." He pointed down the road. "Hospital."

David shook his head; he stuck his hands in his pockets so they wouldn't freeze. "The road's closed," he shouted. "Isn't anybody around?" His voice began to go hoarse.

Again the Indian smiled, his gaze drifting up to the mountain behind them. He raised his left arm and, with a shaking, leathery finger, pointed to a spot on the mountain.

At a point barely visible through the blowing snow, David made out a tiny speck near the top—a house, perhaps? At least, he assumed that was what the old man was pointing to: nothing else was discernible against the mound of white.

"White woman," the Indian said again, this time taking his hand and making a zigzag motion, indicating, evidently, the course of the cutoff road David had seen a quarter of a mile back. "Paaree . . . " he said. David looked at him quizzically. What had he said? "Paaarreee . . ." he said again. "She doctor; she take care of you. She take care of people. . . ." The smile began, quickly faded; the eyes, almost totally hidden behind the squinting lids, seemed to brighten. Then quickly he grabbed the handle of the scraper and stumbled, almost falling in the snow. David put out an arm to steady him, but the old man pulled away. He would probably pass out at any moment, and David could see the clinic staff returning to find him curled up on the porch. It probably wouldn't be the first time they'd found him like that. He was undoubtedly kept on out of kindness, or pity, and some ambulance attendant would probably flop him on a cot and let him sleep it off until he sobered enough to finish clearing the steps.

"All right," David said finally. "Thanks. . . ." He really wanted to help the poor guy up the steps, but he had refused. Resentful, David supposed. And why not? . . .

He returned to Kate, who was about to head back down the steps for the car with Brian. Tears were crawling slowly down the outside of her nose. He put one arm across her shoulder and looked at the white face, spotted red from the cold. "Take it easy, hon. He'll be all right."

She shook her head slowly, looking at Brian.

"Yes, he will," David said determinedly, observing what little he could see of the baby beneath the blanket. The cries were all but drowned out by the wind.

"How?" Kate's voice was weak. "How is he going to be all right if someone doesn't see him?"

David glanced at the old Indian trudging back through the snow, then up toward the mountain. "The old guy says there's a house where we can get help. A doctor's. It can't be too far up the mountain, a mile at the most. We'll check the radio, see if the roads into town are still closed. If they are, we'll try to make it up. We've got to find a place to stay. The weather's getting worse; I don't think we can make it back to Sierra Apache." He waited for her to respond, but she just kept staring at the baby. "You want to wait here—"

"We can't wait! He's sick, David, and he's not getting any better, and the longer we stand out here the better chance he has of getting pneumonia on top of everything else."

"All right, all right." He put his arm around her. "Let's get back to the car."

She started down the steps. David hesitated a moment, and then, in a last act of hope or defiance, yanked on the handle of the door, rattling the steel chain. He could hear the banging sound reverberate faintly through the inside hallway. Peering through the glass, he saw a long countertop running the length of the room, and behind it countless shelves containing bottles and jars and boxes. He couldn't see beyond the shelves, or to the left or right of the counter. The only other thing he saw as he stood with his face close to the glass was the reflection of the white mountains behind him, across the highway, and the thick sheets of snow falling rapidly, burying the surrounding terrain in a deep layer of fuzzy white.

Parked next to the Pinto and the Chevy was a tan LTD. Inside, Laurence Griggs chewed thoughtfully on a stick of Wrigley's. Alone.

He hated gum. He hated the initial sweetness and mintiness; he hated the eventual loss of flavor; he hated the way it sometimes stuck to the inner edge of his second-molar filling; he hated the goddamn *work* his jaw went through trying to keep the gum pliant—but most of all he hated the mere presence of the rubbery sonofabitch in his mouth. Yet still he teased and masticated the endless sticks and flavors over his tongue, as if it were somehow right, a compensatory act after years of smoking, a form of penance handed down by his doctor.

He paused. The wiper blades hummed back and forth. In the few seconds since they had arrived, in the short time he had been sitting here, he thought he detected a rapid change in the level of snow on the old Chevy. The snow was beating down now. When he was a kid, in Minot, he'd gotten used to the snow. Learned to live with it. But up here in the mountains, that was something different. There was no telling what a fucking blizzard would do. . . .

The passenger door opened abruptly and ice sprinkled across Grigg's face

"Guess what?" Kavanaugh slammed the door.

Griggs took out the gum, wadded it in a Kleenex.

"The place is all closed up, everybody's gone."

"I gathered that," Griggs said dryly, "when I didn't see their car. What happened?"

"Lift breakdown at the slope. But there's some crazy Indian out there, drunk on his ass, says some people came by a little while ago. Couldn't get nothin' outta him, crazy fuckin' Indian. Kept pointing across the road there, some house, I guess. Anyway, they probably took off back to Sierra Apache."

Griggs thought a moment. "He kept pointing where?"

Kavanaugh indicated the mountains across the highway.

"Well," said Griggs, "I doubt very seriously that they'd try to go back now. And the roads into town are still closed." He looked once again at the towering white mountain. His bones ached just thinking about heading up there. But it was getting late, and they had no choice. "There's a cutoff road, I think, down the highway. Let's check it out. But before we do, we've got to make sure we don't end up sliding off the goddamn mountain, or getting ourselves buried in snow. Where you from, Kavanaugh?"

Kavanaugh frowned. "Encino—why?"

"You ever put on snow chains?"

Kavanaugh shook his head.

"I'll show you how."

It was sheer luck that David found the mountain cutoff. A steep rise in the bordering slope obscured the narrow road, and a layer of fresh snow half-covered the crude hand-lettered sign. Although the snow was falling steadily, and patches of road had already begun icing over, the access road leading up the mountain remained sufficiently firm underneath to give the worn-out rear tires enough traction to carry the car up the path to the bend higher up. David knew that the chances of their making it down the mountain an hour from now were slim; he also knew it was crazy to even attempt the drive without chains. But considering that he didn't have a set of chains in the trunk, and that the next gas station was no doubt in Ruidoso, their best bet was to try making it to the doctor's house which the Indian had pointed out. They could perhaps stay there until the storm let up—which appeared unlikely in the near future. And to top things off, David could imagine Berenson wondering why he hadn't shown up for work Monday morning. They were to finish going over the contracts for the new flat-plate solar-heating collectors Berenson and he had designed. If he and Kate got snowed in up here and he didn't show up on Monday—

—don't think about that now; think about what the hell you're going to do about the fork in the road.

He slowed the car, afraid to stop completely because the wheels would probably end up spinning in a crevice of ice.

"Jesus," he said.

"What is it?" Kate asked, looking up.

"The road forks." He had assumed that as soon as they made the bend, the cutoff path would lead directly to the cabin; instead, one side forked straight up the mountain and the other curved slightly and disappeared behind the trees. Both were steep and, from what he could see of them, in terrible condition: in fact, they could hardly be called roads at all, but rather wide, rocky footpaths.

"Maybe there's a sign," he said.

They both searched for a post stuck in the ground, a sign nailed to a tree, but there was nothing.

"Your guess is as good as mine," he said. The two roads might merge a few yards farther on, or they might lead in opposite directions, in which case he'd better make the right decision because the paths were too narrow and too icy to allow him to turn around and try again. Finally, he said, "I don't think we can make it."

"We've *got* to," Kate said, her eyes fixed ahead.

The wind shook the car. David pressed slowly on the gas and took the road that curved around the trees: it somehow looked more like a continuation of the road they were on.

The tires faltered for a second, then regained control. David caught his breath and gripped the steering wheel until his knuckles ached. Brian was crying nonstop, and Kate simply stared through [illegible]ield, one hand against her lip. A few more minutes, he thought. Just a few more minutes . . .

But it was much longer than that—after they had followed the narrow, twisting road around snow-covered trees, the feeble tires crunching ice underneath—when the feeling began creeping forward slowly from the back of David's mind. He resisted it at first—he was fighting it now—but it came anyway, and as he looked down past the road to the blurry stretch of pines far below and realized how high they'd climbed, the feeling lodged itself with a dreadful certainty. . . .

HE OFTEN thought that when he was isolated on the lonely mountainside, among the massive pines, with their branches reaching far into irregular patches of cloudy sky and rippling gently in a high, hollow breeze, he was in the midst of an unusual sensitivity, as if nature around him possessed the ability to perceive the slightest alteration in its quiet, ordered existence. Perhaps it was because he was surrounded entirely by living things that he could sense their reaction to change—the sudden, broad sway of the trees, the unexpected flurry of wind through the forest, or the abrupt silence of a distant woodpecker. It might have been all of these things or none of them that caught his attention today, despite the rising storm; but somehow he sensed a change.

Then Michael spotted the buck darting into a closely spaced group of pines on the ledge before him.

He'd been tracking the elusive animal since noon, but had lost it an hour ago. Perhaps now he'd have his chance to catch it off guard, the mounting wind and snow serving to deaden his approach. But it was late; he'd already begun feeling the strain of the compound bow in his hands.

The snow beat down harder, borne by the sudden harsh wind that thrashed the tops of the trees and blew small clumps of ice into his raw face. Through the double pairs of wool socks, his toes had stiffened, numb to their constant bending as he forced his feet up another, and then another hill. Inside his heavy outergarments, under the thermal underwear, his body remained relatively warm; yet his movements had become awkward, cumbersome. He knew the day was drawing to a close, that the hunt was nearly over for now and that unless by some miracle he landed the buck in the next few minutes, he would have to return tomorrow. Besides, it was foolish to continue in this wind.

The grayish brown speck of antlers twisted against the snow in the distance. The animal sprinted from the cluster of trees and headed left in an arc, up the ledge.

Michael's left hand took the grip of the bow. Making a conscious effort to ignore the cold and the stiffness in his legs, he edged forward, following the trail. By now his perspective of the spacing between the tree trunks had dulled; after hours of searching and straining, his eyes found it difficult to immediately focus on the group of trees closest to—or farthest from—the animal.

A movement to the left.

The antlered head peeked out from behind a trunk. The buck had climbed higher than he'd anticipated. If it continued in this direction it would eventually come upon the rise where the mountainside met the narrow road below the house.

He reached out, firmly grasped the crest of the arrow nearest him, withdrew the shaft from the mounted bow quiver. Nocking the arrow, he took a careful step forward.

He knew that if it were not for the cover of snow and the drowning wind, the buck would have fled long ago. And his own carelessness, he had to admit, hadn't helped matters. Deer possessed an acute sense of smell, and although the frigid air deadened any odors the wind carried, he would be courting defeat to pretend his scent would drift totally undetected by the creature. As for his carelessness, he knew it to be self-willed: he could, after all, have waited longer between moving on from one spot to the next; and he could, of course, have long ago built a blind in the woods. But he had done neither of those things. From the beginning, almost two years ago, he knew this would not be an easy hunt. He would not allow it to be, understanding that there were certain times when one must surrender caution to risk—especially with a cunning buck like this one. Over the many months the hunt had developed into an almost personal, vengeful stalk.

The muscles tensed below the thick leather belt, and he moved forward. Wind rustled the white treetops; snow began to seriously obstruct the distant view. But just as his vision had dimmed from the snow, he knew the buck's sight would soon be hindered by the slowly gathering flakes across its lashes.

Turning his torso slowly, quietly, feet planted firmly, he looked behind him on the off chance that the animal had circled back. It had done so before, playing with him, showing off its crafty nature, making sure its hunter spotted it before bolting deep into the forest. Then, having scrutinized every open patch, and convinced the animal was in front of him, he turned around and with his eyes searched closely the terrain before him.

He could barely make out the edge of the house high on the mountain across the road. He hadn't realized how close to the path he'd traveled. A few yards ahead and the trees would spread out just below the road and he would find himself on open ground.

He caught a movement off to the right, his eyes fixing on a point just below the ridge. He wished now that there was no wind, no snow, that his ears might detect the faintest crackling behind the trees and his eyes register the slightest speck of color out of place.

The muscles in his legs and near his groin tightened as he gripped the bow handle. And then there was a kind of stillness, a silence in his mind while he stood riveted, waiting, his eyes taking in every individual tree in the distinct green-and-white backdrop animated only by a thick screen of whirling white.

And then he made out a patch of gray under a low branch. Legs . . .

His left hand relaxed as he pressed the base of his thumb against the handle; with his right hand he brought the nock firmly against the string. Bringing the bow to its vertical position, he straightened his left arm, and with the right made the draw. With an almost imperceptible turn to one side, the buck would be visible behind the branch. But *he* would also be visible to the buck. So there could be no second lost; it must be a quick, continuous shot.

He turned.

The deer stood before him in the gap between two trees. Nothing blocked the course of the arrow. If only the wind would die momentarily.

His eyes immediately focused on the animal's chest. The muscles in his back tightened as he drew past the anchor point, ready to release and—

The buck stirred, moved from range.

Why? It was as if it had heard something—but what? The

wind had certainly drowned the sound of the draw, and he hadn't shifted his feet.

All he had now was a split second. He swung to the left, following the moving patch of gray through the trees, up the ridge, and then—no, the buck moved away. He darted quickly to the left, up the crest toward the animal.

The antlered head jerked away and disappeared behind the trees. It looked as though the buck had climbed toward the ridge, an unlikely way to head, but he followed the movement anyway, scrambling up the hill below the road, bow clutched at his side, ready to draw.

There was a noise in the distance, and a dark flash through the upper snow-covered branches of an enormous pine, moving out from behind the trees across a clear gap by the road. His vision blurred for a second; then he brought up the bow. He silently cursed the wind, ordered it to stop.

He drew back, gave the string a final stretch past the anchor point . . .

Rachel sat on the small lavender stool before the dresser, brushing her hair. She debated a moment about taking one last sip of the lukewarm coffee in the cup on the edge before her, decided against it, and continued drawing the brush through her tangled hair. Unconsciously, her eyes drifted to one of Michael's arrows lying next to the cup. Her hand drew the brush slowly through once more, then stopped. She set the brush down and, hypnotically, reached out for the aluminum shaft and picked it up. She remembered Michael's face last night, in the moonlight. He had spoken of the buck once again, and she wondered if he would bring it back. Ever.

A shiver went through her. How many times had she dreamed that something terrible would happen to him out there in the forest? How many nightmares, and hours of anguish when he failed to come home on time? . . .

She began to feel really cold now. Outside, the blizzard had picked up, but that was not what making her shiver.

She continued staring at the black-and-silver tip, remembering . . . Once, when she and Michael were arguing after he had returned home late one night, she had grabbed an arrow he was holding in his hand, afraid he might swing out with it, threateningly. When she jerked back with it, the tip had slightly grazed her cheek. The small cut had healed, however, and she was thankful. Because her face was flawless; smooth, graceful features. She remembered a movie star of the forties, Evelyn Ankers. Rachel thought she possessed those features, the face of Evelyn Ankers: the same high cheekbones and full lips, although her hair was sable, not blond, and cut close.

Memories . . .

Suddenly the aluminum shaft clattered onto the dresser top as she quickly let it go, realizing that she had been absentmindedly tracing circles into the polished mahogany surface. With the sleeve of her robe, she rubbed the spot vigorously until the tiny lines were barely visible.

Composing herself, she stared back into the mirror, angry with herself for letting her mind drift like that. . . . And then, for some reason, she again remembered Michael's face last night. She remembered again the arrow lightly brushing her cheek. How long ago had that been? It seemed like yesterday. . . . And then other memories began creeping into her mind, and she suddenly wished she could forget the things she didn't want to remember. Forget them because of the sheer terror of remembering. . . .

6

BENEATH HIS shirt, David felt the sweat spreading down his back; his neck was sore from rubbing against the leather collar of his coat as he jerked his head from side to side, searching for—what?

Anything. Anything that might indicate where the hell they were, or how far they'd come, or how far they had to go.

Anything.

"We've got to turn back," Kate said. "You must've taken the wrong road; we're getting nowhere."

Something about the *you* rankled him. Why should he accept all the blame for getting lost? How did he know which road to take, for Chrissakes?

"You insisted we try to make it without chains," he said. "You didn't object when I made the choice back there."

"For God's sake, David, what else could we do? Look at him, David, look at Brian. How much longer do you think he can go without treatment? Didn't you listen to that old man at the clinic?"

"He didn't say which fork to take." He found himself getting angry, his voice growing louder. "Look, Kate," he said, softer, "we're up here, and we've obviously taken the wrong turn somewhere. Let's just try to get out of this mess. It's not going to help to argue. *Some*body lives up here."

"All right, but if we've taken the wrong fork, we've got to turn around, go back—"

"We *can't* turn around up here. We'll end up falling off the edge!"

Don't scream at her, you sonofabitch.

He glanced down. The sight made him shudder.

Kate's voice started low, her tone rising determinedly, almost viciously. He could hear the tightness as she clenched her teeth. "Then what the hell are we going to do?"

He didn't answer her. He pressed a little harder on the gas—a dangerous move, but it was reflexive, a reaction to her violent outcry.

When they finally rounded the next bend, however, there was nothing, just another bend, and beyond that no doubt another and another, and Jesus, he wished he knew where they were going.

"Well?" Kate said.

"Well what? I told you we can't turn around!"

And then she screamed. At first he thought she was returning his anger, but then he saw that her scream was one of terror.

"Watch out, David!"

The car hit a mound of snow near the side of the mountain. David veered left and accelerated gently and they were able to miss most of it; but he could feel the tires as if they were extensions of himself, and he sensed they wouldn't make it much farther, there just wasn't any control.

Kate felt it too, for she looked away from David, no longer pressing the question, but dividing her attention between Brian and the view out the windshield.

There was a sheer icy incline directly ahead, and as David felt the tires slipping beneath them he realized how really scared he was. What had begun as a vague sense of uneasiness a few miles back now turned to utter terror, because now ahead of them lay the steepest incline yet. It rose up the side of the mountain and curved sharply beyond. Below them lay an even sharper drop—and at the bottom nothing but a layer of spotted white. Not only had they made a perilous ascent, but they had left any hope of finding the cabin or house far behind. He could not even determine in which direction lay Ruidoso.

No doubt about it. He was terrified.

And in the midst of panic, a surge of guilt.

What have I done? My God, what kind of mess have I gotten us into?

He heard the sobbing beside him, but it wasn't Brian this time. Kate bent her head, the thin, silky brown hair dangling over the blue blanket, the back of her thick jacket rising spasmodically. He twisted back. Through the rear window the road wound endlessly behind them, obscured through blotches of white.

Think. Perspiration forming below the eyes, can't see—

Stop it! You *can* see—now *think*. But his mind was clogged, wouldn't function, pulled in every direction but—

Omigod, they were moving backward, and that wasn't possible, because his foot was on the brake, yet they were still moving backward slowly. So goddamnit, release the brake!—

The only thing he could think to do was step on the gas.

The tires spun once, then gained traction—barely—and they moved full-force up the incline. Near the top he thought they were done for. The gas pedal nearly touched the floor, and the back of the car started fishtailing; but in a matter of seconds it straightened out and they were over the top of the incline.

The road curved up into a dark canyon. Trees bordered both sides, and although there was another sharp curve ahead, the road beyond, as it swept around the mountain, appeared to be more or less straight—for now.

He couldn't believe what Kate said next.

"I'm getting out."

At first he thought she was joking. But then she reached for the door. He leaned over and put a hand on her shoulder as she pulled up on the handle. The door was locked.

"Kate!"

"I can't stand it, David. You're going to get us all killed. It isn't *safe* in here!"

She yanked on the handle again, forgetting the door was locked.

David slowed the car; he didn't dare stop completely.

"Stop it," he said. "Everything's all right now. Look, the road's leveled out—"

"I don't care. I'll wait outside until you find a place to turn around."

"Don't be crazy—"

"I'm getting out, David, let go—"

Her left hand reached up and around and pulled up the lock. Her right hand went for the door.

And David's right went for her; at the same time his left hand steered the car uneasily around the curve.

"Goddamnit, Kate, stop it!"

"Let me out. Please, David."

"No—"

"Then stop the car."

"Not now."

Crying, she opened the door. But David knew she wouldn't jump out, not with the baby in her arms, not at that speed. She seemed to be waiting for him to stop, but he couldn't, at least not until after he made the approaching curve.

Which he did.

Then he reached over farther, placing a firm grip on her shoulder, and as his eyes darted from Kate back to the windshield, he found himself staring—incredible as it was—at a figure just off to the left, below the road—a hunter with his bow drawn, aiming directly at the windshield of the car. *Aiming directly at him.*

Instinctively, he pressed on the brake, turned the steering wheel.

I have to was the thought speeding through his mind. *He's going to kill us.*

But he shouldn't have pressed so hard. He felt the complete loss of control underneath; at that instant the tires might not have been touching the ground for all he knew. Then through the driver's window he saw that the car was straddling the road, and they were sliding back, faster than before. David stepped on the gas, but the tires spun hopelessly in the snow, and they continued to slide backward, toward the edge of the mountain.

This time he *wanted* her to get out.

"Hurry," he said, reaching over and pushing her door open. "Get out—*now!*"

He felt the rear tires bump over the bank of the road. He opened his door.

The shoulder of dirt and snow didn't stop the car from rolling.

Kate screamed, grabbed Brian, and leaped from the car onto the edge of the narrow road.

David looked down.

Below him, the pine-covered mountain wall dropped hundreds of feet to a blurry canyon—

—and Jesus, the car kept sliding back, the rear wheels almost hanging in space—

"David!" Kate screamed. "For God's sake, get out—"

He heard the screams, then he didn't, for soon they no longer registered. Within seconds he had swung out the door on the passenger side and made the terrifying leap to the ground. He fell onto the icy road, banging his shoulder and the side of his face.

His eyes remained riveted to the automobile, which teetered on the brink of the canyon.

Christ Almighty, he thought, looking at the precariously balanced car and wondering when the Malibu would drop out of sight to the canyon below.

He pulled himself up and approached the hanging car, walking slowly, cautiously, as if the mass of steel were an anxious predator about to strike.

"Get back, David!" yelled Kate, the fear in her voice *convincing* him now that the swaying Malibu really was a poised monster of some kind.

He neared the automobile, afraid that any second the powerful wind would send the thing tumbling over the edge. *Where was that sonofabitch with the bow?* He looked around, saw no one. Surely he hadn't imagined the figure. Where was he? He looked down the road, then at the trees below. There was no one.

His feet trudged numbly through the shoulder of snow near the car, his movements almost automatic, as if he were in a deep trance. He blinked quickly, to remind himself that what was happening was real and not a vicious dream.

He stopped before the car's right fender. Just then the car rocked farther back.

Kate screamed again.

He turned and saw her standing on the opposite side of the car, shielding Brian from the wind and the falling snow, her eyes watching him blankly, her scream sounding as automatic as his own actions.

He moved away from the teetering car, joined her near the bank of the mountain. His eyes roamed the lower valley and upper mountainside, searching.

"He's freezing," Kate said quietly, almost matter-of-factly. Then she began crying. "Why didn't you turn back long ago—this would never have happened." The voice sounded numb, like the numbness in his feet and ankles. It was as if it were not Kate at all, but a disembodied voice. "We're in the middle of . . . nowhere. . . ."

David looked straight into her eyes, his mouth tight, his brain trying to fathom all that had happened while at the same time trying to find the words to placate his wife. But the words wouldn't come.

"Shut up," he said finally. Not loud, not angry, but demanding. "I want to find out who's out there."

She said nothing. But she was looking at him strangely, unbelievingly. And then he realized that her eyes were fixed on a point directly behind him, watching.

David turned.

The man was climbing up the ridge to the road. He stopped when he reached the top and saw the car; he turned toward them. David thought he heard the man utter something as he quickened his pace down the road to where they stood.

As he neared, David saw that he was bundled heavily against the cold, his thick leather boots pounding the snow as he approached. He wore a white thermal coat and a black woolen cap over his head, and clutched an odd-looking bow in one hand.

"Is anyone hurt?" he said as he reached them.

David lurched toward him, angrily. "Goddamnit, what the hell were you trying to do? Don't you realize you could have *killed* us with that thing?"

The man glanced at the bow in his hand, turned to Kate, then back to David. "Are you all right?"

The face beneath the cap was young—late twenties, perhaps—and blistery from the cold. His eyes searched beseechingly at David, waiting.

"Jesus," David said. "No, no one's hurt. But you could've killed somebody, shooting toward the road like that." For a moment he felt guilty for screaming; it was obvious the stranger was genuinely concerned. But goddamnit! When he saw that arrow pointed at them as they rounded the curve, he had thought for sure it was meant for them. He might be sitting over there right now with that goddamned feathered shaft through his throat.

"I'm really very sorry," said the man. "I was aiming at the buck."

"Does that look like a buck?" David pointed to the car.

The man didn't turn; he continued watching Kate. "I'm terribly sorry," he repeated. "There haven't been any cars up here all winter. I've been tracking him all afternoon, and your car passed through the trees just as I had him in sight." He looked toward the ridge. "He's gone now."

The merciless wind and snow whipped across David's face; he barely heard the man's last words.

The stranger now turned to the car, which was rocking slowly on the rim of the mountain road. Snow had already gathered on the hood and the windshield.

"Let me help you," said the man, laying the bow down gently in the snow. "Maybe we can push it back on the road."

"My *God,*" Kate said suddenly. "My baby's freezing to death. He's going to die. He's freezing, and if somebody doesn't help him he's going to die!"

"No," David said firmly, confidently. "He's going to be all right."

"Oh . . . God . . ." Kate repeated softly, lowering her head.

The man continued staring at her. There was something peculiar about his expression, but David couldn't define it. Perhaps he was overcome with guilt and really felt responsible for what had happened; but his expression hinted at something else.

"Come on," David said. The stranger followed him to the edge of the road.

The spot where the Malibu was perched proved more treacherous than David had thought. Snowdrifts made it impossible to judge secure footings on the embankment. The car itself was potentially dangerous: the left rear tire hung outward over the canyon; a few more inches and the right rear tire would also be suspended in space. The left front tire was embedded in a snowbank, and David couldn't tell if it rested on earth below or just snow, in which case the slightest movement might collapse the bank.

He shut the door and carefully made his way down the embankment, to the rear of the Malibu. The stranger balanced himself on the rim above, near the right front fender.

"All right," David said. "Slowly. We've got to shove it onto the road. If that right tire's buried in nothing but snow, we're in trouble."

"Ready," said the man, securing his footing.

David nodded.

They began pushing. David braced his feet and shoved as hard as he could. The stranger fumbled with his grip on the fender, then began pushing. The Malibu rocked on the shoulder. Large clumps of snow broke away, tumbled down the mountainside. *Come on, you sonofabitch,* he thought. *Move. . . .*

But then David saw the snowdrift give way under the left front tire, and after the snow broke away, he saw the tire moving back through the layer of white and the bank of dark earth underneath breaking.

"Faster!" he yelled to the stranger. But he could see that the man was pushing as hard as he could.

The undercarriage suddenly scraped over the shoulder, and David knew they could never get the car up without a winch. Provided, of course, that when the two men let go, the car would again lodge itself into the snow and the embankment, that it wouldn't roll off the edge.

"It's no use," he said, easing the pressure off the rear. "We'll need a tow truck to get it up."

But just then his footing gave way, the rear chassis lunged backward. David sprinted from behind the car, up the mountainside, missing the rolling car by inches.

"Move away!" he shouted.

Suddenly, as the stranger moved from the car and as David fought to maintain his balance on the edge of the road, it became clear that they would need no tow truck, no winch, because the carriage caught a terrific gust of wind and the weight of the automobile finally rocked to the rear, switching the balance of the seesawing monster over the rim and sending the car scraping down the hill toward the valley of trees below.

"Goddamnit," David said, watching in awe as the car tumbled through the brush and snow until a clump of trees halted it with a hollow, metallic thud halfway down.

He stared at the distant car for a long time, thinking it was bound to happen. The way their luck was running there was no doubt it would finally fall, and finally it had.

He looked up at the stranger, who now stood beside Kate on the road, staring also into the valley.

David climbed onto the road.

"Goddamnit," he repeated softly to himself. He was exhausted. Defeated. An icy chill surged through his bones, a chill he hadn't felt before, not that cold. His face felt wet and raw; his nose began to run, and he wanted more than anything else to collapse right there in the snow.

The stranger, still looking down the mountain, said, "You'll need a truck now." He turned to David. "But you won't be able to do anything in this weather; not until after the storm has passed."

A cry escaped from Kate as she stood rocking the baby. "He's going to die. My baby's going to die."

"No." This time the response came from the stranger. "Your baby will be fine."

"Can you give us a lift into town?" David asked. Then he remembered that the roads were still closed. But surely the plows would have them cleared before long.

The man's eyes drifted from the child in Kate's arms, past David, out across the surrounding terrain. He shook his head. "I'm afraid not." He bent down and retrieved his bow. "You couldn't make it any farther than you did because the storm's coming up; the roads are too iced over—"

"How the hell do you know how far we could've made it?" David felt the anger building; he pointed at the bow. "If I hadn't seen you aiming that goddamn arrow at us—"

"*Stop it!*" Kate screamed. "Stop it! We couldn't have made it anyway." Her brown eyes were burning now. And then suddenly she turned them toward Brian and began dusting away the heavy accumulation of snow on the blue flannel blanket.

David found himself glaring at her. Jesus, what was coming over him? Why was he mad at her? She was right, of course.

"Please," the man said. He pulled the edges of the woolen cap down tighter over his ears. He had to shout now; the wind had grown to a ferocious intensity, whipping and screeching about them. "I—I can't take you down because I don't have a car. And even if I did I wouldn't risk it in this weather. You can be thankful you got this far." He swung the bow onto one shoulder and pointed toward the top of the mountain. "We live just up there."

David couldn't see the house he was pointing to. The mountain made a steep incline, and whatever lay beyond the curve was obscured by the rising slope of trees. Could it be the same house David had seen from the highway?

"If you'll follow me I'll take you up," he said. "It's a bit steep. . . ." He indicated Brian. "Rachel can help look after the child."

Kate pulled Brian closer to her.

"We—we don't have much choice," David said. He looked at Kate for a response, but there was none.

The man had turned and was looking out over the mountainside. Then he looked at the bow in his hand. When he turned to David, a thoughtful expression came over him. "It would have been a good shot. I think I could have taken him this time, if it hadn't been for the wind, and . . ." He studied the bow a moment, then strung it over one shoulder. He stood for a long time looking at the view below the road, his eyes seeming to search the frozen terrain, until finally he looked at David and said, "My name's Michael."

HE COULD get lost in her.

Trudging up the frozen mountainside, searching for the buck, then seeing her standing there, shivering with the bundle in her arms, Michael thought, I could get lost . . .

He regretted losing the buck; and yet he knew that he would not have followed through with the shot in the harsh wind. There would be a next time. Yes, there definitely would be a next time.

You could've killed us, the man had said.

It was true, he could have. He could also have killed his wife. . . .

Although bundled heavily against the cold, Michael shivered. He could not remember how long it had been since he had seen anyone like her. There had been, of course, the other girl (how long ago had that been?), but nothing to compare with the shivering, dark-haired one with the baby. The other one had been blond, the one in Ruidoso, long ago. He fought to remember her face—the laughing, taunting face—but the only face he could see was the one of the dark-haired girl struggling to keep up behind him.

What was it about her that aroused him?

My baby's freezing, he's going to die.

She had spoken those words to him, he was sure of it, because they were stranded out in the middle of nowhere and he was the only one who could help them.

Michael smiled to himself, and hoped they hadn't seen him: but they couldn't have, of course; his back was to them as he led them toward the house and to Rachel.

Rachel would be jealous. But she would know how to care for the child. That must be why they'd come up this far. The clinic must be closed, the roads into town closed, and they had seen the house. Yes, that must be it. There was no one else up here. . . .

Michael smiled again. Because of the coincidence, the irony of it all. He had been stalking the buck, the sturdy, noble creature with antlers that reached the sky, and he had found her. What had she thought when she saw him coming up the edge of the mountain to the road? Perhaps she thought nothing; she was obviously overwrought with concern for the child. But Michael saw through the concern, and knew her to be (what was her name? had *he* spoken it?) much like the child she cuddled in her arms.

My baby's going to die. . . .

And her husband answered, *No*.

But she wasn't convinced by his words, and when she said

that again, Michael had tried to reassure her by repeating her husband's word, and he said, *No*—but his answer carried a conviction the other man's had not, because Michael knew that Rachel would care for the child when they reached the house. And she would be surprised to see someone after all this time. It would not be comfortable at first, and she would be surprised—

—like that girl in town—

Michael's jaw clamped tight, his teeth grinding into each other until he heard the scraping grittiness of bone, because he suddenly thought of something else. That day long ago. Long *before* that girl in Ruidoso. So long ago that he wondered if that day had ever really happened. But it had; and what happened that day would continue to replay itself in his mind as if it were happening now. . . .

He was sitting very still.

Cold, yes. It was always very cold.

He plugged in the tiny heater, but because the place wasn't insulated, it took a long time before he felt warm—

—like her, she was warm—

Years ago he would not have dared touch the brown, square aluminum housing with its three rows of winding coils, would not touch it because of all those times she had warned him.

You mustn't touch that, *she would say, pointing.* It's electric.

And when she had first said that, he remembered thinking, Yes: E-l-e-c-t-r-i-c, I understand. That means the tiny square works with wires, wires that carry 'lectricity and make the silver coils orange and hot and make the place warm—

—like her—

After he plugged in the heater, he thought that she could make him warm now if she were here. But she wasn't—couldn't be—here because He was keeping her at the house, talking loud, with words he could not totally understand, and spilling the bottle—

(—where's the goddamn bottle, bitch? where'd you put the goddamn bottle, I said—)

—spilling it sometimes on Himself, sometimes on her, and when He did, He got madder, starting to hit hard all over, and—

—and that was when he ran. Even though he wanted to stay with her (to always stay with her), he ran, because what else could he do? He had tried in the past, tried to face up to Him because, after all, she had told him that he was A Man Now; but it didn't seem to make much difference to Him, since the huge, gnarled, hairy fist just pounded harder, not caring if he was A Man Now or not, just hitting harder and harder, coming down like a big iron ball, pounding into his cheek, his eye, pounding deeper, pounding—

(—I asked you a question and you didn't answer, good-for-nothin' sonofabitch, I asked you where's the goddamn bottle, you don't hear so good, I said—)

—like a monster, beating on him now because the bottle made him (what did she say? crazy?), made him crazy. Crazy man, crazy man, crazy—

Then one day she had told him Things would Change. Since he was A Man Now she would tell him Things that he would be Better Off Knowing, and which were important for his Survival.

*(—you mean it will be different? is something going to happen? are you leaving? leaving me—*oh, baby, no, not that, not leave you—*)*

Change, changing. Things were going to Change.

And that day, they had. . . .

Michael jerked back, afraid for a moment the couple behind him had disappeared. But when he turned around he saw them dragging behind him, the girl clutching the baby tighter to her breast. He wanted to stare longer, become lost in her, but he turned back around and continued trudging up the side of the mountain. Yes, he thought, Rachel would be surprised to see someone after all this time. And she would be jealous, too, just a little. Wouldn't she? . . .

8

DAVID RUBBED his sleeve across his cold, wet nose and inhaled deeply. Big mistake. The icy air surged through his lungs, shaking his body. His knees felt as if they would stiffen any second, and he'd end up freezing like a statue right here on the edge of the mountain, a kind of national monument to forever stand on this silly mountain path.

They had been following Michael up a path that cut through the trees above the road for about five minutes now. Most of that time David had been trying to think of alternatives, and it wasn't easy trying to concentrate when your nose felt like a dripping wedge of ice stuck to your face and your feet were frozen numb, the snow clumping around the ankles and melting and trickling through your socks.

What the hell were they going to do?

Their car lay stuck at the bottom of a ravine, and even if a truck with a winch were available to them, he doubted very seriously if the car could be raised and hauled to the road with the ice and slush covering everything and making the operation—even with chains—dangerous. Besides, it was getting impossible to see through the driving snow.

Kate's padded jacket bobbed before him as she struggled to keep up with the man, faltering now and then, regaining her footing in the snow. She must be frozen, as David was, and Brian must be chilled to death beneath the blanket.

Chilled *to death* . . .

He remembered Kate's words and no longer felt cold. He wouldn't let himself think about that. Brian was going to be all right once they got to the house. Surely it was the same house he'd seen from the highway. What had the Indian told him? The old man had been drunk, hard to understand. But he *had* pointed to a house in the mountains, David was sure of that. Was it Michael's house? Was this man who had been hunting deer, and who had almost shot an arrow through the windshield of their car, almost killing them, a doctor of some kind? And could he treat Brian? Regardless, David knew he felt a somewhat irrational anger at Michael Whatever for scaring the hell out of him, and a very rational, deserved anger directed at his own stupidity for trying to make it up a goddamn mountain road, in the snow, in a ten-year-old Chevy with nearly bald tires.

Stupidity, plain and simple.

And what if he'd stupidly misinterpreted the old Indian's words? What if the old man was just pointing to *any* cabin—not a doctor's, where there would be someone competent to treat a sick child, but just some mountain resident's? They would still have to get Brian to the clinic when it reopened.

One thing that struck David odd was that Michael had told them he had no car. How the hell did he get up and down the mountain? Jesus. David would have to call a service station or a wrecker service—or the clinic, if it had reopened, for an ambulance—because somehow they would have to get into town.

The sun would be sinking in a few hours. If by some chance they could get to Ruidoso tonight, they could take the bus into El Paso—but not before tomorrow morning. Provided, of course, the roads were clear. Provided Brian was better.

Up ahead, through gaps in the trees, he saw the house. He had envisioned one of those A-frame, condominium-style structures, but the building before them was a large, old-fashioned log cottage. It lay at the top of the rise where the mountain leveled off, and was sheltered by a thick cluster of snow-covered pines. As they drew near, David saw that a path led to the front door; the walkway had no doubt been cleared of snow earlier, but now the new snow was quickly burying the walk in a blanket of white. To one side of the cabin, at the rear, was a dilapidated structure that must have been a single-car garage, and to its right, even farther back, was a wooden shed, probably housing stacks of firewood.

The front of the cabin appeared to be in a minor state of disrepair, evidenced mainly from the peeling strips of dark green paint bordering the windows and the front door; the logs, however, seemed sturdy enough, and the rust-colored roof looked as if it had recently been repaired or repainted. A rock chimney, set into the logs at one side, ran from the ground up, continuing for two or three feet above the roof, a trail of thin gray smoke fighting its way from the opening out into the blustery air.

Kate stopped when they reached the top. The edge of Brian's blanket had come loose over his head, and she quickly tugged it back into place. Michael, his back toward them, heard or sensed that Kate had stopped, and turned. He offered to help her, saying something David couldn't make out through the howling wind. Kate shook her head and continued on, following Michael as he turned and went down the walkway to the front door. When he reached it, he turned the bolt and held the door open.

The warm air hit David's face, lightly stinging his cheeks and eyes. He blinked, his eyes began to water. Gradually he felt the warmth make its way through the layered sleeve of his jacket and down through the corduroy pants. His ears and feet were numb. His lungs continued heaving furiously, replacing the icy air with warm, and his heart still pounded from the climb up the mountain.

They were standing in the foyer. Before them was an open hallway, leading to a room from which David detected the aroma of cooking. To their right and three steps down opened the main room—a large wood-paneled den, accented in deep browns and rusts and oranges, the walls lined with mounted deer heads, a shotgun hanging over the mantel. A huge fire blazed on the other side, in the center against the wall, and at the far end of the den rose a stairway to a second landing.

Michael shut the door, said, "Go on in, Get close to the fire. I'll call Rachel."

Kate had already stepped down into the main room, headed for the fire; David joined her as Michael proceeded down the open hall to the room at the end, the room that David suspected was the kitchen, for, as his nostrils began to thaw and he inhaled the warm air of the cabin, the aroma of cooking grew more pronounced. It smelled wonderful.

Kate was kneeling by the fire. A small, smooth-haired gray cat crept stealthily around one of the chairs in the corner.

"How is he?" David asked. He lifted the blanket. Brian moved an arm outward; he had ceased crying long ago and now simply stared up through half-shut eyes. The few crusted patches visible around his neck didn't look as red as they had in the car. That was due to the cold, David thought; even the skin on his forearms had turned a pale pink, almost white.

"He's freezing," Kate said softly. "Like me."

David put an arm around her, with his other hand stroked her shoulder through the nylon jacket. "I know. We're all freezing."

Kate laid Brian on the orange shag before the fire. The momentary silence, broken only by the crackling of the flames, unsettled David. It shouldn't have; after the thunderous beating of the wind in his ears and the heaving of his own breath, a quiet reprieve was an act of mercy. But the silence only seemed to accentuate the emotional gulf between him and Kate. *Of course we're all freezing,* he told himself sarcastically; don't tell her something she already knows.

"I'm sorry," he said. He wasn't sure how the words sounded to her, how she would accept them. How had he meant them? He supposed he meant he was sorry for getting them into this situation. Sorry for taking a dumb chance. But for God's sake, what had been their choice upon finding the clinic shut down? The roads closed? Goddamn the snow, he never wanted to see the stuff again. Ever.

Kate looked blankly at him, as if her eyes could not focus. Then the brown ovals seemed to deepen in color, becoming more intense, as if she were seeing him for the first time since their departure from Berenson's cabin late this morning. The look was one of utter helplessness.

"What are we going to do?" she said.

The same question David had asked himself only minutes before. He had, on the climb up, considered numerous alternatives: which one should he offer her?

Brian began to cry. A little whimper at first, but then, perhaps because he was becoming aware of the sudden change in temperature, the whimper stretched into a continuous wail. David wondered, did the child feel pain? Had the infected skin, once partially anesthetized by the cold, begun to thaw and ache? Watching the baby now as he tossed and turned on the rug, David too felt utterly helpless.

"Warming up?" The voice came from behind. Michael approached the fire, followed by a slender brunette wearing a multicolored caftan. Dark hair curved down around her cheeks, and her features were delicate and smooth, except for faint lines about the mouth and eyes, which would have gone unnoticed by David had it not been for the shadows cast by the flickering flames. She appeared somewhat older than her husband, but that was probably because her face seemed to reveal a maturity which sharply contrasted with Michael's almost boyish looks. She moved forward, past her husband. "Poor child," she said, kneeling next to Kate and looking down at Brian. "Is he—?" She noticed something and turned back the baby's pajama collar, observing the reddish discolorations. She studied them a moment, then said to Kate, "He's got an infection." It sounded like a pronouncement, David thought. Kate, staring trancelike at the small, crying form, barely nodded.

"We were supposed to meet a doctor at the clinic," David said. "But the place was shut down."

The woman rose. "Shut down?"

"There was an accident in Sierra Apache," David explained. "Everyone had left—except for the caretaker. He pointed up the mountain this way, indicating we might find some help."

Michael, the bow still strung over his shoulder, removed his woolen cap; then he drew the bow over his arm and propped the odd-looking contraption before him. "Why didn't you drive into town? There's a hospital there."

David shook his head. "The roads were closed. At least, they were the last time we checked. That's why we headed up here—"

"You said the caretaker at the clinic told you to come this way?" the woman asked. Something in her tone hinted of surprise.

"He didn't really say much of anything. He was drunk. I asked him if there was anyone around, anyone who had remained at the clinic and who could help us, and he shouted something I couldn't make out exactly, and pointed up the mountain. I saw what I thought was a house. I couldn't tell you where it was now. I got so turned around on the drive up that—"

"He must have been pointing to this house," Michael said to his wife; then he turned to David. "We're the only people up here. There aren't any other houses."

The woman glanced down again at Brian. Kate was rubbing more ointment on the infection. Then she looked up, exchanged glances with her husband. "You don't know what this Indian said?"

David tried to remember the old man's exclamations. The wind had been screaming, the guy had been drunk and slurring his words, and besides, the utterances had made no sense at the time. Paar . . . paare . . . paaree . . . something like that.

He spoke the word to the woman, the way he remembered it, and again the two exchanged glances. What was wrong? David wondered. "Yes," the woman finally said. "It was this house he pointed out, and it was undoubtedly me he was referring you to for treatment. I'm Rachel Perry. You've met Michael. He told me what happened. It was a careless mistake—"

"Yes," Michael said. "It's a shame about the car."

"We're both very sorry," said Rachel.

Paaree—Perry—of course; the caretaker must know them.

"I'm David Meredith; this is my wife, Kate—"

"Can you help my baby?" Kate said, for the first time raising her head and looking at Rachel.

Rachel knelt beside her. "I can look after him until you get in touch with a doctor."

"Oh—" David began. "I—I thought . . . for some reason I thought maybe you—"

"I used to work at the hospital in town," Rachel said. "As a nurse. Then when they opened the clinic I worked for a short time on an emergency basis; I've quit altogether now. Perhaps the caretaker remembered me."

"I see," David said. "Well, the doctor in Sierra Apache told us the baby has—"

"That's not hard to figure out," Rachel said. "Looks like impetigo."

David nodded. "He also mentioned something about ecthyma."

Rachel considered a moment. "I'm not sure what medical supplies I have here. First let's move him to one of the back rooms where he'll be comfortable. Mrs. Meredith?—"

There was silence for a while as Kate shifted on the floor, ran a sleeve across her parched face. Rachel extended a hand, placed it on Kate's shoulder, and held it there until finally Kate responded, nodded slowly, bundled up Brian into her arms, and stood.

"That's better," Rachel said. "Follow me."

She led Kate to the hallway that was at right angles to the front door, and they entered the first room on the right.

"I'm sure they'll be all right," Michael said. "Your wife

and son. I'm sure they'll be fine. Rachel was a terrific nurse." He lifted the bow, clasped it in one hand.

"Yes . . ." David answered thoughtfully. He was not so optimistic.

Michael crossed the floor to the other side of the fireplace, made the step up to the second landing before the staircase. Against the wall was a large wood-and-glass case containing china. David watched him as he set the bow on the top of the case and then stepped down into the den. He crossed to David and stopped before the sofa nearer the fireplace.

He had taken off the white thermal jacket and now wore only a light blue turtleneck sweater under what looked like a red-and-navy-plaid Pendleton. He removed the plaid shirt, tossed it on the sofa, and adjusted the end of the blue turtleneck over the top of his beige woolen trousers. His frame was tall and extremely slender. He said nothing for a moment, and appeared to be plunged temporarily into deep thought. The skin on his forehead drew back, accentuating his temples, and David noticed a slightly pronounced vein running from a point above the right eye into the hairline. The hair itself was a dull black, medium in length and somewhat curly, and his features, like his wife's, were delicate and smooth. For a moment his face appeared to border on the feminine; but, as David had noted earlier, the image was more boyish than feminine, and not dissimilar to that of a young Roman god. The two of them, husband and wife, made an extraordinarily handsome couple.

"You're welcome to stay here until the storm passes," he said.

"I hope it won't be that long. Could I use your phone? I'd like to call the clinic; there may be a chance someone's there now."

Michael didn't answer for a long time, just stared at David as if he hadn't even heard the question. Then: "Pardon me? You asked—?"

"About the phone," David finished. "Where is it?"

Michael turned his head slowly to the left, toward the sofa. David followed his glance, saw the sofa and a small end table near the wall; for a second he thought the man was indicating a phone on the end table: but the table was bare except for a porcelain lamp and a small stack of *Outdoor Life* magazines.

"It used to be there," Michael said. "The downstairs phone, that is. We had two of them—another one upstairs in the bedroom. They're gone now."

"Gone?"

Michael was still staring at the end table. When David had spoken the last word, the man seemed to only half-hear it: his face turned slowly back to David; he didn't answer directly but again appeared to be thinking about something else. The tiny, barely discernible vein near his right temple grew more noticeable, and the black eyes looked intensely ahead. He ran a hand down the front of the blue turtleneck, as if to smooth the wrinkles, and said, "We had the phones taken out some time ago. . . ." His face was expressionless. David started to speak, but the man continued, his face slowly coming to life. "I'm sorry—it just occurred to me—your being unable to call—"

David's mind felt suddenly as if it had gone blank, ceased to function: his brain had been bombarded unexpectedly by information which he needed time to fathom, sort out. Thus, momentarily stunned, he fought desperately to call to mind the alternatives he had considered earlier—and finally he realized that every alternative had taken for granted the availability of a telephone to call for assistance. He was wondering what to say next when he found himself looking over at the sofa and thinking about what Michael had said. He turned quickly back to the man. "Taken out? There's not a single phone in the house?"

Michael shook his head; again his face went blank. "I'm afraid not."

"But—why?—" David stopped himself. He was angry: he needed to use the goddamn phone—but something stopped him short, perhaps the thought that it really wasn't his business.

"—why were they taken out?" Michael completed the

question. David said nothing. "It's a long . . . complicated story. We were getting calls. I guess you'd call them . . . obscene calls? You've heard about them, haven't you?" The black pupils came to life again, a hopeful look flickering across his face. "What I mean is, people get them, you know, *other* people. . . . Rachel and I got tired of it." His face became suddenly serious, the eyes glistening with what David thought was a mixture of hatred and fear. "It became unbearable, the phone always ringing, the same terrible things being said . . . *cruel* things about . . . well, we had to take the phones out."

Against his better judgment, but because curiosity prevailed, David said, "Why didn't you just change the number?"

Michael stared at him. "What?"

"Change the number; get it unlisted?"

"Why? Someone would find it, it would get around and we'd have to—"

"But—" David blurted out, he couldn't help it now, "—how do you—"

"Get by? We do. We just do. You see, we don't really miss it—the phone. They're a nuisance, really. Don't you think?"

"Not now," David said bitterly.

"No—of course not." Michael lowered his head slightly. "I'm sorry. You wanted to call the clinic, of course."

A powerful, screaming wind beat across the cabin just then, and the room seemed to shudder; the screens on the windows knocked against their frames, the door behind them creaked on its hinges, and for a moment David didn't feel the warmth of the room, the heat of the flaming fire: his body shuddered with the cabin. He raised the zipper of his coat and, overcome with sudden discouragement, flopped himself down on the sofa. He saw the cat leap onto one of the chairs and lie down.

"Can I take your coat?" Michael said. "You'll feel warmer; it keeps you from getting the direct heat of the fire."

David shook his head. "No, thanks." The flames flickered

across his face; he was aware of the dancing shadows over his eyes. His thoughts became an endless parade of images: the red, blistered tissue on Brian's chest and around his neck . . . the round plastic frames of Dr. Bristol's glasses as they bobbed up and down on his nose, and the doctor's aged, even voice resounding confidently, alleviating irrational fears . . . the long drive toward town, toward the clinic . . . the helpless indignation upon finding the clinic closed . . . the enigmatic smile on the old Indian's face . . . and finally the unmitigated terror of the harrowing drive up the mountain in search of—what?

Nothing.

Nothing.

"You're welcome to stay."

Michael's voice.

"As long as you like."

Like? What the hell? David thought; I'm supposed to *want* to stay here? No way. Storm or no storm, he was going to get Kate and Brian to a hospital, even if he had to drag them down the mountain on a makeshift toboggan made from bedsheets stretched over a wood frame.

"Did the doctor in Sierra Apache give you that?" Rachel indicated the small silver tube in Kate's hand.

Kate nodded, blinked a couple of times. Her eyes ached; they felt as cold and as raw as her face. Rachel held out her hand and Kate gave her the tube.

"Neomycin," she read the label. "I may have something stronger, I don't know; it's been so long."

Kate barely found the strength to speak. "It's . . . it's all Dr. Bristol had," she said, and even as she spoke the words they seemed to dissipate, echoing in her ears—fading, meaningless tones; and her ears, frozen, had registered little since she had stood deep in the snow watching the car slide further off the road: she remembered screaming then, but that was about all. She wasn't even sure where she was now; she didn't remember the last name of the woman standing on the other side of the bed; all she had said was "Call me Rachel." Nor did she know where David was now—was he calling the doctor?

Brian lay on a twin-size bed, crying again, perhaps because of the pain—was there pain?—or perhaps because he was cold.

Rachel handed back the tube. "I'm sure Dr. . . . Bristol, was it? . . . knew what he was doing. The ointment is all right for now, but he's going to need a strong antibiotic." She began pulling the sheet a little closer around Brian. "Well, let me see what I have. I've treated impetigo before."

Kate reached over and took the sheet from Rachel's hand and completed covering the baby.

"He's going to be all right," Rachel said.

"He's . . . so cold . . ." Kate said.

"We'll fix that." She crossed the small room to the wall, bent over, and opened the vent to the heating duct near the floor. "We usually keep the two downstairs bedrooms closed up; we have no call to use them anymore. The heat from the den takes off the chill—but we want him warmer than that, don't we? There—" She stood up. "—it won't be long before he'll be nice and snug." She went to the bed, looked down at Brian, and said, "Yes. Nice and snug."

Kate moved closer to the edge of the bed. Again she felt the sting in her eyes. She leaned over and began stroking Brian's forehead. Then she sat on the bed, absentmindedly adjusting the flowered sheet. In a moment she thought the warmth was finally taking effect, because for the first time when she inhaled she could detect a faint odor: her nose, wet and blocked from crying, recognized the smell of mothballs.

She wanted to repeat reassuring words to Brian—calm, soothing tones to comfort him; but she just couldn't bring herself to speak, and instead continued stroking his forehead and the light, wispy strands of hair. She wondered again about David, if he had contacted a doctor. And then she became aware of something brushing against her hair, at the back of her head. She glanced up and saw that Rachel had moved onto the edge of the bed on the other side and she had her hand around Kate's back, stroking her hair just as Kate was stroking Brian.

"I know how you feel," Rachel said. "But I promise you, your baby will be fine."

Kate felt the muscles in her neck tense, then relax. Rachel's words echoed in the small, silent room, each calm, smooth, reassuring inflection resounding in the still air like a velvet petal. Looking deep into her eyes, Kate felt suddenly suspended in a tranquil vacuum amid a whirlwind of anxiety. And the sensitive resonance of the words *I know how you feel* connoted a tenderness which seemed for the moment to alleviate a portion of Kate's worry, and she remembered that the woman had once been a nurse. Reassuring words came naturally to her, Kate thought, they were part of her job; and yet there was another quality lying beneath the sound of her words, her voice, a tender, motherly quality that imparted conviction to the words *I promise you, your baby will be fine*.

She turned away from Rachel now and lost herself in Brian's flushed and feverish face. Before she could stop it, a sob broke, her mouth tightened, her eyes began to blur. She felt Rachel's hand across the back of her head, stroking her hair, and the soft, even intonation: "You're going to be all right too."

David faced Michael, who sat in a large padded chair opposite the sofa. "You said you don't have a car?"

"We do, actually," Michael said. "But we might as well not have one. It's busted. Haven't used it in ages." He must have detected a puzzled look on David's face. "I guess you're *really* wondering now how we get by—no phone, no car; how do we get into town? Buy groceries?"

"What's wrong with the car?" David asked.

Michael leaned back, crossed his legs. "I'm not sure. I've never been very good with automobiles, mechanical things. It's lucky I can string my bow." A smile crossed his face, disappeared. "But I can." He sat silent for a moment. David was about to speak when Michael said, "Anyway, Rachel and I manage quite well without a car. Our groceries are delivered once a month, and we rarely find it necessary to go into town. When we do, we catch the bus from the ski run; it stops just off the highway, at the foot of the mountain. During the winter, of course, when it gets like this"—he looked toward the window—"the buses don't run. And besides, who *wants* to go out?"

"No one else lives around here?"

"That's right. Nearest building is the clinic; and the closest home is about two or three miles in toward town." A frown appeared. "They haven't begun building up here yet; in fact, we own most of the surrounding land. My father owned it, that is, and now it belongs to me. He was a builder, my father; he built this place. He always prided himself in keeping a step ahead of everyone when it came to buying up land."

David didn't really want to hear any of this. He wondered how Kate was doing, how Brian was. He wanted to get up from the sofa, go into the back bedroom and check on them. But he doubted he could be of any real help, except perhaps to comfort Kate—and Mrs. Perry's ministrations to Brian would accomplish that better than he could. In the back of his mind lay the persistent notion that the three of them could still somehow make it to the clinic. He heard the howling wind as it beat against the house, and from where he was sitting he could see the whirling screen of white outside the window; but his determination to undo his stupid mistake, the dogged optimism to get them to safety blindly prevented him from accepting the present storm as a serious obstacle. He knew this, realized the irrationality of it all.

"Do you think I could have a look at the car?" he asked.

Michael looked at him curiously. He glanced quickly toward the door; it appeared to be an almost instinctive action, suggesting that the weather outside precluded even opening the door.

"Now?" he said.

"I just thought maybe I could look at it. Not that I could fix it or anything; but it's worth a try, don't you think?"

Michael shifted in the chair, glancing once again toward the door, then at the window. "I suppose so," he said.

David stood. "Fine. But first let me check on the baby."

On his way into the hall, he passed Mrs. Perry.

"I'm going to see if I have anything for him," she said.

David nodded, thanked her, and entered the room.

Kate was sitting on the bed. Faint cries sounded from the small bundle on the bed. He crossed to the bed and placed his hand on Kate's shoulder.

"How is he?"

She looked up at him, said nothing. Her eyes were watery and swollen.

David said, "And you?"

She nodded quickly, perfunctorily. Her eyes pierced his, sending an eager, questioning signal to him, and he said, "We can't reach anyone; there's no phone. But they have a car. It isn't running, something's wrong with it, but I'm going to look at it anyway."

Her eyes fell back to the bed.

"Honey?" David said.

She looked up.

"He's going to be all right; you know that, don't you?"

"That's what I keep hearing." The voice was low, barely audible.

"Believe it, okay?"

She nodded solemnly.

"Kate?" He looked straight into her eyes. "Love you."

She let go a tiny, muffled sob and put one arm around his waist.

Michael was pulling on the plaid Pendleton when Rachel emerged from the hallway.

It was useless, he thought, to venture out into weather like this just so this Meredith guy could look at the car. Didn't he believe him when he told him it was busted? Well, it didn't really matter; once they got outside, Meredith would realize that even if the old Lincoln *could* run, there was no way to get down the mountain in a blizzard like this, just no way. It was obvious that he was from the city; the way he was dressed in corduroy Levi's and a woolen shirt proved that. The tanned leather jacket he wore might keep him warm, provided the rest of him was properly layered against the cold: but Michael doubted Meredith wore even an undershirt. Then again, it didn't really matter; once they got outside . . .

Michael smiled to himself and wondered if Rachel had seen him. Poor Meredith would soon awaken to the bitter reality of the storm. And Kate—

—so soon? how could he be speaking so familiarly about her so soon?—

—would not be pleased. No, she would grow distressed, would wonder; she might even wonder if her husband hadn't somehow deliberately forced them into this situation. She would need comforting then, special treatment. . . .

At that thought, Michael felt very warm, almost feverish. Comforting . . . special treatment . . . He knew about those things. He knew how important they could be when you felt truly frightened . . . alone. . . . And he remembered it all so well, that day when Things had Changed. . . .

He heard the rusted latch on the door swing back and saw the old wooden door open. He blinked quickly, a million times, trying to focus on her silhouette against the wooden wall. Her presence warmed the chill; slowly, closing the door behind her and carefully pacing her steps, she approached. She didn't speak. He thought that perhaps he should be the first to speak, but he didn't. Neither of them said anything—not then; not moments later; not until the next day.

And she approached him.

Drawing the sleeve of her right arm across her eyes, she blotted away the tears, until finally when he saw her face in the orange glow of the heater, all that was left of the pain was the glisten in her eyes.

He wanted to cry. Really cry. But then she knelt and stroked his hair, his face, and for the first time he understood—thought he understood—about the Change, for there was a Change about her. Something in *her, in her face, deep within the glisten of her eyes, told him that she was different. It was a calmness, perhaps, although she was breathing quickly. And strangely, his own breathing slowed for the moment, and relief swept through him as the fear had done earlier.*

He looked into her eyes. It wouldn't matter, he thought, if he never saw another tree, another river, another sunrise, if only he could gaze into her eyes all day long, forever, because they were eyes that could feel, could speak silently to him. When she got so close that he felt her breath across his face, he realized that she was feeling him with her eyes—large, glistening ovals, soft, reaching, smiling like her hands. Yes, even her hands smiled when they touched him, brushing over his skin, making him warm, long, delicate white fingers drawing patterns on his chest. They sat looking at each other for a long time. He propped himself against the hard cold bars behind him. What was she thinking? Why was she smiling like that? Her hand swept over the hair on his head and around, down across his cheek to his neck and shoulders. He looked up at her, feeling the warmth of her smooth palm on his skin. And then she began to kiss him. . . .

Something happened then, something inside him that he could not explain. Time stopped them in a blurry frieze, framing them in stop motion until later, when it was all blasted apart in a terrifying shock of white light. . . .

Michael started. Rachel had stepped into the den, was crossing the floor toward the kitchen. When she reached him she paused. Their eyes met. A charge of something resembling electrical energy seemed to pass between them, as it often did, and Michael sensed the tacit message in Rachel's eyes. He had fantasized that she would be jealous of Kate—

—there, again, the immediate familiarity—

—but he now detected in her eyes and her expression the other thing, the thing which he dreaded because it hinted not of jealousy but of fear. And that other thing was silent admonishment: a frightful warning. . . .

9

IT WAS an old battle-scarred Lincoln, '57 or '58, and from the looks of its bent and dented fenders and its scratched and faded purple paint, David imagined it had been driven hard and carelessly. The long, massive body crowded the pine garage which housed it, and contributing to the claustrophobic setting were countless piles of junk: tools, old tires, oily rags, boxes, and empty antifreeze cans. Garage stuff. Lining the walls were dust-covered planks used as shelves, supporting a number of crumbling red-and-white cardboard boxes. Remnants, perhaps, from the days when Michael's father had built the place, for the labels read KEEP AWAY FROM CHILDREN, CLASS A EXPLOSIVES—DYNAMITE, and BLASTING CAPS—CAUTION. David wandered over to the shelves, peeking casually into them as he made his way around the car. Perhaps the boxes had been left over by some subcontractor, or Perry himself had used explosives to clear areas of land. Now portions of the labels had been blocked out by a felt marker, replaced by labels reading WIRE, BITS, RATCHETS, and the like, and in place of their original contents, the boxes contained rusted tools—pliers, hammers, jack bits, wire cutters, screwdrivers, and everything else imaginable.

In fact, the only element lacking in the garage was the odor of gasoline and oil, and doubtless even that existed, although it wasn't detectable through the icy air.

Michael handed him the key. David's fingers could barely squeeze against it, they were so numb. He couldn't believe how the wind had picked up during the last few minutes. He was literally freezing.

"Here," Michael said. He tossed him a pair of gloves from a rack on the wall.

"Jesus, it's cold," David said.

"It's going to get colder."

It wasn't possible, David thought. He put on the gloves. They were large, but anything was better than exposing his bare skin to that temperature. "Thanks." He flexed his fingers; they creaked, he was sure he could hear them. Get warm, he ordered them.

He took the key in his right hand and went to the driver's side, got in, inserted the key into the ignition on the dashboard, turned.

Nothing.

He turned it again.

Not a damn thing. The engine wouldn't turn over, didn't even start to; the only sound was a dull *click*.

"See?" Michael stood by the driver's door. "Busted."

"The battery." David got out, opened the hood, looked down at the ancient battery.

The terminals had corroded over, and large lumps of yellowish acid crystals had hardened over both of the connections, nearly burying them. David searched the rest of the engine, wondering if the source of the problem couldn't be somewhere else, and if it was, would he be able to spot it? Seeing nothing out of order, he jiggled the battery cables. The cables, like the rest of the inside, were covered with a deep layer of dust and grease. Then with his gloved index finger he scraped at one of the corroded terminals. The chalky lump didn't budge. He scraped harder; some of the particles fell away.

"I need a screwdriver or a file," he told Michael.

Michael went around to a shelf of tools on the wall and came back with a large screwdriver.

"Here." He handed it to David. "It's the battery?"

"Sounds like it." He scraped away at the terminals with the end of the screwdriver. "How long did you say it's been since you used the car?"

"I didn't. I guess a few years."

Jesus Christ, David thought. The guy was a genuine fucking hermit, had to be, there was no other explanation.

"Even if we can clean the terminals, after this long the thing's probably drained dry." He continued scraping.

"Let me work on one of them," Michael said, going to the tool shelf and bringing back another screwdriver. He began on the positive connection, forcing away some of the corrosion.

The action of David's screwdriver after a while became monotonous, hypnotic, and he found himself working harder because it was cold. His nose was beginning to run, he didn't dare move his lips for fear of cracking his face, and he wondered if he still had his ears—or had they fallen frozen to the ground? The wind blew open the door of the garage and snow began blowing about them. David wiped the sleeve of his coat against his nose and barely felt the leather on his face. He glanced once at Michael and could not help wondering if the man even felt the cold. With his black woolen cap pulled tight over his ears, and dressed in his thick woolen trousers and nylon thermal coat, he seemed to hardly notice the godawful wind. *We're all freezing*, he had told Kate. Wrong. This man next to him, who was politely scraping away at a corroded battery terminal, was not freezing, David was convinced of it. He *was not freezing*. He was nice and warm and secure—like a fucking bug in a cocoon.

"All right," David said after a while, when they had done about all they could. "Now—" He stopped, looked around. "Any pliers?"

"Uh-huh." And Michael brought a pair from the shelf.

David adjusted the pliers, pinched the clasp on the cable

clamp, and lifted off the negative cable. He did the same with the positive one. Then Michael said, "Here" and handed him a ball of steel wool. David took it, surprised Michael knew they would need it. He scrubbed vigorously at the left terminal, and Michael, with another wad of steel wool, went to work on the right one. But the damn stuff wouldn't come off. David worked the wool all over the terminal post, back and forth, up and down, grinding the gloved fingers deeper and deeper into the steel wool and harder and harder against the circumference of the post, round and round. He gave up after a while, knowing they had done all they could with the wool.

"Got any baking soda?" David asked.

Michael hesitated, nodded, started back toward the house.

"And some water," David called after him.

He worked with the wool a little more until Michael returned with the soda and water.

"I've never tried this before," David said. "But it's supposed to work."

He sprinkled a generous amount of baking soda over the posts, and on top of that splashed water from the large tin pitcher. "Soda's supposed to cut the acid," he explained.

And it did. A little. There was still a fairly heavy ring of battery acid around the posts, even after he had gone over them again with the steel wool; but the terminals looked better than they had before. David repeated the procedure on the cable clamps and replaced them on the posts. Then he checked the water, found none, as he expected, and filled the battery with the remaining water from the pitcher. After that he got in, turned the key and—

—click.

Damn.

"Busted," said Michael.

"Shit," David said. He shivered on the torn fabric seat.

"Could be something else."

"It could be *any*thing else. But I don't think so. It's the battery, gotta be. There's no goddamn charge, that's all."

"What about the gas?"

"Three quarters full, I checked. No, it's the battery. Hasn't this happened before?"

Michael shook his head. "I told you—"

"I know. You don't need a car, a phone. Jesus; right now I could use both."

The garage door banged repeatedly against the outside wall; snow had already covered the entranceway, and occasional flakes spotted David's face with wetness. All right, he thought. Try to forget the cold for a minute and muster up some more alternatives.

"Inside—" he began, then stopped as a blast of wind thrashed through the small garage. His shoulders quivered. "—Inside, you mentioned that your groceries are delivered. How?"

Michael looked puzzled. "How?"

"I mean how do you order them, without a phone?"

"Oh. They're delivered once a month—the same things, nothing varies much. We've used the same grocer for years. If we need anything special—you know, special meats, or fruits when they're in season—we let him know when he comes and he delivers them the next day—or I just take the bus into town." Again the puzzled look. "Why?"

"For one thing, I was curious. But I really wanted to know if there was any chance of someone coming up here."

Michael laughed. "Hardly. We got groceries last week. No one ever comes up here anyway—and certainly not in this weather. You'd have to be crazy."

Or desperate, David thought. Michael looked momentarily embarrassed, as if he'd suddenly realized what he'd said.

"I meant—"

"Come on," David interrupted. "Let's go back. I'm frozen."

The wind slapped their faces as they left the garage. The snow had increased again, and from where David stood by the side of the creaking garage, waiting as Michael secured the latch on the door, the cabin made a hazy gray outline against the whirling white screen. Turning, David could make out another outline, this one more distinct because it was closer. The small shed he had observed from the mountain path appeared larger now, blanketed by a steadily mounting layer of snow. It was positioned on a slightly raised stretch of ground. He had thought earlier that it probably housed stacks of firewood. But what else might it contain? Was it perhaps an old storage shed, and mightn't there be spare auto parts, or—

"What's in there?" he asked.

Michael turned, looked where David was pointing. He said quickly, "My—my . . . things." He paused, then evidently realized he should have been more specific. "My archery equipment. I keep it all in there."

"Oh. No chance, then, that there might be a spare battery—anything that might help—a sled, maybe—"

"I told you *no*. Just arrows and strings and stuff. Don't you believe me?"

"Well, are you sure there's nothing else in the garage that—"

"Nothing."

It was practically useless to talk now, the wind blocked out everything. Michael started off. David grudgingly picked up his frozen feet and followed him. But not until after staring a moment longer at the isolated shed, wondering.

"I've got some ampicillin," Rachel said, showing Kate an amber plastic bottle. "But they're capsules." She pried off the white cap and sprinkled a couple of gelatin capsules into her palm.

"Kate looked at them questioningly. "I don't . . . "

"We'll just open them and mix the powder in with his bottle. When was the last time he had any milk?"

Kate thought a moment. "This morning, I think."

"That's all right; but we won't give him any more until the impetigo clears."

"I don't know . . . "

Rachel stepped closer, put a hand on Kate's shoulder. "I know what I'm doing. Really. You trust me, don't you?"

Kate was watching Brian twisting on the bed, his face a deep crimson, his expression blank. He had suddenly stopped wailing: he had probably cried himself out. Where was David? Had he fixed the car? Would—what was his name? Michael—would Michael let them take his car to the clinic?—

"Mrs. Meredith? . . . Kate? . . . "

Rachel's eyes peered steadily down at her. Her mouth was slightly parted, the lips barely curving upward at each corner, giving her face a relaxed yet concerned look.

"You *do* trust me?" she said again softly.

Kate glanced at the amber bottle. Slowly, she nodded. She wasn't sure why—no, she was sure. She *wanted* to trust this woman. She *had* to.

"That's better. We can mix the granules in some honey water. Is that okay?"

She nodded again.

"Good. Do you have his bottle?"

Kate leaned over, got her purse off the bed, searched awhile and found Brian's plastic bottle. She handed it to Rachel.

And then there was a lengthy silence between them in the room. Kate thought she could feel the heat now, coming through the vent. There had been a continual, underlying noise ever since she had entered the room, since she had been sitting on the bed: It was the steady rhythm of the pounding wind outside, beating against the small window on the wall beside the bed—the only window in the room. Kate didn't realize it for a moment, but she was still looking at Rachel, and Rachel was not talking now; perhaps it was the silence that finally brought Kate around to the realization that the woman appeared suddenly lost in thought. In fact, she was staring now out the window. The cool, kind face seemed frozen, the gray eyes slightly glazed. Kate could see the bright white outside the window reflected in those wide gray eyes. Then Rachel's lips moved, forming words which sounded in a monotone.

"It's bad."

Kate's heart quickened, an abrupt fear struck deep in her stomach. Was she referring to Brian? Had she been pretending all this time that things would be all right? Was the "it" she spoke of the rash? Kate searched the face for meaning. And then Rachel added, "The storm."

Kate turned, looked out the window, breathing easier now, her heart slowing. She watched the tossing white specks against the tall swaying pines. Strange, but the scene didn't make her feel cold: it made her feel lonely—and helpless. It reminded her of how far away they were from the clinic, and of the distance between here and town.

What was keeping David? When could they leave this place?

"It's worse than they said it would be."

Kate turned away from the window, looked at the woman.

Odd, she thought. The woman's gaze remained fixed. She must dread the snow, the wind, Kate thought; she seemed so concerned.

"It worries me," Rachel said, still gazing out the window.

"I . . . don't understand. . . . " Kate said.

Rachel looked down from the window; her eyes met Kate's. No longer did her face appear soft and smooth; there came over it a strange harshness, a look of anxiety. The corners of her mouth still curved upward on either side, but, peculiarly, the gentle smile had become almost a grimace, and the gray eyes looked sharply at her.

"I told you," she said, "that I'm convinced the ampicillin will clear up whatever your baby has, but . . . it worries me that . . . " She looked back out the window. " . . . that you may have to stay here longer than you anticipated. . . ."

"Why don't you remain here until the storm passes, and then you could hike down to the clinic and call a wrecker for your car."

Michael stood behind David as David removed the oversized gloves and rubbed his hands together before the fire. When the numbness began to disappear, he turned to Michael.

"The storm could last for days. We can't wait that long."

Silence. Michael removed his coat, sat on the sofa. Why wasn't he shivering, as David was? He just sat there.

David went into the back room where Kate and the baby were.

She was alone with Brian, still sitting on the bed.

"Are you all right?"

She nodded.

"I couldn't start the car," he said.

Kate sagged.

He went to the bed. "How is he?"

"The same," Kate managed. "Rachel has some medicine, some kind of antibiotic. . . ."

He leaned down, kissed her lightly. She didn't move, so he placed a finger gently below her chin and drew her face up to meet his. Finally she said, "Oh, David, I'm so confused, I don't know—"

She stopped.

"Don't know what?" he said.

"I—I hope this is all right, what we're doing."

There was a noise from behind, and David turned.

"Here we are." Rachel entered, carrying a baby bottle in one hand, a blanket in the other. She placed the blanket on the bedside table, handed the bottle to Kate. Kate hesitated, then took the bottle of straw-colored liquid. Her hands trembled.

"It's all right," Rachel said. "I mixed it up good—just honey water and the ampicillin."

David said, "Is that what he needs?"

Rachel nodded. "He needs an internal antibiotic to combat the staph germ. It's perfectly safe, Mr. Meredith."

Brian made a coughing sound, then let out a short, faint cry.

Kate placed the nipple of the bottle in his mouth, and the child began sucking the mixture.

"Of course," Rachel said, "it will be some time before you'll notice a change. And you'll still need to get him to the clinic."

"Yes . . ." David said. He looked at the woman. "Thank you. . . ."

"Not at all. I'm sure he'll be all right." Her expression changed suddenly, and she said, "You looked at the car?"

David nodded grimly.

"It didn't start," she said.

"No. It's the battery." He paused, then added, "Mrs. Perry, your husband said there's no way to get into town—"

"Michael's right. I'm afraid you'll have to walk to the main road and . . ." She hesitated. Then: "You see, it's getting worse outside, and . . ."

"I know. But isn't there a way to reach *some*one from here? Neighbors?" He knew Michael had already answered the question; he repeated it because he found it hard to believe that they really were isolated two or three miles from *any*one.

"I'm afraid not," she said. Her voice quivered. David thought he detected a trace of fear.

Brian continued sucking the honey water, completely occupying Kate's attention. David ran a hand across his face, felt the stubble that had formed on his cheeks. He glanced at his watch. Four-thirty. The sun would be down in a couple of hours.

Sweat soaked his shirt, sticking it to his back. His nose must still be glowing as red as the blisters on the baby's chest. For the first time David felt something other than numbness: a growing thirst had formed in his throat. He could use a drink. Jesus, he could use a drink.

"So—" Rachel said, forcing a smile. "What will you do?"

David looked at her suddenly, somewhat taken aback and not sure why.

"I mean," she continued quickly, "you're welcome to stay, of course. But I'm sure the sooner you can get down from here the better off you'll be—and the better off your baby will be." She smiled again.

David thought of Michael's insistence that they should stay, that the storm precluded any thought of venturing outdoors. He sensed the exact opposite reaction from his wife. Her welcome lacked—what?—sincerity. He sensed that she wished they would leave, that they had never come. And it was a perfectly understandable feeling, David knew, albeit a bit callous. At any rate, it was *his* feeling as well.

He nodded. "Yes. Well, I've got one idea." He squeezed Kate gently on the back of her neck. Brian hadn't tired of the honey mixture; he still pulled eagerly at the nipple: quick, urgent mouthfuls.

David left the three of them there and joined Michael in the den.

This time Perry was standing by the fire. He had removed the Pendleton and stood with his back toward the crackling flames. So he did get cold, David thought.

"How are they?" Michael asked.

"Fine."

"Rachel fix them up?"

Them? The reference rankled.

David nodded.

"I was just thinking about the car," Michael said. "I suppose I should sell it. Never thought of it before. You think with a good battery it would run like new?"

"Not like new," David said. "But it would run. I was thinking about the car too. And since what it needs is a battery, I think we ought to put one in."

"Put one in?"

"Mine."

"But—"

"It's not doing any good where it is. It's just lying down there at the bottom of the ravine. Car's no good, but the battery is."

"You're going back for it?"

"You want to help?"

"Well, sure. But will it fit?"

"I don't know. Maybe we can make it fit; maybe not."

"Well, if you want to try."

"I do. No offense—I mean, we appreciate your offer to stay—but your wife is right, the sooner we can get down from here the better."

Michael's expression suddenly changed; his eyes narrowed. "Rachel say that?"

David nodded, said, "My feeling too. I've got to get in touch with people, my office, and if that damn clinic would reopen I'd feel a lot better. Provided, of course, we can get to it."

"I understand," Michael said weakly. "It's just that I know what kind of storm is building and I don't think you do."

"I've got to do what I can, while I can."

Michael reached for his coat. "Okay, let's go."

"One thing, though. Do you have chains for the Lincoln?"

"Yes, I believe so. They're in a box in the garage."

"Good. No sense trudging down there and back for nothing."

"It *will* be for nothing if the battery doesn't fit."

"We don't know that—yet."

Michael shrugged. The cat meowed. It had made its way over to the sofa. Michael looked at the feline and frowned. "Shut up," he told it. He sounded truly angry. "You like cats?" he asked David.

"Never had one."

His eyes bore down on the creature, his face twisting into a horrible grimace. "I despise them."

After donning his coat and Michael's gloves, David went in to inform Kate of his plan. Rachel was on her way out, and David was glad. He wanted Kate alone.

She responded feebly when he told her.

"And then what?" she asked.

"Then, if the battery fits, we'll head down, check the clinic. If it isn't open, we may be able to make it to town. We'll have chains."

She raised her head. David could tell she wasn't convinced.

"We've got to do something," he explained.

Kate sighed, turned away from him, faced the window. "The snow . . ."

David looked. But he didn't want to be reminded of that

now. He was already beginning to realize that time really *was* running out. In the back of his mind he knew, painfully, that Michael was right, that they would have to eventually accept the Perrys' hospitality. But that time had not yet arrived.

"I'd better go," he said quickly.

Kate turned. They both looked at the baby. Brian had finished the bottle and was finally falling off to sleep. *A blessing;* David remembered Dr. Bristol's words and immediately wished the old man were here with them now.

"Mrs. Meredith."

David turned. It was Michael, standing in the doorway.

"Excuse me," Michael said. "I thought I should let you know that Rachel's in the kitchen if you need her. She's fixing dinner. You must be starved."

Kate just stared at him.

Michael didn't move or say anything; he stood transfixed in the doorway like a goddamn messenger waiting for an urgent reply. David thought it was all Kate could do to finally nod. "Yes . . ." she said. "Thank you. . . ." Michael smiled. After a beat he left the room.

David waited a moment longer, then said, "We'll be back as soon as we can."

She sat there for a while, knowing she should move, perhaps go into another room, try to relax. But instead she just sat there. It finally dawned on her that there was little she could do for Brian right now. It was up to the medicine to take effect, and Rachel said it would take a while. But how long? The thought caused her stomach to squirm, but she deliberated for a moment (the first semblance of rational thought she had exhibited since yesterday), and supposed she could live with the reality that it would take time if only during that time she could see a change. Then she would *know* that he was going to be all right. And then she thought, *If only I could sleep, just for an hour, maybe, if I could get some rest, I don't know if I can even stay awake much longer . . .*

. . . of course she must stay awake, keep alert; if David fixed the car they could leave. . . .

David.

She had begun to feel guilty. Her anger at him had not completely dissipated, but it was on its way. Numbness, an emotional vacuum, had contained it. But now the numbness was beginning to disappear—owing in part, to the feeling that she must trust the medicine Rachel had supplied.

She had said nothing to David a little while ago. He waited, and it only now occurred to her that perhaps he was waiting for her to say something—

—my God, she should have said something, should have, if nothing else, reminded him to be careful, to hurry but be careful; after all, it was a long descent to the road, and although she had only glimpsed the car as it tumbled down; she had heard the dull thud a few seconds later when the car hit what she knew must be bottom—and that was a long way, long and steep. . . .

She reached for a Kleenex on the bedside table and blotted the wetness forming around her nostrils. Then she pressed a couple of fingers to the area below each eye, feeling the puffiness. She knew the eyes were bloodshot, and they still ached when she blinked. She had cried more than she realized . . . and the icy wind hadn't helped any. . . .

Then at once she visualized *his* eyes. Not David's, but Michael's, as they watched her. They were large and perfectly round, of deep, bright onyx, and they seemed to actually enter the room, passing through the doorway where he stood, intensifying, piercing the space between herself and Michael and piercing her own weak, red pupils. Staring at her. Looking at her like . . . like . . . what? Kate could not decide; but she remembered someone else who had looked at her—watched her—like that, and it was a memory she had not recalled in years. It was at the school where she taught, while David was completing his graduate work. The school had been divided into two separate buildings, across the street from each other. Her building housed first through sixth grades; the building opposite, the junior high. She taught third grade and had little connection with the other school. But one day, one of the girls in her class was absent; she'd had the flu and would not be able to return for a few days. Kate learned of the girl's condition through a note her mother sent by the girl's brother, who attended ninth grade across the street.

It was her free period, and Kate was sitting in the classroom alone, working on plans for the next week, when the girl's older brother entered, accompanied by two classmates.

The boy introduced himself and handed Kate the note. As she read it she became aware of sounds coming from the two companions. She glanced up and saw one of them staring at her in a peculiar way, smiling, while the other boy whispered to him. It irritated her: the two boys appeared much too old to be in ninth grade. For a moment she wondered if they hadn't come from another school. When she finished reading the note, she looked up and the brother asked her if there was a reply. She said No, thank you, and there came whispers from the two companions. When she glanced at them, the taller one—who looked to be about eighteen or nineteen—smiled at her; rather, he grinned—a big, wide grin, showing a row of large, crowded teeth. But it was his eyes that really unsettled her. They weren't black, like Michael Perry's, but dull brown, and yet behind them lay the same piercing intensity.

He said, "You're Mrs. Meredith, aren't you?"

Kate nodded politely, said, "Yes," then added, "You know you're not supposed to be here, don't you? Junior High students aren't allowed here without special permission."

"Permission?" the boy said, grinning wider. "Permission—just to look?" He laughed, turned to his friend. Then he turned back to her and continued to stare. Kate felt a hollowness in her stomach, a queasy fear of these two young men, for that was what they were. The girl's brother, in an effort to divert Kate's attention, said, "Thank you, Mrs. Meredith." He turned to leave, but the older boy was still staring at her, and this time she looked directly into his dull brown eyes. Her fear must have betrayed her, because he continued watching her, the grin on his face widening, and yet his was not the expression she found on the faces of men on the street—the hungry but complimentary glance—his was an expression more animal-like, and she found herself wondering, *What's going on behind those eyes?* and immediately answering, *You* know *what's going on* . . . and again the queasiness rose inside her. They left, finally, and she heard muffled laughter outside the door.

Michael Perry had not been crude. He had not been sarcastic. He certainly was not animal-like. But something had been going on behind those eyes. Kate didn't know what, but she knew that the feeling deep in the pit of her stomach had been similar to the feeling she had experienced that day in the empty classroom.

Suddenly, she thought again, You should have reminded David to be careful. . . .

Rachel stood in the kitchen, absentmindedly shelling a last handful of peas for dinner and placing them in a plastic bowl on the linoleum counter top next to the stove. After a while she glanced up out the window, watched the falling snow. She was used to the cold, having lived with it so long; but now she could not keep warm. She felt, also, strangely vulnerable for some reason. It was unusual having someone else in the house. How long had it been since someone had been here? How long had it been since she and Michael had left this place together? He had tried to get her to leave, to go into town with him, but she could not. That was when they had been troubled with the phone calls.

"It will do you good," Michael had said. "It will do you good to get out of the house for a change."

But she had declined.

"What would you rather do, then? Stay here with that?" He pointed to the telephone.

"No," she had said. "We'll have it taken out. That's what we'll do."

And so she never left. And Michael rarely left now, not since . . .

Rachel returned her concentration to the task before her, hoping the Merediths would not be here for dinner, that they would be able to fix the car and leave. She felt uncomfortable with people in the house.

Except for the child. He was a beautiful baby; even in his illness he was beautiful. A lucky woman, Kate Meredith.

And then Rachel blinked quickly; her eyes stung, and she felt suddenly warm. She remembered Michael's face in the den and she felt a sharp spasm of fear in her stomach; and at the same time, strangely, a tear fell unexpectedly onto her cheek. . . .

10

IT TOOK about fifteen minutes to reach the road.

A cold fifteen minutes, during which David followed Michael through pines and over frozen ground, thankful that he could still move trunk and limbs through the whipping sheet of white ice.

Neither of them spoke for a while. If he had, his words would have been jerked from his lips and propelled away by the wind. Just before they began the descent over the side of the mountain and down onto the road, David had struggled fiercely to keep up with the constantly moving white back of Michael's thermal coat. He saw then why the man wore it when stalking prey: When the jacket moved into a position against a backdrop of snow, either against a cluster of trees or against a rise in the ground, it blended away into a patch of white, and at times David could barely make out the figure before him.

Once they reached the road, he saw the full extent of the last hour's snowfall. No wonder he had had considerable difficulty maneuvering up the narrow incline, what with the icy patches here and there and the gathering flakes—but that road, the one he'd been on when he saw Michael, was nothing like the angular ground before him now. Snow covered the road at least two inches thick, and the spot where the car had slid off was barely recognizable.

They edged cautiously through the embankment and saw the Malibu. It had grown a deep mantle of fuzzy white.

"It's practically covered," Michael shouted above the whipping wind.

David turned to him. Michael's eyes seem to question him from beneath the visor of the woolen balaclava he now wore. The man knew how to protect himself against the cold, David observed, and again considered that Michael would eventually prove himself right about the impossibility of making it down the mountain before tonight. Well—damn him.

David turned away, studied the earth below, recognized the unevenness of the ground and the deceptive footing. Then, carefully inhaling the icy air and wishing he enjoyed the protection of a woolen face garment in place of the cap Michael had given him, he turned to Michael, said, "Well, let's go," and started down.

His left foot searched a moment, decided on a spot, and sank into the snowy ledge. He balanced himself, prepared to go ahead with the right foot, jumped the left farther down, balanced himself again, painfully aware now of the snow melting through his guaranteed-waterproof chukkas, but, ignoring the sodden frigidity of his toes, stumbled down the glacial incline—fitfully, fighting for sheer tenacity and praying that any second his foot wouldn't strike a mound of bottomless snow or an insecure rock, the boots flashing before his eyes until they scudded to a muscle-twisting stop countless yards later.

The car lay on its side, propped against a tree, whose lower branches scraped against the Malibu's top. David didn't want to imagine what the other side of the car looked like, the side against the ground. The top looked bad enough, indented by the trunk of the huge pine. He stood immobilized by the sight, overwhelmed by the sheer loss of the damn car, looking disdainfully at it the way one does at a car after a severe wreck, mourning the loss of an old friend.

He moved toward the automobile, aware now of Michael coming up behind him. Michael went to the car and pointed at the top. "We'll have to bring the thing down," he said.

They reached up, got the best grip possible, Michael at one end, David at the other, and began rocking the machine. The balance of the weight was against the trunk of the tree, making the task that much more difficult. David's hand slipped across the snowy surface; he dusted off a layer of snow before again taking hold of the fender. The wind blew the accumulated snow into his eyes. He stopped, cleared them, began again, this time careful to turn his face away from the wind. He couldn't get a secure hold with his right foot, the ground kept slipping away.

"Okay?" yelled Michael, leaning past the edge of the car, squinting through the hooded face protector.

"Wait!" David said, and pushed deep with the chukkas until they found firm ground.

Then he nodded and they tugged.

The vehicle came forward an inch, balanced back, wobbled. They tugged again. The car rocked.

The third time David saw the top side swing forward, coming down—slowly at first, as if in slow motion, then, as the balance switched sides, faster.

He moved back, strutting across the rugged ground.

Michael backed up, the white hood staggering, his eyes watching the potential crash.

And it came. The Malibu collapsed onto the earth with a metallic thud muted by the wind.

David stepped around, looked at the side of the car that had lain against the ground. The same sense of regret mixed with subdued anger surged through him. But it quickly subsided when he went to the hood, anxiously aware now of their purpose.

Michael came around. David couldn't see the man's mouth under the balaclava, but because of the tautness of the skin around his eyes he was no doubt smiling approval.

The hood of the car refused to budge. David yanked on the release, heaved upward. He thought he heard a crunching sound, then saw where the side of the car that had lain against the ground had been bent inward, mashing into the edge of the hood. Michael grabbed the end next to David and together they pulled upward until finally the hood scraped open.

David drew Michael's pliers from his back pocket, unclamped the cables, and began working on the battery, thankful to the underside of the hood for the momentary protection it offered against the wind. In a few minutes he had released the battery housing, lifted the battery out. He dreaded the trip back, carrying the damn thing.

He shouted, "All right," stepped back from the car clutching the battery, and Michael shut the hood.

"Here," Michael said, offering to take the battery.

But David shook his head, hefted the black box closer, and together they walked to the bottom of the embankment.

He started up reluctantly, grudgingly, Michael following.

It was damned hard, struggling up the mountainside carrying the extra weight. He stumbled a few times and occasionally stopped altogether to change the position of his grip. Then a gust of wind swept across them and for an instant he truly thought he would be lifted off balance and sent teetering backward down the slope. It was a good thing Michael was behind him.

The rim of the road above them seemed hopelessly far; he

fully realized now that if they faltered a second too long—if they spent any longer making it back to the cabin than they had spent getting down the slope—his toes would in fact become frostbitten. David had a fleeting image of Doc Bristol coming slowly at him, wielding a rotary saw, bearing down inch by inch toward two rows of dead purplish toes. David quickly wiggled them now in protest.

Michael kept up behind, occasionally almost overtaking him; at those times he slowed his pace, dropped behind. What David felt now more than anything else was the wetness on his face. Blowing snow had soaked the skin; if he opened his mouth he gulped ice water, and when he blinked, moisture stung his lashes, and as he trudged onward the apprehension that continued to rear its ugly, fearful visage was the fifty-fifty possibility that the Malibu's battery wouldn't fit in the old Lincoln: after all, one car was a Chevy, the other a Ford, so there was that possibility that the battery wouldn't work somehow. But at least they had to try.

You'd better work, you sonofabitch.

And so on they trudged, an overpowering pain working its way through David's fingers and arms, a frozen, numb, godawful throbbing in every limb as he hefted the infernal black battery higher and tighter.

But then just at that moment David, despite his numb movement and faltering steps through the mounds of ice, just then he saw the rim of the road closer than it had been before, and his heavy feet found a spark of life he hadn't known was there, and he breathed heavier, panting, a new energy surging through him, he couldn't believe he had the strength, but now the end was near and he knew that when he climbed onto the road he could collapse if he wanted to—so he trudged forward, harder and harder, and now he was right up there, if his swollen feet could make it one yard more—and they did, and he was at the edge now, the battery clutched under one arm because he had to use his hands to climb the rest of the way, to maintain balance, and the gloved fingers dug into the ground and he pulled himself up higher and higher, and then he made it, had reached the rim of the road and was about to command the last surge of energy available to force his dying legs and feet over the top of the ledge when he saw the car stopped on the road a little way down, a car he'd seen before, and then he looked up into the face of a man inching his way toward him, his hand outstretched offering to help him onto the road, and now David recognized the tan LTD and Laurence Griggs–with-a-U with his sidekick standing behind him, and the man was saying loudly, above the roar of the wind:

"I think it's time we had a talk, Mr. Meredith. . . ."

PART II

The Standoff

11

THEY DROVE on in Griggs's car, in silence, David too numb to say anything and too surprised to know what to say. Michael had asked them who they were and what they wanted, but neither of the men had answered. The car was warm, and for the moment that was all that seemed to matter.

Griggs asked, and Michael told him, where the cabin was, and eventually they reached the point where the narrow road curved sharply, making an acute angle upward. Griggs stopped the car just before the house and they walked the rest of the way, Griggs at the front, the burly man bringing up the rear—although David didn't hear the big man's footsteps behind him for a while, then finally they sounded through the wind, as if the man were struggling with all that fat to keep up with them.

Michael offered to carry the battery, and David was more than willing to let him. The muscles in his arms and legs had been wrung out; he could barely move any of his limbs, and when they had to start walking to the cabin, his whole body ached with dread.

Britannica salesmen my ass, David thought.

Whoever they were, they were from the city; like David, they weren't dressed for the cold—at least, not the rumpled-looking one with the moustache. David had noticed earlier that he wore a tattered, unmatched suit, while at least Griggs wore a heavy topcoat and thick gloves. Furthermore, he suspected this smooth-talking gum-smacker with the pilot glasses to be a real sonofabitch. And Jesus, what if the two of them wore guns under their coats? But that couldn't be, it just couldn't, his imagination was getting out of hand.

One thing he did know, and which eased his mind considerably, was that regardless of what these men wanted, he hoped that once they learned the severity of his and Kate's problem, once they realized that there really *was* a sick child involved, they would be willing to drive the three of them down the mountain to the clinic—or, if the roads opened momentarily, to town. David had asked Michael earlier if there was any chance of someone venturing up here—well, someone had, and whatever motive they had for making the perilous drive up, they might very well prove to be the Merediths' salvation. And for that David had to be a little thankful.

Kate was lying on the sofa when they entered. When the door slammed shut she pulled herself up, groggy. She blinked, watching the four men enter and step down into the den. Rachel appeared from the kitchen, looking bewildered.

Griggs spoke to Michael as he set the battery on the table. "This your place?"

Michael nodded. David thought Michael had been acting strangely since his meeting with the two men. Obviously he was confused, as David was, but there was something else in his movements and expression, a certain nervousness, his hands jittery, his eyes quick. Michael introduced himself and Rachel. Then he asked Griggs again, "Who are you? What do you want?"

He got the same response as he had earlier. Silence. The only sound came from the wind outside and the crackling fire. Griggs stepped closer to the sofa. The other man remained fixed at a point behind him, near the step leading toward the door. He was heavy, David observed, but it wasn't tempered muscle concealed below the dilapidated coat, it was fat, and the skin on his face puffed out as if from an abundance of alcohol. He hadn't said a word during the walk up, not even to his partner.

Griggs was looking at Kate. "You're Mrs. Meredith? Katherine Meredith?"

Kate stood up. ". . . Yes. . . ." She looked at David for an explanation.

"You mind telling us what's going on?" David said.

Michael turned to him quickly, surprised. "You don't know them?"

"No." David had been staring at Griggs's back, and that bothered him, so he crossed to the sofa and looked directly at the man. "You told me in Sierra Apache your name was Griggs. But I don't know you. What do you want? Why did you follow us up here?"

Griggs looked at him this time, smiling politely. "Please, Mr. Meredith; no need to get excited. I know this is unsettling for you." He looked at Rachel. "You must forgive us, Mrs. Perry. I know we're imposing upon you, but we won't be staying long, I hope. It's just that we must talk to the Merediths, and this is the only way—"

"How did you get here?" Kate asked suddenly, her voice anxious, breaking. "You must have a car. Can you take us into town? Our baby's—"

"Certainly, Mrs. Meredith. Our car's just outside." He turned to David, smiling. "We had better luck than you did."

"So what do you want?"

"How *is* your baby?" he asked Kate.

She hesitated, began to speak, but Rachel said, "He'll be fine."

Griggs looked uncertainly at Rachel, turned back to Kate. *Where* is he?"

"In the bedroom," Kate managed. "Asleep. Why? What is this? David? . . . "

"Well, Mrs. Meredith, what I've come to discuss is of a personal, delicate nature." He eyed Rachel, then Michael. "As I said, we *are* intruding, but there are extenuating circumstances here, and one of them is time, and so I wonder if Mr. Kavanaugh and I might speak with the Merediths alone?"

Another silence. What could anyone say? Two strangers had popped up out of nowhere with a message of seeming urgency, and in addition to barging in on an unsuspecting household, they now wanted the owners of the house to leave the room—Jesus. . . .

Then Griggs said, "Or perhaps it would be better if the Merediths came with us now?"

"I thought the roads into town were closed," David said.

Griggs smiled. "They're open now."

"Yes," Kate said quickly, "we can leave now, David. . ."

"Of course," Griggs said. "And then on the way down I can talk to you both, without having to trouble these people further."

Kate started to get up.

"No," David said. Something was just too damn smooth about this guy; David wasn't sure what exactly he wanted, but something told him that they'd better find out now. "Say what you have to say."

"But David—" Kate began.

"It's all right. I think Mr. Griggs knows we have a sick

child who needs to get to a doctor; but we can wait just a moment for him to explain."

Kate slumped back on the sofa.

Griggs looked uncomfortable. David knew he didn't want to speak in front of everyone. What the hell did he want? And *why* couldn't he speak before everyone?

"Very well . . ." he said, moving slowly to the fire. He removed his gloves, rubbed his hands together before the flames, as if the action were somehow expected. More likely he was stalling. "Fire's nice. It's freezing out there, must be a record for this part of the state."

Silence. A long one this time.

Finally he said, "Look, why don't we all sit down?"

As a group, they complied, David sitting down next to Kate on the sofa, Michael and Rachel sitting together on the sofa adjacent. Griggs stayed a moment by the fire, rubbing his hands; then he took the gum from his mouth, tossed it into the flames. He took a seat in the overstuffed chair, leaned forward into the group. The burly one—Kavanaugh—retained his pose in the background, watching over them like a goddamned butler or something.

Griggs took off the glasses. "Now, then, you came up here because the roads were closed. What happened to your car?"

Another silence.

Finally David said, "We had an accident. The Perrys have a car, but the battery's dead. We were down there getting mine."

Griggs's jaw was moving back and forth, as if it didn't know what to do without a gob of gum to chew on. The sunglasses off, David noticed the man had extremely tiny eyes—black and set deep. A wide forehead accentuated the smallness of the eyes as well as his mouth. The slightly graying hair was combed back in an attempt to cover premature balding, and the strands were necessarily long, untapered. His black eyes moved over the four of them slowly, surveying what he had made a captive audience.

"Yes, that's unfortunate about the car. But like I said, we'll be happy to take you down. It's amazing the way chains can cut through all that slosh." He looked at David, smiled. "I'll bet you wish you were back in El Paso now, huh? It's nice, we just came from there; temperature a warm seventy, seventy-five . . ." Then suddenly he grew serious. "We talked to the doctor in Sierra Apache; he told us about the child. I'm sorry."

Kate said weakly, ". . . Mrs. Perry gave him an antibiotic; it's supposed to—"

"You're a nurse?" Griggs asked Rachel.

"I was once," she said.

"I see."

Just then Rachel stood up, said, "I think . . . I think I'll get some coffee. . . ."

"That would be fine," Griggs said.

And then Michael said something that sent David reeling, and it wasn't an order for the man to leave, or any ultimatum regarding the subject of his presence.

"Kate—Mrs. Meredith—isn't feeling well now. You should know that. I don't know what you want, but I think you should know she isn't well." He was looking at her as he said it, and David didn't know why the words jarred, but perhaps it was because of the sudden familiarity.

"I realize," Griggs said, "that Mrs. Meredith is under a certain amount of strain right now. However—"

"A certain amount?" Michael interrupted.

"A *great deal*? Is that better?" He turned to David and Kate. "So this isn't going to be easy, not for either of you. It isn't easy for me." He reached into his pocket, pulled out a stick of white Wrigley's, unwrapped it, put it in his mouth.

The cat appeared from behind the sofa, circling its way about the room, meowing neurotically at the newcomers.

"You see, I'm just as concerned about the baby as you are. Of course, I could have waited until you returned to El Paso, talked to you there, but I didn't know how long you were going to be gone, and unfortunately there's the matter of time involved." He grinned. "I probably sound like some

Hollywood producer, huh? But the fact of the matter is that in this particular case, for me at least, and for Mr. Kavanaugh, time *is* money." The grin vanished. "I'm an investigator, Mr. Meredith; from Washington."

David's eyes widened.

"No, no," Griggs laughed, the gum showing, "not *that* kind, not with the Feds or anything. That's not to say the association hasn't proved expeditious in the past—but that's not me. I'm private. I work solo, and I'm working right now. That's why I'm here."

Rachel entered just then with a tray of steaming coffee mugs, set them on the table, handed one to each of them. Kate refused. David wished Rachel had brought something stronger. He wasn't sure his stomach could handle the coffee, but it sure could handle four or five fingers of bourbon—and he felt he would need it because he was thinking, Oh, Jesus, this business of Griggs's has something to do with Brian, and it may be that someone found out about the arrangement with Dr. Murchison. . . .

Kate looked at him. He was pretty certain she was thinking the same thing: she was almost trembling. Michael stood up slowly, as if to stretch his legs, and made his way over to the fire.

"I can guess what's going through both your minds. And again let me suggest that you come with us now and—"

"Go on," David said.

Griggs leaned back, stopped chewing, and finally let it out: "The baby's adopted, isn't that right?"

Calm, David thought, be calm and for God's sake don't be impetuous— on the other hand, don't hesitate so long the guy *knows* you're shaken. He paused for a beat, looked Griggs squarely in the face and said, "No."

Griggs let go an imperceptible smile, but David caught it, and he wanted to maintain the dead-eye stare but somehow he couldn't; he lowered his eyes for a moment, fully intending to bring them back to direct an angry focus on the man, but before he could even blink, Griggs said, "I'm speaking literally, of course. *Legally*, if you will. Are you saying that the baby asleep in that room is legitimately and legally yours?" His jaw began working again; the black pinheads bore down on David like vengeful laser beams, slicing through skin, muscle, and deception. Before David could answer, Griggs said, "Mr. Meredith, I happen to know that's not quite true."

David didn't take his eyes off the man, not even to observe the expressions on the Perrys' faces, and managed a weak "Oh? I don't understand."

The balding man leaned forward. He said in an even, patient voice, "Let's quit the charade, shall we? We're intelligent people. I already told you that Mr. Kavanaugh and I have just come from El Paso, and it must be obvious to you by now that we didn't go there because of the weather. But if you're not convinced, you can call a Dr. Alfred Murchison and he can verify our visit."

"W-what? I—" from Kate.

"All right, so you talked to my wife's doctor," David said. "So?"

"So we're aware of the arrangement made between yourselves and that shining specimen of the medical profession."

Kate said, "I . . . I don't understand. Brian's our son. . . ."

The expression on Grigg's face went sour at the mention of Brian's name.

"The *infant*," Griggs said, "was not—how shall I say?—placed in your hands through the proper channels."

Proper channels? What proper channels? There *were* no adoption papers involved, only a birth certificate, verifying that Brian was legally—*naturally*—theirs.

"*I* don't understand either," David said. "My wife just told you. Brian's our son, and right now he happens to be ill, and if it's all the same to you we would appreciate it if we could concentrate on getting him to a doctor."

The man winced. "In good time, Mr. Meredith. In good time."

Bastard.

"On the surface," Griggs continued, "the infant appears to be yours. On the surface. Legally, if the birth certificate is to be believed, the infant *is* yours. But appearances can be deceiving, especially when the necessary components in creating the façade fail to play their parts completely. Dr. Alfred Murchison *procured* the infant in question through a midwife by the name of Lydia Mendez. For you and your wife, the timing was understandably convenient. No waiting period. No Welfare Bureau hassles. A legal certificate of birth with your names on it as the infant's birth parents. Presto: a healthy baby boy."

Kate had placed a hand on David's knee, was now gripping him harder.

David shook his head, "I don't know exactly what you want, but I'm afraid you've confused us with someone else, another couple."

Griggs shook *his* head now. Said nothing. His eyes rolled up and over to where Michael was standing by the fire. He wasn't standing there for the warmth, David thought; he hadn't even taken off his coat. Then Griggs glanced at Rachel, who was still sitting on the sofa, not looking at anyone, ineffectively trying to appear outside the conversation. David wondered what Kavanaugh was doing.

"No, Mr. Meredith. We're not mistaken. As I said, you can verify our visit to your doctor's office, if you wish."

"Let's suppose, for the moment, that you're correct, that an arrangement between a doctor and my wife was made. What of it? If that were the case, no harm would have been done. The . . . birth mother . . . wouldn't have given up her child if she hadn't wanted to."

"She might have," added Griggs, "if she had no other choice."

"Brian's our son," Kate repeated.

Griggs shook his head slowly. "No, Mrs. Meredith. The child isn't yours. You made an arrangement with this fellow Murchison, who in turn made the arrangement with Miss

Mendez. Won't you level with me? There's no sense making this harder than it already is. I've told you that I spoke with your doctor, and he told me—"

"He had no right!" Kate screamed.

"He had no choice," Griggs said. "Literally, he had no choice when we told him Mendez would testify—"

"Leave us alone," Kate said, covering her face with her hands.

"I can't do that." Griggs sounded concerned. "I wish I could, really I do."

No, you don't, thought David. You're enjoying every goddamned minute of it. "All right, you talked to Murchison. What of it? What do you mean he had no choice?"

"He couldn't take the chance that such an arrangement with a midwife could become public knowledge."

"This . . . Mendez," David said. "She would talk?"

Griggs nodded. "Midwives, unfortunately, border on the poverty level. I took care of that."

"Bastard."

"You're categorizing most members of my profession, Mr. Meredith. The successful ones, at least. I don't expect you to like me; I simply expect you to hear me out."

"Do we have a choice?"

Griggs said nothing.

Michael had moved away from the fire and approached the sofa where David sat with Kate. He looked at Griggs, then at Kate. "Can I get you anything," he asked her softly. "Some coffee or milk?"

She shook her head.

Michael glanced again at Griggs, stepped back toward the fire.

I'd like to ask both of you a personal and impertinent question," Griggs said, "and I won't blame you if you curse me to hell and back. Do you love the child?"

Kate let out a cry.

"Wait," Griggs said. "Allow me to qualify the question. You are both young, new parents of an adopted child, a child that is not biologically yours. Many such couples find themselves at first wondering why they don't immediately love their adopted children—"

"I don't want to hear this," Kate said. "David, I don't want—"

"Please, Mrs. Meredith. What I'm trying to say is that the inability to 'instantly love' an adopted child is a common occurrence, and that accepting a child as your own takes time—"

"*We love Brian!*" Kate cried. "Is that what you want to hear?"

Griggs shook his head. "No, Mrs. Meredith. That's precisely what I didn't want to hear. I expected it, however. You see, I had hoped that during the past few months, each of you might have, on occasion, possessed a mild case of self-doubt, in which case my task would be much easier. You do realize, don't you, that *physically* you are quite capable of conceiving another child?"

"Enough," David said. "Cut the bullshit. What is it you *want?*"

Griggs's face grew stern. "Quite simply, Mr. Meredith, I want your baby."

Jesus Christ, David thought. The explanation of Griggs's presence had hung far back in David's mind, had hovered there dangerously close to conscious acceptance, but never close enough for him to formulate into words. And now the words had been spoken.

Rachel gasped, said something David couldn't make out.

Michael turned, his face blank.

Kate gripped David tighter, her mouth open, unable to speak. Then: "David? . . ." She didn't look at him, she was still facing Griggs. ". . . David? . . ."

He didn't know what to say. He felt he should lash out at the man, scream at him, lunge at him, anything. But he was so overwhelmed that he could do nothing but sit there and finally shake his head, sighing, frustrated. . . .

"I represent the child's grandfather," Griggs was saying. "And I'm prepared to fully compensate you for the loss."

. *fully compensate you for the loss?* . . . The man was insane. How could he *compensate* for the loss of one's son? . . .

"I was hoping," Griggs said, "to better prepare you psychologically for this, but I don't know if such a thing was really possible. I hope that before you speak you will try to understand the feasibility of such a proposition. As I said, Mrs. Meredith is quite capable of conceiving another child, and if she chooses not to, there is always the option of legal adoption. The point is that the child's grandfather wants the baby back. And he's willing to pay handsomely in order to compensate you for the loss. He's not willing to wait, however. Mr. Kavanaugh and I must be back in Washington on Monday—with the grandson."

David shook his head, held Kate tighter. "You . . . can't . . . you can't do this. . . . "

Griggs said nothing. His eyes were focused at a point behind David— possibly at Kavanaugh.

"You're lying," David said. "You don't even know who the child's parents are. They don't tell you—"

"*They*, Mr. Meredith, refers to the Child Welfare Bureau. But you didn't go through them. We're dealing with an exceptional circumstance. I know full well who the child's parents were."

"Were?"

Griggs leaned back, signed. "I'd prefer to stop here. You needn't know anything about the parents or my client. As I said earlier, there is a time factor involved. Not a self-imposed limit but one placed on me by my client. I'm authorized to give you a cashier's check for thirty-five thousand dollars. In return I place the child with a blood relative who will give him the care and love he needs."

Kate's nails dug deep into David's knee. She looked up, glaring at the detective. "He already has that!"

"I don't doubt that for a minute. But knowing now that the child does have living kin who want him back, won't you agree that this move would be the best thing for him?"

"No," David said. "We don't know anything about your client—"

"Understandable. Quite so. Do you want to know?"

Silence.

"Do you want to know?" he repeated.

"No," David said.

"Will you accept the check, then?"

"No."

Griggs's mouth tightened. He looked defeated for a moment, then pulled himself up in the chair. "Then let me tell you about your baby's birth parents."

Kate shook her head quickly. "I don't want to know."

"It might help," Griggs said, "if you knew the whole story. Perhaps you'd change your mind."

"Let her alone," Michael said from the corner. "She doesn't want to know."

Griggs stood, faced Michael. Ignoring the demand, he took a stand by the wall next to the sofa. "The child's mother, surreptitiously, along with three of her friends, had been traveling hurriedly south from Washington. They made their way through Virginia, Kentucky, were spotted in Little Rock and then in Tulsa, all the time trying to keep their identities and whereabouts unknown. Eventually they started down into Texas, finally crossing the Mexican border at Reynosa, their destination. After hanging around in Mexico for a while, they crossed back into Texas. This time they were identified by border-patrol agents. Before they could be detained, however, they took off. After a high-speed chase, they managed to elude police near McAllen, Texas. A week or so later they ended up in El Paso. They hadn't planned on stopping there; they had decided by that time to abort crossing back into Mexico at El Paso and instead continue north, toward the Canadian border. But the girl was pregnant, and suddenly she found herself ready to deliver the child. Finally the baby came, delivered by a midwife whose name she had received while traveling underground. You see, the girl was on the run, a fugitive from justice. And once the baby was born, there was no way she and her friends could care for it, what with the FBI in every state looking for them. So they ended up at Miss Mendez's hellhole of an apartment in south El Paso. The baby was delivered and, because time was running against them, they took off north right away—"

"You can't know this," David protested, but Griggs ignored him, continuing—

"—When the girl reached Orogrande, New Mexico, she telephoned her father. It was the last phone call she would make. She was terribly upset and depressed by the fact that she had had to abandon the child; she wanted it desperately. She told her father where the child had been delivered, and by whom, and her last wish was that her father would find the child and look after it, give it a proper home. She died shortly after the phone call, and a few days later her father hired me to locate the midwife who'd made the delivery. She led us to Murchison and he led us to you." He paused, glanced around the room. His jaw had ceased working on the gum and he looked at David thoughtfully. "The mother's name was Barbara Melchor."

12

GRIGGS WAS looking down upon them, waiting, watching for the reaction—the fallout from his bombshell.

"You may not believe me," he said. "But it's true. Senator Richard Melchor hired me to locate and bring back the child his daughter had to abandon. I'm sure you know who the father was. Although word never got out about Miss Melchor's pregnancy, or the fact that she gave birth, the papers had a field day playing up her affair with Mark Van Pelt."

Kate could not control the crying. She clutched her stomach, rocking on the sofa as if she were about to be sick. David stopped her, squeezed her close to him and brushed back strands of hair that had fallen across her face.

"Mrs. Meredith," Griggs said, "I realize this is a shock. I've been stumbling over my own words in an effort to explain the situation as delicately and as gradually as possible. Senator Melchor, you should know, is not a well man. You see, he blames himself, in a large degree, for his daughter's death. Oh, don't mistake me—we all know how the highway patrol shot up the place—could have even been one of their bullets that hit that gas pump; but the Senator places the burden of the guilt upon himself and his wife, years before any of this began."

"Why have you done this?" David asked numbly. "Why couldn't you have let us alone? He doesn't want the baby."

"On the contrary. He's obsessed with that child. Thinks of nothing else, day and night. What most people don't realize is that Melchor and his daughter were extremely close at one time. They went everywhere together; he would take her to work, show her off, they were inseparable. She was a beautiful girl, and he spoiled her rotten. Then, of course, she met Van Pelt, started in with the drugs—that was later.

"After that, things fell apart. You know the rest from the papers. But—" Griggs stepped closer to the sofa. "—What you don't know is that—according to Melchor, anyway—his daughter was about ready to give herself up, as well as play informer. That's right. She and Melchor—contrary to public knowledge—had, prior to the Orogrande incident, kept in close contact. The newspapers, you may recall, quoted Melchor as saying that Barbara had called him shortly before the shoot-out, saying she wanted to come home. They didn't say *why* she wanted to. It was because of the child—and her growing distrust of Van Pelt. She wanted the baby back, though. And the thing is, Van Pelt never knew what she was up to. If he had, he would have shot her right there at that phone booth before those highway patrolmen got to them. Barbara Melchor was going to blow the whistle on all of Van Pelt's drug dealings—his contacts here and in Mexico. Supposedly, she had pulled herself together, quit the whole drug scene. And then a couple of off-duty patrolmen open fire and kill them all. That's how Senator Melchor sees it. To this day he is convinced that his daughter would somehow have escaped Van Pelt and his gang if she'd only been given half a chance.

"Anyway, the sordid details aside, Melchor wants to fulfill his daughter's last wish. He wants the child. He's willing to pay for him, as I told you, but he's not willing to wait. I told you he was obsessed. Either I deliver the boy within the allotted time or he gets himself another man. And I must tell you that I haven't come all this way to go back empty-handed. Now—what do you say?"

Kate was sobbing uncontrollably now, her breath coming in quick, hard gasps. David's brain felt like an overloaded circuit. Too much too fast. His eyes took in the Perrys in turn, scanned the den, stopped for a moment to let the flames of the fire play upon his vision like a hypnotist's swinging gold watch, then blinked at the cat as it curled up in a corner of the room, oblivious to everything but the paw he was licking.

What do you say? the man had asked.

Goddamnit, what the hell *could* he say?

But when the time came, it wasn't David who spoke. Kate raised her head. She was still shaking, her cheeks red and glistening. Slowly, she pulled apart her arms, which had been clutching her sides, and stared up at Griggs through glossy, blinking eyes. David was about to pull her to him, to comfort her, but it was too late for that.

"*No!*" she screamed at the top of her lungs. "Goddamn you, *NO!*"

And then before David knew what was happening, Kate had risen from the sofa and was lunging for Griggs.

"He's *mine!* You can't take my baby away, goddamn you! You *can't!*"

She went for the detective, her flailing arms striking anywhere, everywhere. Griggs backed off and David rushed to his feet, tried to secure Kate's arms. The abusive screams had ceased now and she had given herself up to painful sobs. David became aware suddenly of Rachel, moving off the sofa and toward them. She took Kate into her arms, said something to comfort her, but Kate continued, "They can't take away my baby, they can't take away . . ."

"All right," Rachel said. She glared at Griggs, then said to Kate, "Come with me, that's all right, come with me."

She led Kate down the hall into one of the rooms.

When the crying was all but inaudible in the background, David turned back to the detective.

No one spoke.

Michael was still standing by the fire. His eyes were fixed on the detective, burning.

Eventually Griggs spoke.

"Look . . ." he began, his hands spread. "I'm sorry about your wife. It's unfortunate. I didn't know she'd take it this way. . . ."

"How the hell did you expect her to take it?" David said. He backed away from Griggs and fell to the sofa, his body and mind numb. His ears barely picked up the faint, muffled cries from the back bedroom. For the moment he wasn't even aware of the two detectives or of Michael standing quietly by the fire. Through the numbness in his brain pierced a single, terrifying thought. *This was it, it had to be, the final, crucial blow to send Kate over the edge forever.* . . . Too damn many setbacks . . . and now this . . . the bottom falling out . . .

A form moved before him; it was Griggs crossing to the chair, sitting down. When the detective's angular frame was seated, David expected to see Michael standing behind the chair, but he had moved off beyond the fire.

"Your wife will be fine, I'm sure," Griggs was saying. His jaw began working again. The tiny black dots that were eyes flashed, settled on David. A sound came from behind, and David turned this time—he couldn't stop himself—and watched Kavanaugh shift the weight of his bulky body, maintaining his stance by the door.

"Consider this, Meredith," Griggs continued. "How about if I can guarantee your name doesn't get stuck way down the list of applications for adoption? I'm talking legally now, if you decide to try an agency. You won't have all that waiting. Now, don't ask me how I can do it; but remember, Mr. Melchor will do about anything to . . . compensate, you know. . . ."

"*Compensate?*" David said. "Jesus . . ." And then, in the most determined, peremptory tone he could command, he said, "No."

There was a long silence. Griggs fidgeted. One hand moved up, stroked his jaw. His eyes shot past David toward the front door. Kavanaugh cleared his throat. Something moved on the sofa next to David, brushed against him; he saw the cat quietly inspect the cushion below him and then curl into a small gray ball.

" 'No' what?" Griggs said. " 'No'—you don't want the advantage when applying for adoption?"

"I mean 'no.' To everything."

The detective shifted uncomfortably. "My turn, is it? Okay, I'll play my next card. Fifty-five thousand."

David took a deep breath, said again, "no."

"I'm afraid I'm not authorized to inflate the sum any more without consulting with my client."

"Fuck Melchor."

"Are you trying to tell me you don't need fifty-five grand? I'm talking about an infant that isn't even yours—"

"I told you no," David said again, tired of hearing the word.

"But what about the kid? He's sick, right? This way, we'll take him down, get him to a doctor—"

"*I'll* get him to a doctor. We'll get down from here somehow."

He thought he heard a muffled laugh behind him and

turned around. Kavanaugh hadn't moved. But before David had turned back around he caught a quick but full glimpse of the burly man's stained and rumpled excuse for a tweed jacket. He'd noticed earlier that Kavanaugh was hefty with fat, but from this angle he thought he saw a bulky outline near the left armpit. David had criticized his imagination for running amok, for thinking these two jerks might actually be hiding guns—but that was before he learned they were detectives. . . .

Griggs rose slowly from the chair, held out his hands. "Don't you see it all yet, Meredith? Don't you see the kind of position your Dr. Murchison is in? That Mexican midwife is ready to tell everything for a couple of grand, and Murchison's wondering if he'll have a practice once this hits the ethics board. You see, I've got his hands tied."

David shook his head. "I don't care. You're talking about my son. If I have to, I'll . . ." He didn't finish; he couldn't, and Griggs knew it.

"You'll what? Go to the Child Welfare people? The police? You'd expose yourself?" He shook his head. "You'd be cutting your own throat. Christ, once the CWB finds out how you got the child, it will get custody of him before you know what's happening."

"The birth certificate—"

"—won't be worth anything when this thing goes to court and Mendez testifies—"

"—it'll be her word against Murchison's—"

"—not so. I thought I made that clear. She's got more than enough evidence to discredit Murchison."

Jesus . . .

The windows banged in their frames, shaken by another blast of wind.

He has *your* hands tied too, David thought.

"You've got to understand, Meredith, what kind of man the Senator is. I say this off the record, of course, and Mr. Kavanaugh can vouch for my observation, but the Senator, well, he really isn't himself anymore. He's throwing his entire soul into the search for his grandson, and it's . . . how can I say? . . . it's diminished his mental faculties, as well as his health. I told you before that he is an obsessed man—I mean, why else would he demand the return of a child within so many days, stipulate such an unreasonable time limit?—and he thinks of nothing else day and night—except, of course, when he begins to drink. . . . Well, I shouldn't be saying this, but I think you should know the extent to which he'll go; he believes that that child is the last thing left of him here on earth. He doesn't even talk to his wife anymore."

"The *child,*" David said sarcastically, "has been ours for the past three months, and is going to stay ours. I don't know Mr. Melchor. I don't know who his daughter was, I just forgot. Give me some time and I won't even remember who *you* are."

Griggs signed, took a few steps forward. "You've forced me to play my last card, Meredith. I wouldn't have to, you understand, if you would just accept the best offer of your life. Instead, you'd rather be stubborn and foolish. I mean, hasn't it occurred to you yet that Melchor's *throwing* his money away on you? He doesn't have to feel obligated to compensate you and your wife *at all*. Because ultimately you have no choice. No choice at all." He was moving toward David now, coming around the sofa.

David sat frozen. He didn't turn his head, but his eyes followed Griggs as the detective approached. When he was five or six feet directly before him, he stopped. David hadn't taken his eyes off the angular, balding man; and at this distance his nostrils picked up the flowery stench of cheap cologne.

"You lose everything, then," Griggs said. "The money too. Because we're taking the child."

David heard Kavanaugh's footsteps come to a halt close behind the sofa.

Griggs unbuttoned his coat.

Omigod, I was right, they do have guns—

—and Griggs's hand inched deeper into his coat, and David really knew what helpless meant now, he just sat there—the cat uttering an annoyed meow at the figure closing in on its private space—wondering if they might all be dead in a couple of minutes, because if Griggs decided to kill them all it wouldn't make any difference to Melchor, since the bodies would never be found, not up here in the middle of nowhere, and—

"Please don't move."

The voice came from the other side of the den.

"Please don't either of you make the slightest movement."

The hand stopped inside the coat. From the look on Griggs's face, David thought that the detective was debating whether or not to quickly complete the reach for the gun and swing around; but evidently he decided against it, perhaps because of something in the tone of the voice that had made the command, or simply because he wasn't one to take unnecessary risks. He stopped his hand and began removing it from beneath the coat.

"Slowly. Very, very slowly."

Griggs started to turn his head.

"Slowly. Turn around slowly and take your hand out even slower. You too."

That to Kavanaugh, David thought; evidently he hadn't already drawn his gun.

When Griggs had turned halfway around, David could see Michael standing by the case in the corner, the bow in his hands drawn, the long gold shaft of the arrow pointed straight at Griggs.

"What the hell—" Griggs said.

"This is an Alaskan hunting bow," Michael interrupted, "with a drawing weight of fifty pounds, and with a razorhead arrow at nearly full draw, aimed directly at your side. Turn farther, please."

Griggs did, his back now to David.

"Now the arrow is pointed directly at your breast. If Mr. Kavanaugh would remove his hand from his coat, I'd feel a lot better."

David turned and watched Kavanaugh drop his hand to his side.

Griggs stood rock still.

"If you want to," Michael said to Griggs, "You could try going for the gun. But I should tell you that I'm very accurate with this thing. Of course, the strain is getting to me now, I can't keep the draw forever. And if I let go, this aluminum arrow will cross the room at about two hundred feet per second. If my aim is good—and as I said, I'm very accurate—the razor-edged broadhead will shatter your breastbone on impact, probably puncture your heart, and cause an awful lot of bleeding. You'll be alive, Mr. Griggs, long enough to hear the sound of the shaft through the air and feel the shock of the impact before the loss of oxygen to your brain causes you to black out. But you'll probably be dead before you hit the sofa."

"You're crazy," Griggs said.

"Yes, and my right arm is growing very weak. I don't know how much longer I can hold the draw—"

"All right, all right," Griggs said. "Jesus." He slowly withdrew his hand completely from inside the coat.

David stood up.

"Mr. Meredith, if you would take those guns . . ."

Stunned, David pulled aside the detective's coat, reached in, cautiously felt around until he found the leather bulk that was the holster, then the stiff wooden grip of the gun, and pulled it out. He held it awkwardly, his fingers clenched around the walnut checkering on the handle, and for just a second stared at the damn thing as if it were a live explosive—and it was, potentially. David didn't know much about guns, but he knew enough to know that this was an automatic, and didn't automatics go off, sometimes, when you didn't want them to? He pointed the barrel down, switched the gun to his left hand, rounded the sofa to where Kavanaugh stood with a scowl on his face. When he reached inside for the gun, the heavy man mumbled something to Griggs.

"Mr. Kavanaugh seems to exhibit little concern for your health," Michael said.

Griggs turned, looked fearfully at his partner, his eyes pleading for Kavanaugh to make no hasty moves.

David searched, removed a smaller gun, a revolver, then walked back around the sofa. He was standing before Griggs, closer than he had ever been to the man. The smooth, pale face reeked of cologne; the eyes remained fearful, but the twisted lips spoke rage. David wanted to land one hard blow dead center.

Michael sighed. The right arm that had drawn the string relaxed, releasing the tension of the draw. But he continued holding the bow vertically in his left hand and pointing the arrow at Griggs.

"That's better," he said.

"Meredith," Griggs said, "Can't you see the absurdity of this? This isn't doing you any good. Why don't you tell your friend here to put that thing down, and we can talk about . . . alternatives? . . . "

"Alternatives?" David said. "What alternatives? I thought I didn't have any."

"Maybe we can work something out."

"Such as?"

"A . . . mutual agreement."

"Fine. Such as?"

"I shoulda pounded your ass," Kavanaugh said, then looked at Griggs. "You shoulda let me."

David looked at the guns in his hands.

"Why don't you put that thing down?" Griggs called to Michael. "You got our guns. We aren't going anywhere."

"That's entirely up to Mr. Meredith."

David thought a moment.

"Come on, Meredith."

David looked toward the back hallway. What if Kate and Rachel were to come out now? And now that he had these two creeps, what was he going to do with them?

You're going to get rid of the bastards.

He switched the guns in his hands, placed the revolver on the end table. In his right hand he raised the automatic and, careful to keep his index finger just off the trigger, aimed the gun at Griggs. Then he turned to Michael, nodded. Michael lowered the bow.

"You were wrong," David told the detective.

"What?"

"You *are* going somewhere." He raised the gun higher, pointing it at the man's head. "You're both going out that door. But first—" He held out one hand. "—the keys."

"Now, look, Meredith—"

"The keys, damnit."

Griggs reluctantly reached into his trouser pocket, handed David the car keys.

"*Now,*" David said, "you're going out the door."

Griggs hesitated. "You sure you don't want to just . . . *talk*? . . ."

"Would it change things? *Any*thing?"

There was a long pause. Finally, Griggs shrugged and turned, headed for the door, reached slowly for the knob.

But just as he did, Kavanaugh's huge arm came from out of nowhere, crashing down across David's forearm. The gun hit the floor. Griggs spun around and went for David at the same time that Kavanaugh dived to the floor, scrabbling for the gun. With a swift kick, David sent the gun clattering a yard further down the hall.

Griggs was on him now, tearing at his throat, trying to make it down the hall to the gun. David thrust up his arms, blocking the detective's blows, and then turned and went for Kavanaugh—but Kavanaugh had too much of a lead, he was almost to the gun—

—but just before the big hand pounced on the weapon, there was a flash, and the thick arm jerked back, accompanied by a scream of pain.

"Jesus Christ!" Kavanaugh cried. He was clutching his arm ferociously, and David now saw the blood spreading through the big fingers. An arrow was sticking from the leg of the entry table against the wall.

David registered this.

He also registered a movement from the left corner of his eye—Griggs—bounding for the end table.

But the leap, the timing were impossible.

David was too close; he jumped to the right, scooped up

the automatic, and aimed it at the rushing man.

"Hold it," he said.

Griggs caught himself, froze. His eyes darted to the end table where the revolver lay, and he was perhaps considering his chances of reaching it, but he remained frozen. The end table was too far away, and besides, Michael was standing in the middle of the den now; he had placed another arrow in the bow and was aiming it toward the front hallway.

Kavanaugh stumbled to his feet, blood dripping and hitting the wooden floor in tiny red splotches. He appeared to be in a state of shock. Jesus, David thought, Michael was right, he *was* good with that thing. The arrow had sliced just through the fat of Kavanaugh's arm, traveling on until it hit the table.

"You'll live," Michael said from the den.

David was trembling. Even standing there with the advantage definitely back on his side, holding the gun on the detective, he still shook. He thought he had sounded convincing earlier when he'd ordered the two men out; he thought he'd gotten the message across that *I mean business;* he'd felt certain he had scared them. And maybe he had scared Griggs, but Kavanaugh was stupid—a big silly mindless goon who probably didn't know the meaning of fear.

And that scared David. He wanted *both* of these creeps out of his life forever.

He stepped forward.

"Easy, Meredith," Griggs said.

David turned from Griggs, approached Kavanaugh, stopped within two feet of the big man. He placed the barrel between Kavanaugh's eyes, firmly into the skin at the top of his nose. He deliberately made his hand shake—just a little, enough to show this fat slob that here was one nervous sonofabitch who was holding a loaded gun right between his eyes and if he blinked it might scare him enough to jerk back on the trigger.

He pressed the tip of the barrel deeper into the skin until it was making a strong indentation. The detective's eyes were growing bigger, his lips drew back tight. David clenched his teeth and pressed even deeper. He was about to say something—not that he thought it would do any good, because even now he doubted this little display of force could faze the stubborn oaf, but he was about to say something when he heard a soft, quick "My God."

He turned around, keeping the gun pressed into the wide forehead.

Rachel was standing in the entranceway to the back hall.

She just stood there. His eyes questioned hers, and for a moment she simply remained there dazed, then turned and went back down the hall.

David turned to Kavanaugh, lowered the gun, stepped back. "Now—out the door. Slowly."

Griggs crossed to the door, opened it. Snow swirled into the room, along with a freezing blast of wind. It was dark outside. Kavanaugh, clutching his bleeding arm, glowered at David, then trailed sluggishly out.

David picked up the battery on the table, held it with one arm against his side. He turned to Michael, asked him if he would really miss the old Lincoln. Michael smiled, shook his head. Then David told him to pick up the revolver on the end table and follow them.

13

IN THE cold, cramped garage, David handed the automatic to Michael and said, "If they move, kill them."

He had ordered the two detectives to stand against the wall at the back. Because the garage was so small, and the space on either side of the Lincoln so narrow, it was highly unlikely that either of the men could charge the length of the place and get near Michael before he could get a couple of shots off.

David worked with the battery. He could see right away that the battery from the Malibu wouldn't fit right, but that didn't mean he couldn't connect the terminals and tie the box down.

Which was what he did. He found some rope and secured the battery in the engine block; then, because the damn thing was sticking up above the hood, he tied down the hood with some more rope, but only after he'd taken the key from Michael, inserted it into the ignition, turned.

The lincoln hummed. It whined. It coughed. It didn't want to start at all. *I'm old,* it seemed to say, *let me alone, I don't want to start, this is my grave and I want to lie right here as I have all these years—*

—start, you sonofabitch, David thought—

—again the engine coughed, choked, rumbled; but then the rumbling got louder, steadier, until pretty soon the thing feebly came to life—not enjoying it, perhaps, but coming to life anyway, rumbling hesitantly at first, and then as David gave it more gas, it didn't hesitate at all, just roared loudly, and David thought he heard Griggs say something from the wall.

He got out of the car, looked at the two men.

"You're not serious, Meredith," Griggs shouted above the roar. "You can't be serious." He was coughing himself now because of the fumes, the exhaust.

David took the automatic from Michael, motioned for the two men to come forward, get into the car.

They moved around the Lincoln. Michael opened the passenger door for Kavanaugh, ordered him in.

"Can't we just talk—" Griggs began.

"Get in the car." David began to shake. It was cold, sure, but he was shaking because he wondered if he really had the guts to pull the trigger if it became necessary.

Griggs got into the car, closed the door.

David stepped out of the garage, motioned with the end of the gun for Griggs to roll forward, which he did, then stop.

Griggs rolled down the window.

"Look, Meredith—"

"You look. I'm going to watch you until I see these taillights far down the mountain—"

"My God, Meredith, this car won't last that long, there're no chains—"

"That's right, no chains, and the tires are old, and you're going to be lucky if you get down alive, but I can tell you one thing: you won't make it back up in this junk heap, I know that. I know you'll make it down, but not back up."

"What about *my* car?"

"I'll leave it in Ruidoso for you to pick up tomorrow, I'll park it at some service station, you'll find it, I don't want your car, I just want to get my son to a doctor and then I want to go home, that's what I want, you understand?"

"Think about it a second, Meredith. I told you about Melchor, he's obsessed, this isn't going to stop him. What am I going to tell him?—"

"You can tell him that his daughter's baby was born sick. Real sick. Tell him that it died, you did all you could, but it was too late, the baby died—"

"Aw—?'

"*Tell him that it died!*" David shook violently. He'd had his fill of these two bastards. He shook more when he felt his finger tighten around the cold metal trigger. He brought the gun closer to Griggs's face. "Tell him whatever the hell you want to, but make him believe it, because if I ever—*ever*—see your face again I'll—" He stuck the gun closer. "—I'll blow your goddamned head off!"

"Easy with that, Meredith, you don't know how—"

"Drive."

Griggs looked at him a moment as if he were crazy, then sighed, shook his head, put the car into gear, drove slowly down the rise, sliding over the snow and ice until the car hit the road. David and Michael followed them on foot until the old purple Lincoln reached the brown Ford. Griggs had difficulty maneuvering the car around on the narrow road, and as the Lincoln rolled past the LTD, the two cars scraped sides, but finally Griggs eased the old car past, and David stood in the middle of the road and watched the unsteady monster cut uncertainly through the snow. He knew that if Griggs wasn't careful, the car would slide off the road, the old Lincoln was that wobbly with those nearly bald tires—and of course there was no way David was about to mention to Griggs that the chains to the tires were sitting in a box in Michael's garage.

He watched as the taillights rounded the curve below. The car fishtailed as it came out of the turn, and David smiled: it would be impossible for them to make it back up once they were down.

He continued watching as the taillights now appeared far in the distance, tiny red specks in the night. Then he headed off down the road.

"Where you going?" Michael called.

David didn't answer him but kept on down the road, the wind not blowing as strongly as it had earlier, but still cutting through his clothes, chilling him. The snow spotted his face with moisture, and he was wondering if he should continue, but he did, he kept walking until he could see the road curving far below. He watched for the tiny red lights in the distance, but he couldn't see them. He stood there for a long time, snow pelting his face, eyes burning. And then finally something flashed below and he saw the lights of the Lincoln far in the distance, and he was certain now that the two detectives had descended past any point where it might be even conceivable for them to begin back up. There was just no way.

But he waited a little longer, still watching, until the lights were barely visible, until the Lincoln had curved around another and then another bend, finally descending out of sight.

Then he felt in his pocket, withdrew the keys to the Ford, jingled them in his frozen hand. We can go home now, he thought.

14

BRIAN LAY asleep in the small bedroom. Heat from the lower duct had insulated the room from the cold outside, lending the place a mellow, secure warmth.

Kate sat in a ranch-style chair in the corner, weeping silently.

David went over, sat on the corner of the bed before her.

"They're gone."

She looked at him through red, puffy eyes. "They're not taking our baby." Her voice was weak, about to crack, but beneath the weakness lay determination and anger.

David shook his head. "No. No one's going to take him."

Then her voice cracked, the strength and anger gone suddenly as she said, "Why has all this happened? Why, David? . . ."

Their eyes locked; he saw the confusion and desperation in the normally bright brown ovals. The look was familiar, it sent through his mind a fearful déja vu, and for a second he was back in the hospital, bending over her bed and looking into the same questioning eyes, and the eyes saying to him "Why?—after all our planning, all the hope. Why did this have to happen?" That's what she had said a few days before he'd discovered the half-empty bottle on the nightstand—

—stop it—an accident—Murchison said so, an accident.

He now looked into those same pleading eyes, realizing that he had not yet answered her, and realizing too that he couldn't because he didn't know the answer. He lowered his head, shook it. Kate wiped a Kleenex across her nose.

"Dr. Murchison said—" she began.

David held up his hands. "That doesn't matter anymore. It's beyond his control. We have no legal grounds." He explained briefly, delicately, what had happened after she had left the room.

"But he's *our* baby," Kate said.

David nodded. Then: "It doesn't bother you, change things, knowing what they said?"

She shook her head. "They're lying." She got up, went to the bed, sat down next to Brian. "He's ours. They're wrong; they're lying."

He joined her at the bed, placed a hand gently on her shoulder and slowly turned her so that he could see her face. She *wanted* to believe they were lying: but how long could she delude herself?

He lowered his voice so as not to wake the baby. "No, Kate. They weren't lying." And before she had time to either turn away angrily or spill more tears, he added, "But it doesn't change things. He's our son, isn't he?"

She bent her head and began weeping again. Long, intense sobs. That's all right, he thought: Cry. Cry until you can't any longer. But for God's sake—Jesus, Kate, for all our sakes—hang in there, this isn't anything we can't handle, somehow we'll get through, we have in the past and we will now, so please don't fade on me, Kate, hang in there *please*. . . .

Then he showed her the keys, told her about the car.

"It's outside?" she said hopefully.

"Just where they left it. I'll need to bring it around."

"We can leave now?"

He nodded. "If you feel—"

"Yes, now, I'll get—"

"Wait," he said, holding her. "I want you to calm down; this isn't going to be easy."

She nodded slowly.

He held her like that a moment, then said, "Okay. You wrap Brian up and I'll go get the car, bring it up."

Again she nodded, and David left her, went into the den.

Michael was walking in the front door, carrying a couple of logs, just as David started out.

"We're going to need lots of this tonight," he said, taking the logs to the grate, setting them down. "Where are you going?"

"To get their car."

Michael looked surprised. "You're going to try leaving tonight?"

David said yes.

"You'll never make it. I don't think *they* can make it. Why don't you start in the morning?"

David opened the door. "I've got to try tonight."

Michael sighed, took a flashlight from the mantel, started for the door. "I'll go with you."

David got inside, put the key in the ignition, turned.

And nothing happened.

"What's the matter?" Michael asked from the open driver's side.

"Don't know." He tried again, pressing the edge of the key tight into his index finger. Nothing. The car didn't start, it didn't do anything. It was as dead as the old Lincoln had been.

"Any gas?" Michael asked.

Jesus Christ, David wanted to scream, of *course* there's gas, I'm looking right at the goddamned dashboard, I'd *know* if there wasn't any gas, and besides, those two guys weren't stupid enough to start up here without gas, they even had *chains*, for Chrissakes, and David shuddered when he reminded himself again about how smart those two goons were.

But something was wrong with their car.

He got out, opened the hood, looked around in the light from Michael's flashlight.

After a while he said, "Goddamnit! Goddamn those sonsofbitches!"

Because the fucking distributor cable was gone. Jesus Christ, they'd taken the fucking distributor. *When? Why?*

"What is it?" Michael asked.

"They took the damn distributor."

"What's that?"

"That was our last hope of getting down," David said, but he was thinking about that balding, unctuous Laurence Griggs, smooth-talking sonofabitch, *Christ!* And his eyes searched out over the mountainside, but he knew they'd gone, those bastards, they couldn't have come back, so they must have taken the damn thing before they had started up the hill to the Perry cabin, maybe a safety precaution, a procedure Griggs went through all the time, a habit—hell, Griggs didn't get to where he was by taking chances. Probably Kavanaugh had slipped the thing out when they were starting up the mountain—he'd been at the tail end, after all—*goddamnit*, and that was why Griggs had sighed and driven off so—what?—so confidently? All the time he'd been protesting, stalling, asking why they couldn't talk things over again, all that time he knew David would get nowhere in their car. Shit. And what was Griggs thinking about all that time? There was no way he and Kavanaugh could make it back tonight, that David knew, so did that smooth sonofabitch figure he'd come after them in the morning?

"What now?" Michael asked.

"I don't know."

And he didn't know.

Maybe that fucking detective thought he'd get a car by morning and come up for them—although that was doubtful, because by then the snow would have buried the entire mountainside—or maybe he planned on waiting for them at the foot of the mountain, asking them when they got down, "Won't you reconsider, Mr. Meredith?"

Well, fuck him, that wasn't going to happen, because by the time Griggs got near this place again, he and Kate would be gone. David would make it down to the clinic—surely it would be open now—and he'd get a chain-equipped ambulance up here to get Kate and the baby. If nothing else, David had the night.

And he would use it.

When he told Kate about the car, he thought she would truly break, fall apart, but strangely enough she sat there on the bed in Brian's room and just stared at him, partly in disbelief, he thought, and partly in resignation, because she knew that once she got her hopes up, they were bound to fall; and so she just stared at him for a long time, then lowered her head and began to weep.

He put both arms around her, wondering what he could say now, realized there was nothing, he would have to wait until she had cried herself out, and then thought that maybe he could get her to drink something, a brandy maybe, just a little to calm her down. He could use something too. He kissed the back of her neck, got up, and went into the den.

Michael was still standing where David had left him, near the sofa on which lay his bow. His wife stood next to him, and before they heard David's footsteps, they had been arguing. Or so David thought. He had caught a brief flare of angry tones as he was coming down the hall. When he came into the den, his first sight was that of Rachel, her hands firmly on her husband's shoulders, eyes wide, lips moving quickly, saying something in hushed but nervous tones; it was Michael's voice, he thought, that had sounded angry. And the two of them were standing extremely close, looking intently into each other's eyes. When they heard, or sensed, David entering the den, the exchange ceased abruptly. They turned to him and Rachel said, "Mr. Meredith. Anything I can do?"

David thought for a second. "I was just wondering . . . do you have anything I could give her to, you know, calm her down? Brandy, liquor of some kind?"

Her face grew sullen. "I'm sorry. We don't keep liquor. But I may have something; come with me."

She turned, headed for the kitchen on the other side. He hesitated a moment before following her, stopped before Michael and said, "I didn't get to thank you for helping me with those two men."

Michael glanced at his bow, then back at David. The tiny vein near his eye leading into the hairline appeared larger in the flickering orange light; the black eyes had lost some of their brilliance, and he looked drained. For a second he looked about to smile. But he didn't. His face grew serious. "I'm sorry about your baby," he said.

David nodded.

Michael looked toward the back hallway.

"They'll be back, you know," he said firmly.

I've cried in my sleep before, she thought.

Her thinking was racked by choking sobs; she could barely breathe. The pain in her chest had become almost unbearable, she could feel her ribs and lungs battered about, and she wondered if the difficulty in breathing wasn't because her lungs were on the verge of collapsing; she fought harder to bring in the air, but there just wasn't time between the moaning sobs. The blood in her head seemed to be bubbling furiously, all of it having gushed to her forehead, her eyes, and the puffy circles below her eyes. *God in heaven* . . . her face was about to explode. . . .

But I've cried in my sleep before, she managed to think as she let out a low, agonizing moan. *I have cried in the middle of the night for the unborn child I had lost and the child I would never have—* so why shouldn't this be just another nightmare, a bad dream? Yes, that's it, a bad dream. Those two men don't exist, they never did, you're imagining this because you can't believe that Brian is really yours—and after all that's happened it's just a little hard to believe that you really have a son, so you're imagining the worst, and those two men weren't here, they don't exist—

—But Jesus God, they do. . . .

She cried harder. Through blurry eyes she made out Brian's tiny sleeping form, and she wondered how much longer he would be asleep with all her crying. Perhaps it was the medicine that allowed him to sleep through all of this. Maybe she should take some too, so she could sleep . . . sleep forever . . . beyond forever . . . for . . .

She felt something on her back. David? Was he still there? Had he been watching her all this time?

It didn't matter. She didn't care. He had seen her like this before.

So she didn't turn but kept crying. She pulled at the soggy, shredded tissue in her hands, brought it to her nose, blotted the wetness from her nostrils; she didn't care about the tears, let them fall, they had already drenched her face and clothes and no doubt the sheet as well.

Again David touched her back, then her shoulder. *What can he want of me now? My God . . .*

Then from out of the corner of her eye she noticed David moving around to her side. She lowered her head into her hands. Please go away, she thought, I can't talk, I can't listen, please let me have this out. . . .

She sensed him standing before her now, just off to the side, and she felt him place a hand on her shoulder.

"Kate?" His voice was barely audible, almost a whisper.

But it wasn't David's voice.

She stifled a sob, blinked a few times, the aching eyelids swimming in large globules of tears as they fought to stay open, and then she raised her throbbing head. Her eyes blinked rapidly now, the light from the bedside lamp flashing prisms of light through the tear-filled pupils, and she strained, focusing her eyes on the face of Michael Perry.

Kate vaguely remembered the man addressing her by her first name earlier this evening, in the den, as she had sat dumbfounded and frightened during the monologue of the tall, slick, balding man standing over them,

(Jesus God, they do exist)

and remembered Michael asking her something, and even then, in the midst of all that fear and agony, she thought it strange that he should use her Christian name.

"Mrs. Meredith?" came the sound from the blurry face, and Kate felt more comfortable when he addressed her that way, because it reminded her of the heavily bundled man who had come upon them in the snow after the car had gone over the edge and had offered to take them to his house—the tone was the same, she thought, not like—

—"Kate?" he said.

—not like the way he'd spoken it just now.

She rubbed the back of her hand across both eyes, wiping away some of the tears, and tried harder to focus the man's face. When she could see him more clearly, she managed to get out a watery "Yes?"

He leaned his arm on the headboard.

"Can I get you anything?"

Kate shook her head, lowered it, ran a couple of fingers under her eyes, catching tears. She didn't want anything, except perhaps for him to leave. Couldn't he see that she didn't need anything and didn't want to talk to anyone?

She heard her name again, the tone of his voice a little clearer now, a little stronger. She looked up.

"Do you mind?" he said, indicating the space on the bed next to her.

My God, did he actually want to sit down? Look at me, she wanted to say, look at my face. Can't you tell that I want to be left alone?

That was what she thought, what she wanted to say. But she hadn't the strength; her whole body ached and was about ready to collapse. So she turned, looked about her absently, then eased back on the bed, farther from the edge, adjusting the covers around Brian and praying he would not wake.

Michael brought himself down gently on the edge of the bed near the headboard, sitting upright, one foot on the side of the frame. Kate looked away from him, her attention on the tiny sleeping form in the middle of the bed. He still seemed to be sleeping soundly; the lesions, though still red, had cleared just a little. She thought she had better rub some more ointment on him, and was about to reach into her purse for the tube when she considered that if she were to touch him now he might wake up, begin crying again, so she decided against it.

"You okay?" he said.

Kate managed, barely, a nod. She saw his hand move toward Brian, toward the blanket, then return.

"Sleep's good for him," he said.

I know that, Kate thought. Won't you please leave me alone?

"You ought to get some yourself," he added.

Simple, mindless amenities. I might *try* to get some if you would go away. Is that all you have to say? Simple, mindless . . . and then she thought, he's only trying to help, offer a little comfort, so why do you feel hostile toward him?

A good question. But she dismissed any notion of probing for an answer because she already knew the answer.

It was his eyes.

She recalled those eyes looking right through her.

But men had looked at her like that before, *eyes that stripped you naked,* she had been there before, no big deal—

—except these eyes looked further than that, *these eyes stripped your soul, your mind*. That was why she felt this way. That, and the instant familiarity in his voice. *Kate? Kate?* It had a strange, reverse effect: her own name was beginning to sound unfamiliar to her.

So won't you please leave me alone?

"You mind me calling you that: Kate?"

She lied and shook her head. Why, she didn't know, except that maybe it was easier than nodding, because then he might ask for an explanation and she wasn't sure she could explain.

She lifted her head to wipe away new tears, and when she did she noticed he was smiling.

"That's good," he said. "I'm glad you don't mind. Some people would, you know. I mean, we haven't known each other long. . . ."

She quivered, perhaps because she was cold; but no, the room was warm, she knew it was.

We haven't known each other long. . . .

A chill went through her.

And we aren't going to know each other, she thought. It would not be possible. Because she and David were leaving this place as soon as they could, they were going home.

Home. She choked out one last sob, began wiping her eyes again.

And Michael Perry placed his hand on her shoulder. Left it there.

"Easy," he said. "You'll be all right."

She lowered her head.

"Look at me," he said softly.

But she didn't want to. She wanted, first, for him to take his hand off her and, second, she wanted him to leave.

He did neither.

"Look at me."

She raised her head, blinking away the tears, trying to get her eyes to focus.

"I didn't know about the baby," he said.

Kate's mouth parted; eyes squinting, she made herself look into his frightening eyes. "Wh . . . what? . . ."

"I mean I didn't know it wasn't yours. You should've told me."

Kate's hand holding the tissue went to her lap. Anger began building insider her, her stomach twisting now, a nausea coming over her as if she were about to get sick. But before she did she thought she would scream.

He must have noticed.

"It's all right, I mean. It doesn't matter."

She held her mouth tight, tried to suppress some of the anger before she spoke because if she didn't she really would scream, and that would surely wake Brian.

"*He's my son,*" she said evenly, but with hatred unmistakably suffusing itself through every syllable.

"All right," he said. "Whatever."

God, what did he want? She didn't need this right now.

"But I wanted you to know about those two men, those two detectives. I stopped them."

She looked at him curiously. David had told her what had happened, basically, but he hadn't gone into any of the details. Not that she wanted to hear them.

"I stopped them," he repeated, smiling. "With my bow.

Wounded the big ugly one. Oh, not seriously, or anything like that, he'll live. But that's just it, that's what I wanted you to know. . . ."

She looked confused.

"Don't you see?" he said. He moved his face closer to hers, his hand still on her shoulder, pressing firmly now. "What I wanted you to know was that *it could have been serious if I'd wanted it to be*."

Kate remained perfectly still. He saw her eyes drift toward her shoulder: he looked at his hand, then self-consciously lifted it away. A frown crossed his face, disappeared; then a smile began to form—not a wide, pleasant smile, but a tight, self-assured grin. He gazed at her expectantly, as if anticipating a response; but Kate said nothing, she was too confused. His black eyes seemed to shine. He leaned even closer.

"Don't you see? I could have killed that guy. Both of them. I had them trapped. David—Mr. Meredith—was sitting there on the sofa, and this slick guy was going toward him, about to reach for his gun, and I could see the ugly one was taking his cue, so I inched—literally *inched*—my way to the case. They were too busy planning their move on Da—your husband, and when they weren't looking I got the bow." He paused. His left hand reached hesitantly outward, toward her, and he touched her shoulder. "There was nothing he could do. Your husband, I mean. This slick guy nearly had his gun out. If he had pulled it out he would have held it on us, all of us—on *you*—and taken the baby right then and there. And if we had tried to stop him he would have shot us all. I know his kind. But he didn't pull it. I stopped him before he could."

There was a long pause now. Kate didn't know what to say. If what he said was true, she should at least thank him. If he had been instrumental in forcing those two men out, didn't he deserve some kind of acknowledgment?

So why didn't she say something?

Because, face it, you're . . . afraid . . . of him. . . . And to thank him, she thought, would establish her as some kind of—of—consort, or something, would somehow bring her into agreement with him, and that, in turn, would somehow bring her closer to him.

And that wasn't possible. They were leaving here, going home; even if that car didn't work, David would get them home some way.

"Kate?" he said. "You're not looking at me. I wish you would, because this is important."

She looked at him. His eyes were very bright now. She considered brushing his hand from her shoulder, but decided against it when she saw the eyes.

And then his hand moved upward, toward her cheek. His palm was touching her hair now. The muscles in her neck tensed. "I . . . please . . ."

"I would have killed them," he said. "I would have killed both of them before I'd let them touch you."

Slowly, he moved his hand back down, brushing lightly against her neck. Kate cringed, her eyes moving with his hand until it rested once again on her shoulder. Jesus . . . her head was spinning . . . what was going on . . . why was he acting, speaking so strangely? . . . She wanted to cry, but she held it in and managed to say weakly, "They don't . . . want . . . me . . . they want . . . my baby. . . ."

Michael's hand tightened on her shoulder. "I don't trust them, Kate. You never know. . . ."

"No, they don't . . ."

"But don't worry. I would have killed them both before I'd let them touch you. And I will, too. . . ."

Kate shivered, forced herself to look directly into his eyes. "Will?"

He nodded. "See that they don't touch you. Because . . . well, I don't want to frighten you, but . . . I think they'll be back. . . ."

It really sent him reeling, it was all so goddamn strange, him sitting there on the bed next to Kate with his goddamn hand on her shoulder. *What the hell?* . . . he wondered, standing there in the doorway, about to enter. Jesus, he felt as if he ought to knock or something. What did Michael think he was doing? It was a cliché scene from a bad movie, David standing there like that, wondering if he should maybe cough or clear his throat or just creep stealthily in and wait to be observed.

Finally, David just walked in. Michael saw him, jerked his hand off her shoulder, and stood up.

"Excuse me," he said. "I was just . . ."

David went to the bed. In one hand he held a half-filled glass of water and in the palm of the other he carried a couple of capsules. He set the water on the night table and held out his open palm to Kate.

"Here," he said.

Michael walked out from behind the bed, hesitated a moment, then left the room.

"What—what are they?" she asked weakly.

"Sleeping pills."

She frowned. "But—"

"Just take one," he said. "Mrs. Perry gave them to me. One won't put you to sleep, it'll just relax you. It looks like we may have to stay here tonight. Later, if you want, you can take the other." He sat on the bed. She had been crying a lot, he thought; her cheeks were bright red, water-stained, raw. He wiped away a tear that was about to fall, then cupped one side of her face in his hand. She bent her head sideways, into his hand, began rocking slowly.

"What . . ." he said, ". . . what was . . ." He didn't finish, but glanced at the door.

Kate suddenly seemed to tense. She pulled her head back slightly. She didn't look at him directly, but stared blankly ahead. "I . . . I don't know. . . . He's . . . I don't know. . . ." She began to shake. David leaned back, handed her the glass of water, took the second pill and placed it on the night table, gave her the other one. She took it, swallowed. He leaned over and kissed her forehead, held her to him. He wanted to say, "Everything's going to be all right," but he couldn't because he wasn't sure he'd be telling the truth, and he never lied to Kate. Maybe he left things out occasionally, but only when he thought it was for her own good, and that was during those . . . bad times . . . and over the past few months he had come to wonder if he had any right to make decisions for her, to decide what was for her own good . . . so he just held her now. He glanced at Brian and saw that he was still asleep, and that meant Kate would be more inclined to lie down for a few minutes herself, get some desperately needed sleep. He could use some himself, but there were things to do. Of course, the next-best thing right now would be a tall bourbon, but Mrs. Perry ("'Rachel,' please," she had said while searching for the pills), Rachel said they didn't have any—no, she'd said, "We don't keep liquor," that was what she'd said. Sounded ominous; maybe she and Michael were ultrareligious types or something. Anyway, he could sure use a drink, Jesus.

And then Kate said softly, "What . . . what are we going to do? . . . David? . . ."

He didn't answer her at first. He was suddenly thinking about what Michael had said about those two guys coming back. There was no way they could, not tonight—however, if they weren't lying dead at the bottom of some ravine, David was sure they'd try making it back in the morning.

"I'm going to try making it to the clinic," he finally said. "Then I'll try to get an ambulance up here and get us down."

"But . . ."

She didn't finish, but he knew what she must be thinking. What if Griggs was waiting for them? A number of things came to mind. If Griggs showed up at the clinic, David could always call the police, try to get the guy locked up somehow, bring charges against him or something. That was unlikely, though. David couldn't go to the police without Griggs spilling the story about Brian—but maybe by then he and Kate would be on their way to El Paso. No, David considered, it was unlikely Griggs would show up at the clinic, because he wouldn't know that David and Kate had already made it down the mountain.

"Don't worry," David said. "We're going to be back in El Paso before anything can happen."

"But that man . . ." Kate said. "He . . . he said Dr. Murchison . . ."

"Murchison told them who we were because he was afraid of what that midwife might say. But I can't believe that, it's probably a ploy of some kind. Trust me, Kate. Dr. Murchison's been around a long time; they can't discredit him that easily. Besides, we've got the birth certificate, remember?"

Kate nodded slowly, not entirely convinced.

"It's her word against Murchison's," David continued. "And What's-her-name—Mendez—can't have that pure a reputation."

And if by some chance she did, David thought, maybe something could be worked out with her, the way Griggs had underhandedly worked something out.

"Look at me," he said, and Kate raised her head reluctantly. "Nobody's going to take our son away, understand? If I have to I'll spend every last cent I have on the best lawyer we can find." He suddenly remembered what Griggs had let slip about Melchor's drinking, his obsession. Jesus, if he had to, David would dig up every goddamned piece of muck he could find on the man, everything that would discredit his name as a fit parent.

Kate turned away, nodding slowly.

"No one," David repeated assuringly, "is going to take Brian. That's a promise."

But the first thing they had to do was get down from here.

David glanced out the window and shuddered just thinking about making the long trek in the cold. He was wondering what he should take with him. Michael could perhaps lend him some warmer clothes, the balaclava he'd been wearing earlier. What else? The gun, of course. He'd take the automatic, leave the revolver for Michael, because Michael would have to stay here, guard the house just in case. And then David suddenly thought about the old shed at the rear of the cabin. Was there anything in there he might be able to use? Christ, if there were a pair of skis in there he could ski down the fucking mountain—except that *he didn't know how to ski*. A sled, maybe? Forget it. His mind was slowly cracking.

He gently released Kate from his embrace, stood up.

"I've gotta go."

Her eyes pleaded with him.

"I want to talk to Michael," he said. He looked at Brian. "He's okay for now. I want you to get some rest."

She started to shake her head.

"Please," he said abruptly. "You need rest, Kate."

She finally nodded, looked at the baby.

"He'll be fine," David said.

She nodded again. She looked worse. The blank, resigned expression on her face looked all too familiar.

David stood for a moment just looking at her, then took a step back. For the first time since Griggs had shown his face at the top of the ridge an hour ago, David was aware of his sodden feet. He wouldn't be surprised if both feet would have to be amputated after what they'd been through. Tonight he'd have to leave the drenched boots by the fire so they'd dry before he set out down the mountain.

He turned to go. He wanted to stay with her, but he knew she needed rest, and she wouldn't rest with him there.

He also wanted to talk to Michael. *(Why was he acting so familiar with Kate? He didn't know her, they'd hardly exchanged a complete sentence. . . .)* It must get to you, David thought; living up here, just the two of them, it must affect one's personality, his sense of perspective. It had to—which would explain Michael's odd behavior. Strange. . . .

15

SHE HAD wanted to slap him. Michael was sure of it. The look in Rachel's eyes said that she wanted to slap him. But every time that look appeared, it quickly vanished, because she could never strike him. They both knew that. She couldn't because she never had. *Did that mean one day she would?* . . .

"I know what you're thinking," she had whispered to him in the den, before David Meredith walked in.

"Do you?" he had replied.

"Yes. I always do. I don't know why, but I always do."

"I got rid of those two men, didn't I?"

"Only because of her."

"They're gone, aren't they?"

Rachel said nothing. She turned her head; her features were profiled against the light from the lamp in the corner. He gloried in that profile, the gently sloping bridge of her nose and the full, curving lips.

She turned back to him.

"This is none of our business," she said. "I wish they'd never come."

"Who? The Merediths or the two men?"

"All of them."

"You think it's my fault."

"*Yes.*" The whisper rose then into almost a scream. Then she caught herself. "This business with the baby. What are they going to do?"

Michael shrugged.

She said, "Are they coming back? Those two men?"

"They didn't get what they came for."

"Why didn't *they*"—she pointed toward the hall—"why didn't *they* go with them? The child needs to get to a doctor."

He shrugged again. "They want to keep the kid."

She nodded. "That's why you chased them off. But not because of him, and not because of the child. Because of her."

He put his arms around her, leaned to kiss her, to reassure her.

"Michael." She pulled back. "What's going to happen?"

"I don't know."

"But you're thinking something, I know it. I don't know how I know and I wish to God I didn't, but you're thinking something." She sighed. "How did we ever get mixed up in this?"

"I startled them, their car went off the road."

"But what's going to happen now?"

"Why don't you ask *them?*"

"You want them to stay, don't you?"

"They may have no choice."

"Before, it was different. Before this adoption business, those detectives."

He smiled at her.

She paused. "No, you're right," she said resignedly. "It wasn't different before. From the moment I knew it wasn't just him, but her as well, I knew then you'd want them to stay." She looked frightened. "I . . . I don't want anything to happen to that poor baby. . . ." Then she stepped closer to him, ran both hands through his hair, around his face. "Michael . . . please . . ." Her face was very close to him now, almost touching. "Don't you see, darling, I love you . . . that's all there is, that's all that matters."

"But what if it isn't?"

"It is, believe me."

He smiled. "I knew you'd be jealous. I told myself that. I

said, 'Rachel would be jealous; just a little, wouldn't she?' "

She held his face tight. "It isn't that, not in that way—"

"—it *is*. Say that it is. *Tell* me you're jealous." His voice was loud.

"All right, all right, but . . . lower your voice."

"I don't want to. Are you telling me what to do again? We've been through that—"

"No, darling, not that, I just don't want—"

"Then tell me you're jealous."

"Michael—"

"Tell me!"

Her hand tightened over his face. "All right. I am."

He leaned his head toward her, thought of kissing her, when she said, "But we have each other. I *know* that."

"We always have," he added bitterly.

She glared at him.

He said, "Why won't you ever admit it?"

"Admit what?"

"That you're jealous?"

"Because . . ." Her hand dropped slowly away.

"Because why?"

"Because I don't know which I am more. . . ."

"What?"

"Jealous or afraid. . . ."

At that moment Meredith had walked in. Michael wanted to kill him for coming in just then. An intrustion. Rachel wanted him, he thought. He felt himself growing hard: and he wanted her. He was about to touch her, perhaps to distract her fear. But then he walked in. A vile, calculated intrusion, Michael decided, when he saw Meredith's sturdy figure, the mussed blond hair falling in long strands across his forehead. A handsome man—but he quickly dismissed the observation. He realized then that he truly hated this man. Man, he thought, capitalized, because Meredith no doubt thought of himself as a Man; all his kind did. But he wasn't. The kid wasn't even theirs. Why? Had they adopted it because they were one of those couples who feel they should give unwanted children a home and family? Or had they done so because he couldn't give her a child? Or was it because . . . no, not because of *her*. Hadn't that detective said she could have a kid, that she was capable of having one? Of course he had. That left him, Meredith, to blame. So when Meredith entered the room and Rachel began talking to him, Michael turned away so Meredith wouldn't see the smile forming on his lips as he thought about the baby who was not his (Meredith's), and the baby who had brought her (Kate) all this grief. He had mumbled in agreement with Rachel, who was expressing sorrow for what had happened, for the two men who had threatened to take away their—

—the—

—baby.

And then he thought: what was it about Meredith that Kate found appealing? No telling. . . .

He knew, of course, what it was about her that he himself found appealing, and what had attracted him to her.

She was . . . vulnerable.

And he had been glad when Meredith had gone with Rachel into the kitchen to get the sleeping pills—

(—no liquor, we don't keep it—)

—because it had given him an opportunity to be alone with her.

Yes, vulnerability, that was what it was.

Michael smiled again. That scene on the road earlier was right out of an old Mary Pickford film, Kate standing in the snow, looking around helplessly, clutching a bundled baby in her arms (which wasn't hers), it was classic, it really was. It was perfect.

He had dreamed such scenes, but never had he thought he would be an actual participant. The last time he had tried to render such a scene real, it had not worked out, and everything had gone wrong.

He had told Kate what had happened with the two men, how he had stopped them and would kill them if they tried to touch her.

But they wanted the kid, and if they took the kid they wouldn't touch her; so maybe, if things got rough, she would have to give up the child, or they would take it—but even then they probably wouldn't let her alone, because they would think she would talk, generate a lot of publicity, and they wouldn't want that, so what would they do then? . . .

—and why is that baby so important to her; she doesn't need it that much, she only thinks she does because up until now it was the only thing she had. She didn't really have him, Meredith, because he couldn't even give her a child, and she wouldn't miss it that much. . . .

He really hadn't wanted to frighten her by telling her he thought those two detectives would be back; but he thought she should know what was on his mind: more important, he wanted her to know he was there, that she could count on him to protect her.

And that he would do.

So why had she looked at him like that when he touched her? He thought he'd actually sensed her cringing when he put his arm on her shoulder! Perhaps it was because she didn't really know him yet, not the way she would; she would behave differently when they became close friends, it would be different then, especially when she found out that her . . . husband . . . could do nothing for her.

Michael stared into the flames of the fire. Her face (not Rachel's) floated in his mind like a delicate, softly etched cameo. Because she was beautiful. And not a woman, really, she wasn't that old, but a girl—

—not that kind of girl, not a little girl, like the ones who—

(—"Michael Perry! Michael Perry! Michael!"—)

—not that kind, that was long ago, you shouldn't even *remember that now—*

—but he did. . . .

(—"What's the matter, Michael?" they chanted, three ten-year-old-pigtails, standing on the corner outside the Reelstate Office, white knees–white hightop sox–skinny cotton bodies, standing there in unison, "Mother won't let you play, gotta have Momma's say-so to come out and play,

to go to town, go to the bathroom, is that true? Why don't you ask Daddy instead, oh-oh"—)

—not that kind of girl, those were little girls, chanting, giggling there on the street corner by the Reelstate Office while he was waiting for her—

(—"Why don't you ask Daddy? You think he's gone and left you? Not so, not so, we just saw him, didn't we? down at the Buckaroo Lounge, down the street at the Buckaroo Lounge, yes yes—

> *Mister Perry gone all day,*
> *Michael can't come out to play;*
> *Daddy's stayin' out till two,*
> *Drinkin' at the Buckaroo*

yes yes"—)

—NOT that kind of girl—Kate wasn't—

(—"oh-oh, here comes Momma, oh-oh, oh-oh, scatter scatter"—)

—that kind of girl, she wasn't that kind, but she was still . . . a . . . girl . . .

. . . besides, Michael thought, things had changed; he wasn't in town, waiting outside that place, listening to them, watching the stares. He suddenly wished he were not here at this moment, sitting before the fire, but out in the woods, tracking the buck.

I am master now, he thought. Come to me now with your taunts and jeers and chants and pigtails and I will strike you down, send an arrow through your tiny breasts . . .

He didn't like to remember. He didn't like the pain that came with remembering.

And then the cameo of Kate's features came back to him, and he lost himself in the soft white skin, as soft and delicate as a deer's velvet. He considered that those features, that face, might be described as, well, pixielike, and Michael would have to agree, even though the high cheekbones and sprightly nose seemed to contradict the soft cameo image he had conceived. She was a contradiction herself: a paradox.

Yet perhaps she had not yet realized this fact. But she would. He would help her. Eventually she would smile, and he would see the thin, lightly traced lips blossom into a generous, kind, and loving smile; and, shaking back the fine brown strands of her bangs, she would gaze at him with wonder and appreciation, her wide—

(—what if she doesn't?—)

—brown eyes asking—

(—stop it, she will—)

—him to touch her—

(—what if she never smiles?—)

—and he would place a hand on her shoulder and this time she wouldn't cringe or pull away—

(—what if she does? what if she screams?—)

—she won't, she won't cringe, or—

(—what if she claws at your face like an angry cat?—)

—NO, she—

(—what if she tries to tear your eyes out?—)

—THEN I'LL KILL HER!—

. . . no . . . calm . . . down . . . you must realize that that isn't going to happen . . . you are . . . master . . . now . . .

. . . and besides . . . you're forgetting the most important factor involved here . . . the reason you were attracted to her in the first place . . . and that was her vulnerability, remember? . . . Kate Meredith was overwrought, racked by fear and uncertainty . . . so she was vulnerable . . . and that made her . . .

. . . accessible. . . .

"I don't know if you can even think about food now," Rachel said, after David had walked into the den. "But dinner will be ready in a little while. Both of you need something in your stomachs."

David nodded a thank you. He was hungry; it had been six or seven hours since he'd eaten a late brunch at the Berenson cabin.

Then Rachel said, "I'm . . . I'm sorry about everything. . . ." And then she turned quickly, went into the kitchen.

David walked over to Michael, who was standing by the fire. He seemed to be in another world, his face blank, eyes glossy, almost as if he'd been crying. He continued staring into the fire.

David told him of his plan to hike down in the early hours of the morning.

"You'll freeze to death," Michael said.

"Not if you'll lend me some clothes. I was hoping I could borrow another coat, an undershirt, maybe the balaclava."

Michael thought a moment. "You'll never make it."

"I've got to try. Besides, I think I can, and I don't think it'll take as long as I thought. It looks like the wind's dying down a bit."

Michael shrugged. "I guess I could lend you a few things. But what about . . . your wife, the child? They'll freeze."

"They're not going."

"Oh?"

"Not yet. I can make it down before there's any chance of those two guys coming back. But just in case, you'll be here. Is that all right? I mean, you've got one of the guns—and the bow."

"Yes, of course. Of course I'll stay here, watch over things. It would be silly for us both to go."

David nodded, then said, "I was wondering. You don't by any chance have a CB radio or anything like that, do you?"

Michael looked at him curiously. "CB radio? No, I don't think so."

"But you're not sure?"

"What?"

"I was thinking about all those boxes in the garage—anything in them?"

Michael shook his head. "Just tools."

"And the shed out back?"

He blinked quickly, stared at David. "What about it?"

"Nothing really. I just thought, I don't know, I thought there might be something stored in there you've forgotten about."

Michael shook his head. David thought he detected a look of fear mixed with anger in his eyes.

"Maybe something your folks left."

"No, I told you. It's just my stuff."

"You want to check, just to make—"

"We're not going out there!" He began to tremble; then suddenly he seemed to recover, and said, "I told you what's in there. Why don't you believe me?" His eyes were bright.

"All right," David said. "I was just trying to consider everything."

"Well, you have," he said calmly. "You're hiking down in a few hours, and I'll give you some clothes, okay?"

He nodded. Michael turned back to the fire, continued watching the flames.

David turned away. The aroma of cooking opened his nostrils, and he heard the sound of clattering dishes from inside the kitchen. He walked slowly across the den, took the step up to the main hall, went over to the window, peered out through the curtains toward the tiny shed—only in the outline against the snow it didn't look so tiny. He couldn't see very well through the reflection of light off the glass, so he cupped his hands around his eyes and could then see the place more clearly. He wondered for a moment why the windows were boarded over; the windows of the garage were not. Then he looked at the tall pines swaying in the wind, and again noticed that the wind actually *had* died down. The snow was falling more heavily than ever, but it seemed to be really *falling*, and not being beaten about like the dust during a mad El Paso sandstorm.

He took another quick glance at the shed, wondered what it was in there that Michael Perry didn't want him to see, then turned away when Rachel announced that dinner was ready.

16

THEY WERE seated at the large dinner table at the rear of the main room and to the right of the swinging double doors leading into the kitchen.

Rachel had prepared a simple but delicious meal. Thick slices of roast beef, scalloped potatoes, peas, and biscuits. David was starving. He had persuaded Kate to come to the table, because Rachel was right, they both needed something in their stomachs; but so far Kate hadn't touched her plate.

David thanked Rachel for the hospitality, and again apologized for the situation they'd put them in. But Rachel shook her head.

"No," she said, "it's not your fault." She paused for a moment, then said, "I've fixed up the back bedroom for you. Next to the baby. Is that all right?"

"Fine," David said.

"I thought . . ." Kate began. "Shouldn't I stay with him? With Brian?"

Rachel reached over, put her hand on Kate's arm. "You need to get some sleep. Don't worry about the baby; I'll watch over him."

Kate looked down at her plate, said nothing.

"He'll be okay," Michael said.

They ate awhile in silence. The wind no longer beat against the house, but it seemed to have grown colder inside, and when David looked across the den he noticed that the fire had gone down. He had interrupted Michael earlier when he was collecting firewood, and now those logs were gone.

The silence continued, the monotonous sound of forks and knives scraping across plates filling the uncomfortable void.

Then Michael asked David, "You said you were from El Paso, right? What do you do?"

"I'm an engineer. Mechanical. I work for a construction firm, on solar heating."

"Ah," Michael said. "Solar heating. That's the thing these days, isn't it?"

"We think so."

"That's interesting. I guess El Paso's the place for it, too—sun always shining."

David took a sip of water. Rachel was looking at her husband curiously. She appeared uninterested in the conversation; David didn't think Michael was truly interested himself, but he decided to respond to his comment because anything was better than sitting in silence.

"It seems that way," he said. "Logically, El Paso's an ideal place, but actually much more work is being done on solar energy here in New Mexico."

"Really? Tell me. How does it work? I mean, I've always wondered how the sun heats the house. That's what it's supposed to do, isn't it?"

David nodded, hesitated, then said, "Well, basically, you collect the heat from the sun's rays by setting up collector plates on the roof of the house. Then, if you're using an air-type system, you blow air through the absorption panels, which have trapped the heat, and then into your house."

"I see," Michael said. He turned to Rachel. "Interesting, don't you think? I know nothing about these things."

Rachel managed a quiet "Yes" and continued eating.

"And you install these systems?"

"The firm I work for has been retrofitting—that is, installing new systems in old buildings with conventional heating systems—but lately we've gone into experimenting and producing our own new type of flat-plate collector—the panels that collect the heat."

"Mm. Do you enjoy it—your work, I mean?"

David thought a moment, then said wryly, "Well, let's say that at this moment I'd rather be doing that than anything else."

At that, Rachel looked up, smiled sympathetically. Michael's face was expressionless. A moment later, she changed the subject.

"What time do you plan to leave?"

David took a sip of water. "As early as possible. I think I'll try to get maybe a couple of hours of sleep; I'll need it if I plan to make it down without collapsing first. Three o'clock, perhaps. No later than three."

"Michael," Rachel said, "are you going?"

Michael shook his head, looked at Kate. "I've got to stay here, in case those two men . . ."

He didn't finish, evidently not wanting to upset Kate. David noticed her shifting uncomfortably in her seat.

Rachel said quickly, "I'm sure we'll be all right here, won't we, Kate?"

"Y-yes. . . ."

"No," David said. "Michael needs to stay here."

Rachel looked at him for a moment, then whispered, ". . . yes . . . of course . . ."

Watching her, David realized what a graceful woman she really was. She was certainly a few years older than her husband, but David thought she was one of those women who age beautifully. She was always poised, her movements smooth and decisive. In a moment she put down her fork, turned to Kate. "After supper we'll see how he's doing and we'll refill his bottle."

Kate nodded.

Silence.

Then Rachel said, "He's going to be all right." She said this to Kate, who was still staring down at her plate; she hadn't touched a bite.

David said, "Yes, I'm sure he will, and I know you've done everything you can, Mrs. Perry—Rachel."

Then Kate said weakly, "Those two men . . ." It was as if she had been thinking of nothing else ever since Michael had brought the subject up. ". . . what if they do come back? . . ."

"They won't," David said with assurance. "They can't."

"What if they follow us?" Kate said.

"No."

"What if—"

"Please—" Rachel interrupted. She forced a smile. "I know this isn't any of my business. I don't really know anything about those men—"

"They want my baby," Kate said.

"I heard some of it, of course, but what I'm trying to say is that . . . well, that they're wrong. He's your child, after all. I don't see how they can . . . can force you to do anything you don't want to do. And besides, whatever happens, Kate, I know you won't let anything happen to Brian, I know you won't." Her face grew stern. "No one can take away something that belongs to you, that's the only thing you have."

Michael pushed away his plate. "Would anyone like some more?"

David shook his head, but he was looking at Kate and Rachel. Their eyes were locked, it seemed. Kate appeared almost mesmerized by the woman.

"I'm sorry," Rachel said at last. "It's none of my business. Would you like anything else?"

David again declined. Kate shook her head, leaned back in the chair.

"You're not finished, are you?" Michael asked her.

Kate nodded.

"But you need the energy."

"Excuse me. . . ." She stood up. "I'll be right back, I want to check on him." She crossed the den and disappeared into the back hallway.

Rachel got up, began to clear the table. Michael remained

seated, looking lost in thought, so David offered to help with the dishes.

"I was trying to reassure her," Rachel said when they were in the kitchen. "I hope you didn't think me presumptuous or anything."

"No," he said. "She can use the reassurance, thanks."

"You really do plan on leaving early in the morning?"

"Yes. I just want a couple hours' sleep." He was stacking the butter plates in the sink. "It's still hard to believe there's no phone, no car."

"Yes. I suppose it is. I'm sorry." Then she gave a slight laugh. "This is the first time in years we've needed either."

"It was a delicious meal."

"Thank you. I hope it was enough. I'm not used to cooking for four people. But there's still a little more if—"

"Oh, no, I've had plenty, thanks."

She placed the last of the utensils on the drainboard. She stopped suddenly and looked at him with her large gray eyes. "Michael said he thought those detectives would be back. Do you agree with him?"

"No. I watched them leave."

She stared at him. The corners of her mouth edged downward, the full lips parted. He wasn't sure what was going on behind those piercing, expressive eyes, and he wasn't sure why she was staring at him for so long; but he didn't mind. She was beautiful. David couldn't understand how she could be married to someone like Michael; they were so different. Not in looks, but in personality, attitude.

Neither one of them said anything for a moment. She continued staring at him until he found himself growing uncomfortable.

"What are you thinking?" he had to say.

She paused. "I was thinking I wish you could leave now."

Kate folded the edge of the blanket under Brian's chin and felt his forehead. It didn't feel warm as it had an hour ago. Then, knowing she should keep him covered but curious to see if there was any marked change in the lesions on his chest, she drew back the blanket and slowly unbuttoned the front of his pajamas.

She wasn't sure, but she thought some of the reddish, crusty patches had gone down; they looked less swollen than she remembered them. Perhaps it was the light that was playing tricks with the shadows, but she thought he actually looked better. Still not good, she knew, but it was something. She would have to show Rachel; she would know.

Rachel . . .

With all that had happened, Kate had to be thankful for Rachel. She made her feel . . . better. . . .

No one can take away something that belongs to you, that's the only thing you have. . . .

Those were strange words for her to say, Kate thought, but they were the exact words she herself had been repeating over and over since those two men had shown up. Maybe Rachel had been there before. Maybe someone had tried to take away something from her before, because those words echoed experience as well as conviction, and strange though it might be for a virtual stranger to say something like that in the midst of all that had happened, it nevertheless made Kate feel better.

She buttoned the pajamas and drew up the blanket. Brian turned his head, yawned, groggy with sleep. But he didn't open his eyes, he wasn't about to cry.

She got up from the bed, turned the bedside lamp to low, started for the door.

"Hey."

She was startled by the black outline in the doorway. The voice was Michael's. Her eyes adjusted to the figure before her. He stood in the middle of the doorway, one arm across, blocking the entrance.

"You scared me," Kate said.

"I didn't mean to."

She tried to pass, but he wouldn't lower his arm. The muscles in her neck tightened, as they had before, when his hand . . .

"You okay?" he asked.

"Yes." She started forward again. He didn't move. She began to feel queasy.

"Just a second, huh?" He looked past her into the room. "He okay too?"

"Better."

"That's good. I guess."

Kate looked at him, puzzled. What did he mean "I guess"? She didn't understand; he sounded differently than he had at the table, as if he were contradicting himself. She sighed nervously. The whole evening seemed full of contradictions.

"I brought you something," he said, and handed her a small cold object. She was afraid to take it, but he forced it into her hand. She angled it into the light. It was a plaster sculpture. She couldn't make out the design at first; then, as she turned it in her hands and the furrows and indentations caught the glow from the hall, she saw that it was a shell-like background with the raised outline of a winged man in the center. In one hand he held a bow at rest, and in the other a cluster of what looked like foliage but what, upon a second glance, were actually arrows. The craftsmanship—if you could call it that—was crude. The colors were bright and obtrusive, and the object itself looked as if it might have been purchased in some curio shop.

"I got it a long time ago," Michael said. "It didn't cost much, and it really *isn't* much; but I want you to have it."

She didn't know what to say. Her nervousness (fear?) had suddenly subsided, and she wondered if her imagination hadn't gotten the better of her, because for a moment, my God, she felt touched, and her first impulse was to say, "Thank you." But she didn't. And again she felt so damned confused. There wasn't anything in his voice or his look to indicate that there was anything to be afraid of.

"You see," he was saying, "you might think this is crazy, but you may leave here tomorrow and I may never see you again." He smiled. "Not that you would ever want to see *me* again, because you want to forget about this place, this whole experience. But I want you to have something to remember that we met. Because I meant what I said earlier, Kate, about not letting those guys touch you, and so I guess this is sort of like a memory of that, if you know what I mean?"

She looked back down at the archer standing against the shell-like background. Strange, but there was a certain innocence in Michael Perry's voice that indicated an almost childlike sincerity. So why couldn't she believe in the innocence, thereby dissipating the nervousness and the fear? Instead, the fear was building, and she didn't know exactly why, she didn't know why she didn't say something to him, at least thank him, because he was looking at her now with his intense black eyes, and even though he wasn't entirely visible in the light from the hall, she was almost certain that he was about to cry. For that reason she didn't want to look directly into his eyes, and she was about to turn away when she realized that was it, his eyes, that was what had kept her from accepting his innocence, his sincerity. Those eyes haunted her. The eyes and the memory of his hand against her neck. . . .

She finally managed to get out a "Thank you, it's very nice," and started to walk past him. This time he lowered his arm, but followed her down the hall. Before they reached the entrance to the den, he put a hand on her elbow, turned her around. She started.

"You don't have to like it," he said.

"No, it's very nice, thank you. . . ."

"You're probably wondering what it is."

"No, I—"

"I don't know what the thing itself is called—the plaster, I mean. But that's supposed to be Eros holding the bow and arrows. You know anything about mythology?"

She nodded, wanting to turn around.

"Then you probably know about Eros."

Jesus, Kate thought, stop him now. She knew what he was going to say and she didn't want to hear it.

"Yes," she said quickly, and pulled away gently, so as not to make him angry. "Thank you. . . ."

"It means something," he said, following her into the den.

David was warming his hands before what little was left of the fire. He looked around for another couple of logs to toss onto the dying flames, but he didn't see any, and the brass fire basket was empty. Rachel was in the kitchen, getting coffee. He was still thinking about her last words (*I wish you could leave now*), trying to figure out how she'd meant them. There certainly wasn't any bitterness in her voice, and after a while David decided that she had made a simple declarative statement—what was more, one that he agreed with. He wished they were out of this place now, that they were back in El Paso, that Kate was at home with Brian and he was at the lab tinkering with Berenson's new designs. He wanted to be anywhere right now but where he was. *He wanted to be out in the sun*—if not working on the new housing project or in the company lot, then simply at a poolside somewhere, basking in the golden rays.

And then he saw a movement from the hallway and saw Kate walk in.

Not Kate, he realized. *Kate and Michael*. Jesus, he'd thought Michael had gone upstairs to his room or something, he'd thought Kate was alone in there with Brian. In fact, he was just about to go in there with her and see how Brian was. But Michael had been in there with her; either in there or in the bedroom adjacent that Rachel had prepared for them. Christ, what would he have found if he'd gone on in there before stopping to warm his hands by the fire—

—*stop it*—what's wrong with you, you're not the jealous type, you're letting your goddamn imagination go berserk again. Besides, you've got other things to worry about, like—

—like what was that Kate was carrying in her hand?

She came up to him, placed whatever it was on the mantel.

"Where's Rachel?" she asked.

"Getting coffee. How is he?"

"I don't know. I think maybe better. I don't know." She flopped down on the sofa by the fire.

David looked at the object on the mantel. It was a brightly colored sculpture of some kind. He wanted to reach for it, examine it.

"Fire's out?" Michael asked.

David nodded. "I looked for some logs."

"I'll get some more. They're just out back."

He pulled on his coat and gloves.

"I'll help you," David said, reaching for his coat, which was draped over the back of the sofa Kate was sitting on.

"No," Michael said, going for the door. "It's nothing, I won't be a minute."

He opened the door, went outside.

David picked up the object off the mantel. It felt like plaster. There was a winged figure holding a bow in one hand and in the other clutching arrows, against a rippled surface like that of a seashell.

"Where'd this come from?" David asked.

Kate's head was tilted back against the sofa, her eyes shut. Apparently she didn't hear him. He repeated the question, and this time she opened her eyes, looked at him.

"What?" And then she noticed the sculpture. She groaned. "I don't know, he gave it to me."

"Why?"

She shook her head.

He went over to the sofa, sat down, kissed her on the cheek. She looked as if she could conk out right here and now. If she closed her eyes for a couple of minutes she probably would.

David turned the plaster object in his hand. He could guess what the figure was—a cupid, maybe?

Kate rested her head on his shoulder. He felt her tremble.

"David?"

"Uh-huh?" Whatever it was, why had he given it to her? And why had he been so quick to decline David's offer to help bring in the firewood?

"I'm scared."

He ran his other hand over her red cheeks. There wasn't a whole helluva lot he could say in response. He could come back with a tired "There's nothing to be scared of, don't worry"; the trouble with that was that he didn't necessarily believe it himself. Because tomorrow there would certainly be things to worry about.

"David?" Kate said.

"Yes?"

"I really am. I . . ." She didn't finish, but pressed her head against his shoulder.

"Do you want to take that other pill?" he asked.

She shook her head quickly. "Not now. Rachel has to fix his bottle. I need to talk to her."

She started to get up. David held her lightly.

"She'll be in soon, you can talk then."

She let herself fall back onto the sofa. David held up the sculpture. "Strange, don't you think?"

She said softly, "He's strange."

"He didn't say anything when he gave it to you?"

Kate groaned again. "He told me what it was." Then she let out a sigh. "He said it meant something."

"What?"

"The figure."

He looked again at the archer. He had a pretty good idea what it stood for, what it was supposed to mean.

He saw Kate's eyes move from the colored object to his face, and then to the low, dying flames in the grate. She said again, as if to no one but herself, "I'm scared," and David wanted to say, "I am too," but he didn't for two reasons: first, because he didn't want her to *know* he was scared, and second, as he began to consider all the things they had to be fearful of, it suddenly occurred to him that Griggs and his sidekick had phased out of the picture to some extent, had become a slight blur in the background, giving way to another, strangely nebulous and intangible fear. During the last six hours or so, he believed he had been through the gamut of emotions for one day; but now he felt something he had not previously experienced. He felt alone.

It didn't seem to matter that he and Kate were guests of this couple, that they had been in their company during the day, and would sleep in their house tonight. He and Kate were alone. This realization rocked him, because he didn't understand it. He was tired, of course; they had been through an agonizing day, and tomorrow looked to be no different—so it was no surprise that his brain wasn't working at its full capacity. But that wasn't it. They were alone, and by that he meant that some obstacle existed between him and Kate on the one hand and Michael and Rachel on the other.

This business with the sculpture. It reversed the roles David had assumed of everyone. Sure, Michael had practically saved their lives tonight, coming to the rescue like that with that bow of his. So David didn't know why he felt the way he did right now; he hadn't even *known* that he felt like this until he sat down and analyzed his feelings, which he wasn't doing such a good job of—after all, Jesus, a piece of plaster, a crude sculpture, that didn't mean anything in itself, and besides, he knew his imagination had short-circuited somewhere along the way, he wasn't the jealous type—but something was making him feel like this, compelling him to question the threat posed by the two men from Washington and making him pause to consider who the real enemy was. . . .

PART III

The Stalk

17

THE DOOR creaked open. Michael could hear it clearly, so Meredith was right, the wind had died considerably.

He flicked on the overhead bulb and was surprised to see how low the wood supply had become. As soon as the storm let up—if the present supply would last that long— he'd have to cut some more. The winter wasn't over yet, and he had learned not to try to predict the weather up here.

He was, of course, very good at predicting the *effect* of the weather. Which was why he had tried to convince Meredith that he would freeze to death if he tried hiking down to the road. The guy just didn't believe him, or if he did, he would no doubt choose to ignore the advice when the time came, because he was so anxious to get the kid—*which was not his*—to the clinic. And Rachel didn't believe Meredith would freeze, or if she did, she chose to ignore it because she believed the only reason Michael had brought up the subject was because he really didn't *want* them to leave—not Kate, at least. Not yet.

And Rachel was right.

Michael inspected the stacks of wood lying in the sawdust. He grimaced thinking about lugging back three or four logs.

The shed was cold—colder, he thought, than it was outside. He looked around, at the small desk in the corner, the narrow tables with his bow tackle—finger gloves, armbands, sharpeners, cable silencers, along with old strings, quivers, nocks, slings, and Converta-Points, and the ancient recurve bow he had used as a kid. He stepped over to the other side of the shed, where the light from the swinging bulb shone on the bow rack. His eyes roamed across the line of arrows, looking for any gaps, but all twenty-four arrows were there. Then his eyes searched the back of the shed, over tables, through steel, far to the back, eyes straining desperately to pick up the slightest alteration, the smallest item out of place.

Because he trusted no one.

The sun had gone down, the wind had died, but where were those detectives? Had they actually given up, after coming all that way? After all their trouble and expense, and after some exorbitant offer from that senator—did Meredth really think they would scare that easily? Michael knew the extent to which one would go to get what he wanted. *Whom* he wanted. Yes, Michael realized that whenever he looked at Kate. So Meredith was crazy. More crazy, possibly, than Michael himself? . . .

He took another look around the shed, a complete circle. The hollowness in his stomach increased, as it always did. A queasy stab of memory pierced deep within him. The door was ajar, he hadn't closed it; snow blew silently in. White, soft snow. White like wisps of cotton—

—no, like the bright white light swinging back and forth, quick and startling, frightening him with its intensity and movement as it began to swing with the sound of the door yanked open, hitting, crashing against its frame, and the godawful screaming—

Michael closed the door, turned away from it, looked down at the straw-colored floor. Kicked at the dust. The icy air hung like a solid restraint about him, locking in the entire contents of the tiny wooden shed. And the icy shelter contained the odors that aroused the memories, contained and preserved the memories in an icy sheath and would not let them go.

Some of those odors, memories, he wanted to forget. But they were all here.

(*Things are going to change.*)

His mind began to fade, he wasn't sure where he was. Because he knew that things eventually changed—how could they not?—but some things stayed the same, and those would never change, unless . . .

He didn't want to think about it. He made his way about the room, moving around the back, feet shuffling through sawdust, the cold, damp, fusty odor of dead memories circulating through his nostrils. He hesitated when he reached the partition at the rear. He wrapped one hand around the thin cylinder between the wide interstices and left it there while he glanced inside, a sickness building within him. He kicked at the sawdust again, and again smelled the rankness of the place. My God, if Meredith were to come out here . . . And then he smiled, remembering his words to Kate in the bedroom. He had told her, "*You may leave here tomorrow and I may never see you again . . . because you want to forget about this place, this whole experience. . . .*" He had fought to be sincere, and he wondered if she had believed him. She had hesitated when he handed her the engraved plaster object for which Rachel had paid so little years ago in the Apache jewelry shop in town, yet which meant so much to him—yes, she hesitated as if she didn't really want it, and that made him sad, almost to the point of tears. But it didn't matter now because the night was here and the night could change things—

(*—as she had changed him—*)

Then something struck him, and his throat went dry, his heart pounded violently.

What if something goes wrong?

My God, why would he think something like that, he didn't want to think, didn't want to imagine what he was about to remember, so why did he wonder if something would go wrong? *Because it had gone wrong in the past*. He *had gone wrong in the past*.

(*—oh, get up, Jesus, it's no use, for Chrissa—*)

But that was a long time ago—and he had asked for help then, he had asked the blond one for help, but she—

(*—it's me that needs help from picking faggots like you—*)

—she wouldn't help him, and she was all of a sudden screaming and calling him names, some of which he didn't understand (how long ago had that been?), and so in the middle of it all, with her trying to get up and him pushing her back down, he had asked her what those names meant—

(*—what? what's that?—*)

—but she didn't answer him, she just laughed—

Michael's hand gripped tighter, shook the metal. This time would be different. Nothing would go wrong. *He* would not go wrong. Kate was different; she would perhaps help.

His eyes sought out the cold ground, scrutinized the sawdust—the same sawdust he had lain on years ago, after fleeing from the giant fists that had pounded against him, not caring if he was A Man Now or not, just hitting harder and harder, coming down like a big iron ball—

(*—I asked you a question and you didn't answer, good-for-nothin' sonofabitch, I asked you where's the goddamn bottle—*)

—and so he'd fled, and later she'd found him lying in the sawdust, and then her hand sweeps over the hair on his head and around, down across his cheek, and then—

—and then the light fills the room, he can't see, the whiteness blinding—

No. . . . Stop . . . thinking. . . .

He looked out over the sawdust again. He would not move farther toward the back; even from here and through the chilly air the earth gave up its mephitic secrets. He shivered. He had remained out here too long.

He walked to the front of the shed, began piling logs onto his arm. He remembered again his words to Kate, *"You want to forget about this place, this whole experience."*

He smiled. The experience had not even begun. . . .

THE COFFEE wasn't instant, and it tasted good. Rachel hadn't offered any dessert, which was fine with David because all he really wanted to do now was drink his coffee and hit the sack.

They were seated in the den, David and Kate on the beige sofa near the mantel, Rachel on the sofa adjacent. Michael stood by the fire, thrusting the poker into the flames, adjusting the logs.

"I doubt you'd want to build a solar heater up here." He stepped away from the fire, dusting his hands.

"On the contrary," David said, sipping coffee. "You'd be surprised where you can have solar heating."

Michael sat down on the overstuffed chair. He had refused coffee, so he just sat there watching them. Watching

Kate. After a while he turned to David. "Maybe we should put one up here, then."

"Depends," David said.

"On what?"

"On whether you want to go to the expense."

"Expensive, huh?"

"It's not cheap."

"But I thought that was the advantage, that if you're using the sun you save money."

"You do, once you've installed the system. It's the initial installation that scares most people away. That's what we're working on at Berenson's—the firm I work for. Trying to get the cost down."

Michael looked into the fire. The flames were building, crackling loudly now. "Cost. That's always the problem, isn't it?" He turned away, looked at David. "I told you my father was a builder? He was always screaming about cost, the cost of this, the cost of that, screaming at the top of his lungs, and that was years ago, I suppose it's worse now." He smiled. "I wonder, if he were alive today, if he would be building solar houses?"

"Perhaps," David said.

"Interesting. . . ." Michael turned back into the fire. The popping wood grew louder, and his chair was awfully close to the iron screen; he must be burning up, but he didn't move. His head, colored a bright orange in the light, turned slowly around. "Funny. Most people hate days like this—the snow and the cold. Most people except the ski freaks, and even they don't know how to deal with weather like this. They think they do. They bundle up in their parkas and their thermal coats and put on their long underwear and drive up to the ski run and most of them—not all, but most—slosh around in the snow pretending they know what they're doing. But they don't. Because when it's all over they scurry to their lodges to get warm and to drink. They couldn't last in the snow, if they really had to." He paused, shifted in his seat. "I'm sorry, I changed the subject. I'm just saying this because I was thinking about your job, about heat from the sun, and about El Paso. I couldn't live there. I'm not sure I like living here, it's not cold enough, not long enough. Because I enjoy the long winters. Let me have the cold and the snow. You can have the sun." He smiled.

"I'll take it," David said.

Michael's expression went blank again and David knew the room was going to go silent, so he asked, "What about yourself? You work in town?" He wished he hadn't asked the question; Michael couldn't possibly work in town if he never—or rarely—ventured into Ruidoso, and even then he said he took the bus.

"You probably won't be able to understand this, Mr. Meredith. Because I suspect you're the kind of person who works fifty or more hours a week, and who isn't comfortable when he's away from his work for too long. Am I right?"

David pretended to think a moment. "I suppose. I enjoy what I do, if that's what you mean."

"Do you? Or do you just enjoy working—on anything?"

Rachel interrupted. "Michael . . ."

But David went ahead and answered. "I told you. I enjoy what I do."

Michael said to his wife, "I'm just trying to justify myself, darling."

"You don't have to," Rachel said.

"Maybe not. But it doesn't matter." He turned to David. "You see, Mr. Meredith, I don't work because I don't have to. I own an enormous share of my father's old business and collect on it when I have to."

"You're fortunate," David said.

"Do you really think so? What I mean is, do you really believe that?"

David nodded. "Of course."

"Sure? Don't you wonder how a man my age can do absolutely nothing and still live comfortably? Don't you wonder how I keep from getting bored?"

"Not really."

"Well, I can tell you that I never get bored. Rachel and I are perfectly contented here, aren't we?"

Rachel took a sip of coffee. "Yes."

Michael looked at her. "Do you want to tell Mr. Meredith how you feel, not having someone who goes to work every day, who isn't out of your hair for a moment?"

"Michael, please—"

"You'd think she would disapprove." Michael smiled, turned to David.

"Certainly not," Rachel said. "We're very happy here—even if we don't have the long winters." She spoke sarcastically but with humor in her voice, glancing at Michael. "Anyway, I'm quite happy." This time David thought she directed the words more at herself than at anyone else, as if perhaps she might be trying to convince herself.

David intervened. "As I said, you're fortunate that you can live a life like this. Most people would give their right arm to do so."

"Don't mistake me, Mr. Meredith—"

"David, please."

"Don't mistake me, David. We have made sacrifices for our present existence; we've paid high prices."

"I'm sure you have," David said, although he couldn't imagine what they could be, if all Michael had done was inherit his father's business.

"Yes . . ." Michael and Rachel were looking at each other. "High prices . . ." he said.

David put a hand on Kate's knee, squeezed it reassuringly. She hadn't said a word, and David didn't blame her, he just wanted her to know he was there. She should probably take that other pill, get to sleep.

"Don't you want to know," Michael said, rising, "what I do to occupy my time?" He walked slowly over to the chest in the corner, took down his bow, walked slowly and deliberately back to his seat, and sat down. "I hunt. I mentioned earlier, on the road, that I was aiming for a buck when you first saw me. I was. I almost had him when the noise from your car startled him. I spend most mornings and late afternoons looking for him."

"It's an obsession," Rachel said. And then suddenly her face twisted, as if she'd caught herself saying something she shouldn't say, and she looked down at her coffee cup.

"That it is," Michael said.

"All I know," David said, pointing to the bow, "is that that thing saved our lives tonight."

Michael paused. "Oh, the two detectives. Yes." His eyes moved to David's right, to Kate. "Yes, in the right hands a bow can be as effective, if in some instances not more so, as a gun. Did you know that Bob Markworth, the trick archer, once joined a friend in challenging members of a police force on their target range? An equal number of bullets against an equal number of arrows." He grinned. "The arrows scored higher."

He laid the bow across his lap. "I'm not fond of target archery, though. It means nothing to me. I'd much prefer the breast of a deer in my sight than a black paper bull's-eye."

David took a sip of coffee; it was warm, getting cold, so he was glad when Rachel reached for the pot sitting on the end table. He nodded and she refilled his cup. She was about to refill Kate's when she noticed the full cup resting on Kate's lap.

David sampled the steaming liquid. "I know a little about archery, but I've never seen a bow like that before."

Michael ran his hand along the black metallic midsection. "One of the finest compound hunting bows you can buy. I had to special-order it, of course, and they aren't cheap; but it's never failed me in its accuracy." He withdrew an arrow from the green quiver mounted on the bow, twirled it around in the flickering light.

"And those," David said, pointing to the three sets of small black disks at either end of the bow, "they must function as . . . eccentric wheels?"

"Exactly. Like a system of pulleys. When you pull back the string of an ordinary bow the weight increases as you continue to draw. When you pull back on this bow—" He set the arrow down on the floor next to him, brought the bow to its vertical position, and began to demonstrate. "—it reaches peak weight just after you start to draw. Which means you can hold a shot at full draw for a longer period of time without tiring." He released the string and grinned. "I lied a bit when I had those detectives in my sight." He placed the bow once again in his lap. "And of course, a bow is much more fair when it comes to stalking game—certainly more fair than that shotgun on the wall—my father's shotgun."

Yes, that bow was a superb instrument, David thought, a piece of fine craftsmanship. He could tell now by looking at it how it worked, and with six eccentric wheels he suspected the let-off in force to draw the damn thing must be thirty or forty percent. Maybe fifty. Nice machine.

A log crashed in the grate. Michael went over, shoved the poker around, set it down, then sat on the floor before the fire, the bow across his legs. He pointed to one of the mounted heads above the mantel. "I dropped that one two years ago. An easy mark, really, and not entirely rewarding. You ever hunt?"

"Only once, when I was a kid," David said. "Shot a quail with my uncle's twenty-two. He made me eat it for dinner the same night. I got sick."

"I don't blame you. I don't like venison. I wouldn't eat it if I did."

David looked at him curiously. It was an odd thing for a hunter to say. After all, wasn't that part of the hunt, some kind of code among hunters, to eat what they killed?

"Other hunters would chastise me for that, for not eating the meat, but that's not the reason I hunt."

He was quiet all of a sudden, so David asked, "Why do you, then?"

Michael raised his head slowly. From his expression, David thought he had turned inward, was thinking about something else, but then the black eyes lit up, he suddenly came to life. "For the heads, of course." He looked up and around the ceiling at the collection of antlered deer heads. "Beautiful, aren't they? Not many of trophy quality, but I don't go in for that either. I'm not trying to beat any records.

But . . ." He edged over the wood floor toward the sofa where they sat. Rachel watched from behind. She looked nervous. "But if I wanted to—if I really wanted to show off, register a rack, break some records—I could do it." His face was burning brightly now, and David knew it wasn't just the result of his sitting so close to the fire. His whole being had become animated as he spoke. "If I wanted to, I could bring in the most beautiful ten-pointer anyone has ever seen." He nodded. "That's right, the buck I was stalking when you came along the road. The largest, most magnificent antlers I've ever seen on a muley. And he must be at least six or seven years old." Suddenly the excitement in his eyes faltered, his look became sullen as he said, "I'd like to think I could take him this season; but the truth of the matter is, this buck's the smartest I've run across in a long time. Do you know I've been stalking him for almost a year now? We *know* each other, you see. I respect him and he respects me. That's why I don't care about records and winning; I don't like the idea I'm competing with anyone else. I'm competing with him—and only him. It's just the two of us out there, and there's this respect, and that counts for a lot because when I drop him—and I will—it's got to be good, the best shot I can ever hope for. I don't want him taking off, bedding down in some thicket to die; and I only want one try. I keep thinking that I could have taken him this morning if it hadn't been for your car; but I doubt seriously if I would have risked the shot in that wind. So . . . I'll just wait."

"What if he outsmarts you?" It was Rachel's voice, from the sofa at the back, her tone derisive, almost scornful.

Michael turned, faced her, then shifted his position once again until he could see everyone. "Strange, but I was thinking that same thing this morning. I was thinking that sometimes I wonder if this muley isn't more clever than I am. He may be, to some extent. But I'll down him. I'll down him because I want his head."

Rachel made no reply. Kate eased back on the sofa and rested her shoulder next to David's.

"I'm not sure I understand," David said. "What's the

fascination, all these trophies—heads, I mean—if you're not interested in—"

"But they *are* trophies, they're *my* trophies." He glanced at the heads on the wall, smiled. "I'm the eccentric art collector who covets his masterpieces, refuses to lend them out. To me, those racks are *personal* possessions; they're a constant source of wonder—each time I look at them I marvel at their beauty and meaning, their size and color." He paused. "Do you know anything about deer?"

"Only that they seem to frighten easily and apparently harm no one. I couldn't bring myself to kill one."

Michael shook his head. "You know virtually nothing, then, and I doubt I can describe to you the overwhelming excitement of hunting them. Especially the mule buck—a curious creature who will stop at times and stare me right in the eyes. And that's the way I'd like to take him, though I doubt I'll be that lucky."

David looked at Rachel. She was fidgeting with a napkin, looking nervous. Perhaps she'd heard this all before and maybe she thought Michael was tiring them—especially Kate, who David knew should be going to bed. Something was nagging David, however, so he had to ask, "What do you do with them, then? After you've . . . killed them?"

"I take their heads, and as I have no use for the carcass, I leave it there."

David's stomach felt queasy. He frowned.

"You don't approve?" Michael said.

"I don't know."

Michael turned directly toward the sofa. He looked right at them, first Kate, then David, and again his face seemed to glow. "The power, you see, is in the rack. When that is removed there's nothing left."

Out of the corner of his eye, David saw Rachel squirming. He thought he heard her call her husband's name, but she was silent now.

"The power?" David asked.

Michael's eyes sparkled. The vein leading above his right eye into the hairline became more pronounced. "Potency, you might say. A buck's antler growth is controlled by the testes: they are an extension of his sex. And isn't sex equated with power?" He picked up the arrow, ran two fingers along its shiny length.

David said nothing; his stomach continued to send a kind of warning signal that things were out of tune down there.

"I told you," Michael continued, "that I respect the buck. But there's something more. I *envy* him as well. I envy his power and the outward exhibition of that power." He stopped, thought awhile, said, "Can I tell you something about the buck?"

David set his cup on the table before him, looked at Kate. "I . . . it's getting late, and—"

"It won't take long." He was looking at Kate. "But you asked about the fascination; I think you should know."

David leaned back. Kate felt her forehead, said, "I don't know, I—"

"It *is* late, Michael," Rachel said, "and they've had a horrendous day; perhaps—"

"You see," he interrupted, ignoring her, "during the mating season he is a totally sexual creature, and those antlers, while they apparently have no actual sexual function, they're nevertheless a manifestation of his prowess. Because he only grows them for the rut; and no one really knows *why* they're grown, they just are."

David said, "I thought they were used as weapons—to fight off other deer."

Michael let out a laugh. "They're not grown just for that; a buck rarely needs or uses them in that way." His face grew sullen, his tone fervid. "They're so tiny at first, those little knobs forming on the top of his skull. I've studied deer, observed them in detail; and it's a remarkable process, the growth of antlers. There's all these blood vessels that send blood to the bone. And while the bone is developing, one set of these arteries is a soft velvety covering that protects the antlers, and when finally the bone becomes hard, the buck sheds the bloody velvet. What's left is the sturdy, pointed shafts of antler beams, forking, branching into the air. And then—" He moved even closer to them, his breath quickening, face feverish. "—then when the velvet's gone, the hormones are through with controlling the antler growth and can then concentrate on the testicles—"

"Michael?" Rachel asked. He didn't seem to hear her; she said again, "Michael? The Merediths are tired, they—"

"—they enlarge before the rutting period, they swell and pulsate—"

"—Michael?—"

"—and so he's ready when the time comes, he searches for the odor of a doe in heat, working himself into a frenzy—"

Rachel was sitting on the edge of the sofa now, the napkin crushed in her hand, her hand pressed to her chin. Kate stirred next to him. There was a sound from below and David saw the cat enter their little circle from behind a chair.

"—and to locate her, to let her know he's ready, he makes a scrape in the ground; he finds a special place and paws out the soil with his hoofs, urinates in it, and then rolls in the urine because it is the odor of his virility, and he keeps pawing at it, hoping the doe will find it, then she'll know he's ready, and he grows more frustrated, fighting to protect his private space, and then one day he sniffs the air and the scent is there. . . ."

He glanced quickly up at the row of mounted heads. The glassy eyes in their gray-brown sockets peered down at them through changing shadows. To his right, David sensed Kate turning to him. He looked at her; her expression said that she wanted to get up, leave, but Michael, eyes widening, almost fighting for breath, started up instantly again.

"The scent drives him wild and he comes upon her, and she's ready—"

"—please, Michael"—the words from Rachel, pleading.

"—and he follows her around awhile, sniffing her—"

Looking only at Kate now, his face a burning crimson, the skin pulled back taut against his forehead and cheekbones, the vein pulsing, enlarging, he began directing this little drama at her, and she was shifting uncomfortably on the edge of the sofa, looking at Rachel, then David, biting her lip, turning around once quickly toward the back bedroom where Brian lay asleep, but no one said anything; David cleared his throat and Rachel inched nervously off the sofa, calling her husband's name again because the situation was becoming damnably uncomfortable, there was no stopping him—

"Then he bounds toward her, she stands for him, and he mounts her, driving himself—"

"—I don't feel—" from Kate as she looked into his burning eyes, his complete concentration focused on her—

"—driving himself in deeper and deeper—" The pupils enlarged, his onyx eyes burned furiously. David put an arm on Kate, was about to speak, end this.

"—riding her—" The vein near his eyes engorged, about to burst.

"—no—" from Kate weakly, rising—

"—thirty, forty seconds—"

—Kate standing awkwardly now—

"—until he explodes—"

—Kate shaking her head, her hands to her face, rising, turning, catching herself, walking then running across the den and disappearing into the hall—

"—until, lust and fury sated—"

—David getting up, about to turn, but Rachel already there, following Kate's path, telling him to sit, it's all right, David complying, sitting, looking angrily at Michael, who was now clutching the arrow tightly in his hand, digging the tip hard into the wooden floor madly, like some crutch holding him up. The cat meowed, Kate's flight had disturbed it; the creature moved out away from the fire, circling around Michael.

"—until, lust and fury sated," he finished, "it leaves the doe in search of another. . . ." The glowing feverish face lost its tautness; his body seemed to relax. "I . . . I upset her . . . I didn't mean to."

Bastard, David thought. He sat rigid on the sofa.

"I didn't mean to," he said again, "but if only you could know the power . . ."

"You meant to," David said; "don't say you didn't."

Michael shook his head.

The cat had maneuvered around him, was coming up close in front of his legs. For no apparent reason it let out an annoyed cry, and David gasped as Michael angrily brought up the arrow, whipped it outward across the head of the furry creature—but the cat was faster, and darted away, hissing.

19

SHE WAS running before she knew it, not sure if she bolted because she couldn't stand to hear any more or because she thought she would be sick, and so, without pausing to think, she ran until the darkness enveloped her, until she reached Brian's room, where she pushed open the door, staggered across the rug, came to a painful halt against the wall that faced the headboard.

Goddamn him, she thought; *goddamn him, goddamn his eyes. . . .*

She started to cry. It wasn't what he'd said—God knew that biological play-by-play was nothing—but it was *why* he'd said it, the *way* he'd said it. Those damned eyes of his looking through her, she knew what he was thinking all the time, he was thinking about her. She thought she had cried herself out, but here she was again, starting to choke because everything had been comparatively calm at dinner, comparatively civilized and decent, and she gratefully welcomed the interval to simply sit and let anxiety and pain drain from her, allowing her to unwind so she could sleep without that pill. But then he had begun what she thought was a subtle attack on her, *why* she didn't know (*yes, you do*), and it was the irritation that caused her pain to fester until it exploded—

("*—harder until he explodes—*")

—and that was why she was crying—that, and the fact that she had been raped by him as he visualized—visualized . . . stop . . . it . . . stop. . . .

She pressed the back of her head against the wall. Brian was tossing on the bed, his tiny arms thrashing about. She was aware of another movement in the room. Rachel was rushing toward her from the open doorway.

"I'm sorry," she was saying, coming up to her, "I just can't tell you . . ." She hugged Kate, saw the tears, pulled another tissue from the box on the bedside table. "Here." She blotted Kate's cheeks, continuing to apologize. "Are you going to be all right?"

Kate nodded after a while. "I'm . . . I'm just tired is all. . . ." Her cheeks burned.

"I know, but there just wasn't any excuse, I tried to stop him."

"I'm just tired. . . ."

Rachel blotted the last of the tears on Kate's burning cheeks and around her eyes; it was odd, Kate thought, watching her, but there was fear mixed with sympathy in the woman's expression. "There was just no excuse," she said again. "He gets so . . . carried away. . . . I . . . here, let me get you something." She started to turn.

"No. Please; nothing."

"Something to calm you, let you sleep?"

Kate shook her head violently. "For the baby, please. Could you fix his bottle, the medicine?"

Rachel smiled. "Of course; I'd almost forgotten. Here." Rachel led her to the bed. "Sit down here awhile; I'll just be a second."

She took the empty bottle from the table, left.

Kate watched her son moving from side to side, eyes barely open. He yawned once, began to frown as if he were about to cry, but he didn't. Kate tried to smile down at him, but it was difficult, so she contented herself with simply watching him and feeling terribly proud of him—and frightened to death. She whispered, "You ready to go home, baby? You ready to go?" She caught herself before she started to cry again.

Rachel returned with the bottle full of the golden liquid, handed it to her.

"I increased the dose," she said, and then, seeing Kate's concern, added, "it won't hurt, it'll be better for him; trust me?"

In answer, Kate placed the nipple to Brian's mouth. Although groggy, he took it eagerly, began sucking.

"Be right back," Rachel said, and left the room again. Kate heard some moving about in the hall, a closet door being opened, shut, then Rachel coming back, carrying something. It was a small folding crib.

"He'll be better off in here tonight," she told Kate as she spread open the crib, placed the mattress down, wheeled it over to the bed.

Kate got off the bed, looked at Rachel, confused. "I didn't know . . ."

Rachel went to the bed, said "May I?" and Kate nodded while Rachel picked up Brian, placed him down into the crib. "You were wondering why I have this thing?"

Kate nodded.

Rachel grew somber. ". . . I had a child once; not for long, I lost him. . . ." She ran a finger under one eye, turned to Kate, her face fighting to regain composure, to forget the memory.

"I'm sorry," Kate said.

"It was a long time ago. Here." The memory apparently gone, she smiled, took Kate's hand holding the bottle and nudged it forward. Kate leaned down, held the bottle to the baby's lips. Rachel placed a hand on Kate's head, stroked her hair. "He's a beautiful child; even looks like you." Her tone was gentle; Kate liked what she said, it made her feel warm.

A long silence. Faint, moist sounds from Brian's lips were all Kate could hear. She wanted to ask Rachel about her baby, but decided it was best left undiscussed for now.

Rachel knelt beside her; she watched the feeding, watched Kate. Kate's eyes began to water, and in a moment Rachel reached up, streaked away a single tear that was about to fall, gently caressed her skin. "You fight for him, Kate. Don't let anyone touch him. He's your baby, and you protect him."

Kate looked up into the soft gray eyes. Loving eyes. "Yes. . . ."

"I'm sorry about everything," Rachel said. "Michael becomes so . . . obsessed with that animal, he goes crazy sometimes; and you see, there's very little else for him to do, so . . . well . . . I'm sure he'll apologize."

Kate shook her head.

"He'd better," Rachel said.

"I don't think so, I don't think he will."

The fear in Rachel's face was unmistakable now. "I don't understand."

Kate felt helpless. "*I* don't understand, but I don't think he will, because . . ."

She didn't finish, didn't want to; she hoped she could leave things like that, she didn't want to have to tell this woman that her husband had approached her, and so she hoped Rachel would let it drop, but she didn't, she said, ". . . because? . . ."

The blood was rushing to Kate's head. What could she say—no, *how* could she say it?

"I mean . . ."

Again the words would not come, and there was another long pause as Rachel watched her, waited, and as Kate observed her the fear on Rachel's face grew more pronounced until another look appeared: recognition. And

Rachel said, "I . . . I think I know what you mean. . . ." She drew back a little way. "Unfortunately, I think I know. . . ."

Kate felt suddenly overcome with sorrow for her, felt ashamed. She wanted to say something—but what?

Then after a moment determination came over Rachel's face and she said, "Just the same, remember, no one can take your son away from you, no one, and you should never hesitate to do anything that will save you both." She paused, thinking; then: "Do you know what I think? I'm not trying to lay down a law of nature or anything like that, and I'm probably wrong, can't prove it, but I've thought for a long time that of all the animals on earth it's a human mother who will kill more quickly and resolutely before letting someone—even her husband—take her child away. . . ."

Outside, the wind had all but died completely, but the snow continued falling, blanketing the enormous pines.

The faint light of the hidden moon, reflecting off the white terrain, was the only light the driver of the car allowed himself as he carefully maneuvered the tires up the incline. It was extremely difficult, and although at times he was tempted to use the headlights to aid him during the more precarious curves, he dared not do so. He had lived in this kind of weather all his life, and had developed a confidence in his ability to feel his way through such conditions. So he continued guiding the small car up the narrow, treacherous road, creeping slowly, the chains of the car cutting quietly through the icy slush.

They still had a long way to go. . . .

20

HE SAT on the edge of the bed. Exhausted. Numb.

He had looked in on Brian a little while ago; Kate was with him now, giving him the last of his bottle. The Perrys had retired upstairs—Michael first, and Rachel only after she had apologized for her husband's behavior after dinner. And David was still cursing himself for not stopping Michael in the den. Goddamn him for going on like that. Something was very, very wrong.

The room was chilly, but Rachel had promised to turn up the thermostat before she went upstairs, and now David could feel the heat blowing out from the vent at the baseboard below the bed.

Jesus. His head throbbed, his muscles ached, he felt terrible. No doubt looked terrible, too. He was almost afraid to shuffle into the bathroom across from the bed and look at himself in the mirror.

He wished Kate would hurry up. He had talked to her for just a little while in Brian's room, where Rachel had set up an old crib (—Why did she have it?—), and Kate looked all right, he supposed, but they didn't talk very long, or very loud, because she was trying to get Brian to go to sleep, which he was on the verge of doing just before David left.

The room, under other circumstances, would probably have been quite comfortable. The furniture was ranch-style, the bed a queen-size, and Rachel had entered a little while ago with an old pair of her husband's pajamas (which didn't look as if they would fit), one of her gowns and a robe for Kate, toothbrushes, and some shaving things. But right now he doubted he could appreciate these comforts; all he wanted to do was crash.

"He's alseep," Kate said, entering. She looked as bad as he felt.

"Here," he said, moving over so she could sit down on the bed.

But she shook her head, indicated the bathroom.

"You go ahead," he said.

She picked up the flannel gown that Rachel had left lying across the bed, went into the bathroom, shut the door behind her. After a while he heard water running. Then silence. David set the small alarm clock on the bedside table.

More silence.

The silence stretched on until he realized, after a while, that she had been in there a long, long time.

Kate washed her face. It was too late to take a bath, she could take one in the morning. Then she brushed her teeth, rinsed, looked at herself in the mirror, at the swollen eyes, the thin, limp hair that needed washing, the flushed face. She got into the gown Rachel had left and looked again into the mirror. Leaning against the sink with both hands, she bent her head, stared down into the sink, and tried to collect her thoughts. She wasn't really thinking about anything, and that was what bothered her. Her mind had been going in all directions for so long that she wanted to stop the random thoughts, try to control them: *she wanted control over herself for a change.* Today had wrung her inside out and back again, and the time had come to pull herself together.

And she had reason to.

It was hard to believe, but Brian was definitely better. She didn't think time was so important a factor anymore; that didn't mean, of course, that he didn't need to see a doctor, but Kate knew Rachel's medicine had done the trick, if just for now—and that was all she could really hope for, wasn't it? And so, without that crushing, overwhelming element—Time—beating against her and weighing heavily on every inch of her body and mind, she thought she might be able to pull herself together.

But she also had reason not to.

Those two men. And yet Rachel's words had helped her there; her words had helped summon more than a little renewed determination and something more important—anger. She could combat them with anger; it was fear that she dreaded, because she couldn't handle it, she would fall apart. And though it sounded trite, it was fear of the unknown that destroyed her the most—like not knowing what was wrong with Brian, like worrying about complications that hadn't arisen, and like not knowing if he would live or die. But he was alive, that was a fact, and he was getting better, she was sure of it—so there was no Unknown. And those two men, they weren't *unknown*, they weren't intangible, *they were real*, and even though they scared her, Kate thought she could perhaps deal with that kind of fear.

Pull yourself together.

She was still staring down at the sink, immobile, in a dreamlike state that puzzled her: her body refused to react to the thoughts sent by her brain.

Move anyway.

Her eyes drifted to the right of the basin, where Rachel had left various toilet items—toothpaste, soap, the brushes, razor and blades. Her hand reached out and touched the razor. It was an old, tarnished gold double-edge type, the blade inside terribly rusted around the edges. She twisted it in her hand, twisted the handle until the top parted. It was a senseless action, and the only reason she was doing it was that she wanted *to have something to do*—after all, if David decided to shave, he could fix the razor himself. But she opened it, not thinking really; if there had been a wrapped bar of soap on the basin she would have unwrapped it just for something to do. So she removed the blade, held it carefully—it had been a long time since she'd seen one of these thin double-edged blades; her father was the only person she'd known to use them, they were more dangerous to handle than the new ones, harder to find a place to hold because they seemed sharp all the way around, so she held it carefully by the slit in the middle, and then she heard a noise like the door opening, and she turned around.

He would never have walked in there like that on her, he never had in the past, but he'd knocked a few times and she hadn't answered him, and he got worried.

When he saw her holding the razor blade he wanted to scream and rush toward her—a succession of images hitting him hard and fast, and he really wasn't sure what they all were, but one of them was him sitting in the back of the ambulance with Kate as they rushed her to the hospital, after he'd found her with the pills. . . .

But he didn't scream and the images quickly disappeared. He stood there looking at her, and the look on his face must have frightened her. She stared back at him, looked down at the blade in her hand, back up at him and said, "What?—What're you—?"

David approached slowly, he couldn't keep his eyes off the damn blade. "Kate?" he said softly.

"David? What's wrong?—"

He reached out for the blade, and as he did so she pulled away and looked at him as if he were a total stranger. Then her face changed and she said, "Oh, no, David—"

"Honey? What—?"

She knew what he had been thinking, he was positive.

"No, David, no."

"What are you doing with that, Kate? What are you doing with that razor blade?"

She began to break, like a jigsaw puzzle knocked off a table, she began to go. "You couldn't think—"

He went to her, put his arms around her. "It's all right."

"My God . . ." She dropped the blade into the sink, fell back against the rim, and trembled until he felt really scared.

"Kate?"

"I'm that bad," she said lifelessly, a deep monotone. "I can't believe you really thought . . ."

"It's all right, Kate—"

"No, it's not, it's not all right, you see what I've done?"

"What are you talking about?"

"You thought—"

"I didn't think anything."

"Your face . . . if you could have seen your face . . ."

"Come on, let's get—"

"No, don't you see, it's what you think of me. My God, what's happened to us, David, what in God's name has happened to you and to me? I was taking out the blade, for no reason at all, I don't know what made me do it, but don't you see, you thought . . . you . . . you don't trust me. . . ."

"I trust you."

She twisted her head, looked at him funny. "You never believed about the pills, did you? You never believed me about—"

"Stop it, Kate, that's over, I believed you—"

"Oh, David, what's happened? For you to even *question*—for *you to be capable of that expression on your face* when you walked in—how could you?—"

"I knocked. I knocked two or three times, there was no answer, I was worried."

"About what?"

"About *you*, damnit."

"What about me? That I might have done something like I did that night when I took those pills, is that what you were thinking?"

"Stop it, Kate, goddamnit, I was just worried."

"It wasn't my fault then and it isn't my fault now!"

He didn't say anything. Not for a long time.

Then: "Kate?—"

"Listen, David, you've got to listen to me." She was crying. "I'm so afraid, David, you don't know how afraid I am, and it's not that I'm afraid of those two men or of Brian not getting better, it's that I'm afraid for us, David, I'm so goddamned afraid for us."

"Kate?—"

"—Hear me out, please." She put her hands on his shoulders. "I'm afraid of the way you think of me, David. After that time with the pills, I knew you hadn't believed me about it being an accident. And even after the doctor told you it was an accident I didn't think you were a hundred percent convinced, and you know why? Because I don't think *he* believed me a hundred percent. But then after a while I thought maybe you had come around, you didn't treat me so . . . strangely . . . like some kind of live bomb that was about to go off, we even *argued*—those arguments made me happier than anything, can you believe that?—and so I thought things were getting better, at least as far as your doubts were concerned. But then when the doctor told us about the baby—*before he'd told anyone else*—I knew why he'd done it, and then you started acting strangely again, but before long even that changed and we were back to our old selves—and the more arguments I could pick with you and the meaner you got, the happier I got, because you weren't so careful with me—*so why in God's name do you have to walk in here like this and start things all over again?*"

She stopped, held him tighter, moved her hands to his neck and made him look at her. "When will you believe me, David? When will you trust me? I love you, you know, and I love our son, and that's just too much to ever give up."

They stood like that awhile. A long while.

There wasn't anything he could say; she had assessed his behavior, his feelings accurately. He *had* been treating her with kid gloves, he *had* been worried, all the time afraid that if Murchison hadn't been entirely convinced that the overdose was accidental, then that must be grounds for his own doubt.

He supposed that now, given the method, the means, and the opportunity, he could very well do him*self* in. Certainly he had the motive: his lack of faith and trust in his own wife—so he deserved to go.

But he was too selfish. He loved this woman a lot.

Then why couldn't he answer her now? . . .

21

MICHAEL STOOD in his underwear before the dresser. The index finger and thumb of his right hand grasped the plastic nock of the arrow and slid the alloy shaft against the thumb and finger of his left hand. It was one of the finest hunting arrows made—a Metric Magnum made by Bear, with a large diameter and a Super Razorhead tip, and it was perfectly matched to his bow.

He set it on the top of the dresser, across the corner, with the broadhead lying off the edge.

He heard Rachel coming out of the bathroom. He turned, faced her. The light pink nylon gown hung loosely over her, almost translucent. It was an old gown, he realized, and needed replacing. Perhaps the next time he went into town he would buy her a new one.

She said, "I apologized for you tonight."

"You needn't have. They're leaving in the morning."

"I did anyway. You shouldn't have started that. It was obvious what you were trying to do."

"And what was that?"

"With Kate Meredith. Looking at her like that while you were talking."

"Where should I have looked?"

"You know what I mean. Why didn't you quit earlier? Why describe something they didn't want to hear?"

"*I* didn't know they didn't want to hear it."

"You knew *she* didn't."

He shook his head. "Not true."

She sighed. "It was embarrassing, Michael."

"For her or for you?"

"For both of us."

"That's hard to believe." He grinned.

She came nearer; they were face-to-face. "Your teasing her like that—"

"—Is that what you call it?"

"Your flirting, then? Your oral rape? Whatever. No doubt both of them think it was a reflection of a bad marriage. And there's something else, isn't there? You must have done or said something earlier. What was it?"

"I simply gave her a token . . . a token of remembrance. You remember that Eros sculpture you picked up years ago?"

"Jesus, Michael—don't you see what that gesture must have appeared like to her? To them?"

"The inconstant lover, is that it? The unfaithful husband? So what else is new?"

"Stop it. I'm used to that by now. But why make it so obvious?"

"All right; perhaps I shouldn't have in front of him."

Her eyes widened; there was fear in them. "Nor in front of her. You can't do this."

He blinked. "Do what?"

Her face closed in on his. "I told you before, you're planning something, I'm not sure what or when or how, but you're planning something—with her. These are good people, Michael. All they want to do is go home."

" 'Good people'? That depends on your point of view. I doubt those two detectives would agree with you. Good people? That's not even their kid. *He* couldn't give her one."

"You don't know that. Besides, I've talked to her, Michael; I've seen the way she acts around the child. She *loves* that baby, Michael, and that's all that matters, don't you see? That in itself means it's hers; no one can take away that kind of love."

"They *can* take it away and they probably will.

Anyway . . ." He thought about the words carefully. "You're not the one to talk about love, are you? I mean, you're not the one to apply *your* definition of love to *her.*"

She slapped him. Hard. After all this time she was finally able to.

"Goddamn you, Michael. Don't you ever say that to me again. Not *ever.*" Then she began to cry. "My God, what have I done?"

He brought her to him, pressed her close.

"I'm sorry," he lied. He lied because he wanted her tonight. He pressed her breasts closer, feeling them against his bare chest, through her flimsy nylon gown. "It was cruel, I'm sorry." He kissed her forehead.

"I like her, Michael, I *like* Kate Meredith. She reminds me . . . she reminds me in some ways of . . . of myself when I was younger." The glistening gray eyes widened. "I'm frightened, Michael. I'm scared to death because I know that something's going on in your mind. I know that you want Kate Meredith. And what frightens me is that I think I know what will happen if you try. . . ."

He backed away, his hand went up; he wanted to strike her as she had struck him. But he clenched his teeth, lowered his head, and said bitterly, "Don't you mean what *won't happen if I try?*"

"Michael, I didn't mean . . . I just don't want anything to happen to her." She stepped close to him until they were touching again. In a tone that was admonitory as well as ominous and fearful, she said, "Remember what happened to that girl. . . ."

Michael's eyes hurt, his head throbbed, it was suddenly very warm.

("*—oh, get up, Jesus, it's no use, for—*")

"Yes . . ." he said. "How can I forget? . . ."

(*—But she didn't help me, she wasn't the right one—*)

"Of course not," Rachel said. "And that's over, it's in the past. But I like Mrs. Meredith, I don't want anything to happen—

(*—Kate is different—*)

—to her, don't you see? What's past is past." She pressed herself against him. Her breasts almost touched him. "She doesn't matter, Michael. None of them do. Why should they? I'm always here. . . ."

She moved against him. He put his arms around her, pressed the silky pink gown against the small of her back until her breasts and pelvic bone squeezed into him, the loosely hanging nylon below her navel meeting the bulge in his underwear. The familiar frenzy stirred in his loins.

He smiled. "Always have been, always will."

He hovered above her, kneeling on the bed between her parted legs. Sweat stained the alloy shaft of the arrow he gripped in his right hand. His fingers relaxed around the aluminum length and he brought up the broadhead and held the arrow with the fletching pointed toward the bed, the Razorhead toward the ceiling. Rachel's eyes watched him, as they always did, with a mixture of remorse and resignation. And guilt.

It was part of his ritual. She despised it, but conceded; she knew it was too late to change.

(*—Things are going to change—*)

And things did change, but not this—not this part of the ritual which he had conceived out of necessity and to which they were bound.

"This is what you want, isn't it?" she said. "*She* can't give you this."

He turned the arrow until the Razorhead was pointing downward. "No," he said, again lying, because he was thinking, *She can give me this and more*.

Clutching the arrow in his right hand, he moved the vertical shaft forward until the Razorhead was suspended over her chest. Her breasts were soft white, the nipples extended. The abdomen and chest were of the same color and texture—except where the tiny, hairlike scars, some red (the recent ones) and some white, marred the otherwise velvety flesh. Slowly, he lowered the tip. He thought she was about to say something, perhaps a plea for him to be careful, but she refrained. She hated those scars, he knew: hated them yet bore them, because they were her atonement. He would, of course, be careful, he always was. Because he loved her. And he hated her. He had to.

The Razorhead lightly touched her skin midway between the breasts and navel. Her breathing, once heavy, stopped as he barely increased the pressure until the shiny, honed edge at the chisel tip almost imperceptibly broke the skin. The muscles in his groin tightened. Rachel's warm gray eyes looked at him anxiously. She was waiting for the ritual to be over. And it nearly was.

Gradually increasing the pressure, he ran the razor tip down her abdomen for two or three inches.

His groin was about to explode.

Then finally he lifted the tip of the broadhead from her skin and she began breathing rapidly again, soft flesh rising and falling spasmodically.

Her trembling hands reached out for him. . . .

Lying on his side, arm around her, David kissed his wife good night. He heard the quiet ticking of the alarm clock and doubted he would get much sleep—if, indeed, he was able to fall asleep at all. It was already after midnight.

He didn't immediately remove his arm from Kate's side because it felt peaceful like this; the bed was comfortable, and the steady drone of warm air coming through the vent on the baseboard just below Kate seemed almost hypnotic.

"David?" Her voice was soft.

"Mm."

"He's a lot better. Did you see him—Brian?"

"The fever seems to have gone down."

"His skin looks better, too."

She didn't say anything for a while, and David thought maybe she had fallen off to sleep—which was what she needed badly.

Then: "David?"

"Yes?"

"I don't want you to leave me here with him."

"Michael?"

"He frightens me, David."

"Someone's got to stay here."

"Rachel—"

"I'd feel better with him, Kate."

"It's his eyes. I can't look at them because of the way they look at *me*. There's something . . . I don't know, something strange. . . ."

"I know. He's weird, no question about that. But he can use that bow—and a gun."

"That story he told after dinner. About the deer . . ."

"I should have stopped him."

"I don't think you could have."

"I should have tried."

"All the time he was looking at me I knew he was talking about me, that I was the—"

"I know. I told you he's weird."

"Not just him. They're both . . . I don't know . . . they don't seem to go together."

"I thought the same thing. . . ."

"But it's not just that they don't go together. I mean lots of couples don't seem to go together. It's something else. . . ."

"I didn't know they had any children."

"You mean the crib?"

"Uh-huh."

"They did once, but she lost it."

"Oh."

"And David?"

"Yes."

"She knows about it. Him, I mean, Michael. She knows about the way he's been looking at me since we got here."

"She talk to you?"

"Not really." A lengthy silence. Then: "I don't want to be left alone with him, David."

"Rachel will be here."

Another silence.

"Kate? I said you won't be alone, there's Rachel."

"I know . . . but I don't think that makes any difference. . . ."

"You'll be all right. And once I get the ambulance up here we can all leave, go home."

He kissed her again, then turned over so they could both get to sleep.

It was quiet for a while, the steady drone of air and the faint ticking of the clock the only sounds. David was slowly fading away, his muscles relaxing and his mind clearing, when Kate said, "You know what I think?"

He barely heard her, grumbled a "What?"

"I don't even think they're married. . . ."

She tugged on the covers, pulled them up around her and rolled over onto her stomach. Perhaps the sounds had drawn her to the edge of the bed.

Kate blinked in the darkness. She must have been asleep an hour, maybe less, she had no way of knowing. The bedroom itself sounded different: rather, the *silence* sounded different; clearer. Eventually her foggy brain registered that it was because the thermostat had gone off temporarily and there was no longer the steady whisper of air through the vent.

But there were sounds. And they weren't whispers, but something like cries.

Omigod—Brian—something's wrong—he's crying—maybe he fell, but no, he's lying in a crib—

Those were the thoughts racing through her mind—racing so quickly, in fact, that when she realized that the sound wasn't coming from the room adjacent at all, she had not yet lifted her head from the pillow.

She lay there in the darkness, head pressed near the edge of the bed, listening; because the cries or whatever they were came from beneath the bed, and that wasn't possible, was it?

Blinking madly, as if clearing her eyes (which could see only blackness) would somehow help clear her head, she lay perfectly still, muscles tensed. She could tell from his deep breathing next to her that David was sound asleep.

Again she heard the sounds, and now she realized that it *was* possible they were coming from below; they were coming through the silent heating duct. Hollow, tinny sounds. They must be coming from the Perrys' room.

And then, although it was barely audible, Kate recognized what the sound was. It wasn't someone talking or screaming, they weren't having an argument. It was the sound of rapid breathing—high, almost shrill female gasps. They were making love.

Kate grew warm, uncomfortable; she wished the thermostat would come on again so she didn't have to hear them, didn't have to be unwillingly aware of what they were doing. She turned over, away from the wall.

Rachel forgave quickly, it seemed. . . .

22

GODDAMNIT TO HELL, he thought, trudging through the frozen slush, barely able to see. The moon helped considerably—without the moon they'd be sunk. And he had his flashlight, of course, he could always use that if he had to, but he'd try to avoid it.

He wasn't cursing the snow. Jesus, he'd been raised in the snow, and that didn't necessarily mean he liked the stuff, sure he could do without it, especially now, but usually he just didn't give a damn. He was cursing that goddamn David Meredith and his goddamn foolish wife.

And that prick with the bow and arrow.

Kavanaugh was nearly psychotic about the damage done to his arm. He'd wrapped it tightly, and most of the bleeding had stopped; but it still throbbed, and the cold didn't help any. He'd probably want to deal with that asshole himself. Fucking Robin Hood, Jesus. No matter. Robin Hood hadn't met Laurence Griggs on his own ground.

He had detailed the plans with Kavanaugh in the car going down. Christ, they nearly hadn't *made* it down, what with the goddamn car sliding all over the place, creeping dangerously close to the edge. But when they got to the fork in the road, he knew they were home free, and it wasn't long after that when they reached the highway. Jesus, they'd had more trouble on the fucking highway than they'd had coming down the mountain. The ice along the shoulder was deadly; that junk heap of a Lincoln almost spun completely around when Griggs tried to make the turn onto the highway, and finally *did* spin completely around when they got to the clinic and he tried to cross the street.

Griggs had parked the car right there on the shoulder of the street above the clinic. The place had reopened and there was a lot of commotion inside, as doctors and attendants rushed about caring for accident victims.

It had taken less than a minute to start the old Pinto parked in the clinic lot. There'd been two cars to choose from, the Pinto and the Chevy. The Pinto had chains. What had taken all the time was scraping off the snow; the goddamned thing was practically buried in the stuff. Luckily, the car was parked around the side of the building, and no one saw them, even though occasionally an attendant had rushed out to an ambulance and back. It turned out to be a three-speed standard stick-shift, and Griggs hated standards; he hadn't driven one in years and he never thought he'd have to again. But it had come back to him, and he eventually managed to back the car from the lot and turn onto the highway, find the cutoff again, and start up.

It wasn't easy. But Griggs knew Meredith would never suspect them of returning tonight—and if neither of those cars at the clinic had been equipped with chains, they wouldn't be here now, trudging through all this slush, unless they had decided to hijack some motorist. And if it had come to that, Griggs thought, he wouldn't have hesitated. Because no one beat Laurence Griggs, no one. He always prepared himself for every eventuality. That was why he hated chances. Chances meant you weren't prepared in the first place. And Griggs was always prepared. . . .

The Pinto was far behind them now. They had climbed higher in the past few minutes than Griggs had thought they could. The snow bit their faces, and their bodies were numb, but still they continued up, stopping every now and then to listen, then trudging farther on. Griggs had been going over their route in his mind, and he had decided that the one thing they would *not* do was head up straight for the ridge below the cabin. Not that anyone would be waiting there for them, but it was a risk they needn't take at this time, and Griggs hated risks because they were the same as chances, and any you didn't *have* to take, you didn't. If they went up to the front of the house they would be exposed to the front windows—and the front of the house was where they would be expected to appear. So he had decided to cut up the mountain and circle around to the back of the Perry cabin. That meant a delay in getting to the Ford, and Griggs had to get to the car in order to get the gun. One thing Meredith didn't know about—Christ, he'd *better* not know about it—was the .45 wedged under the spare tire in the trunk. Griggs had always carried a spare gun in the trunk. A spare tire, a spare gun. You carried one because you never knew when you were going to have a flat, and you carried the other because you never knew when you might need it. And Griggs covered himself from every angle because he didn't like taking unnecessary chances. And Jesus, he was glad the gun was there now.

It better be there.

He stopped a moment, ran his sleeve across his face, waited a moment for Kavanaugh to catch up.

"Slow down. . . ." He heard Kavanaugh's voice behind him.

"We don't have all night," Griggs said.

"Jesus," Kavanaugh sighed, coming up next to him. "That snow hasn't let up yet."

"It's not going to. At least not for a while. There's no telling what this road's going to look like when we come down."

"Jesus . . ."

"Let's go. . . ."

They started up again, Griggs still thinking about what the road was going to look like an hour from now. He knew they would have trouble. But no matter. Griggs was used to trouble. All his life he had known it in one form or another; it was like an old friend. Or an old enemy. Whatever it was, he'd had more than his share this week.

He'd had more trouble with Melchor, trying to come up with a decent fee. Why is it that the ones who are rolling in dough are always so fucking greedy with it? Anyway, he had to admit that Melchor eventually came up with a pretty good deal—except for the goddamned time factor he'd wrapped around their throats, and that was one thing they were running out of—time.

And then suddenly something jabbed at him, hit a nerve. What if something happened and they didn't make it back on Monday morning? Jesus, *if he were to fail*? . . . Don't consider it. No way you're going to fail. Just keep your head and just keep slicing through the mush and begin turning to your right now because you're nearing the cabin now and you don't *want* to near it, not yet, you want to cut to your right, straight up the mountain and around the rear of the place.

He turned and saw Kavanaugh coming up close behind, freezing his ass off. You'd think a big guy like that would have more thick skin to protect him from the cold, but no, there he was, shivering all over.

"Jesus . . ." Kavanaugh gasped. He stopped, propped himself against a tree. "My feet . . ."

Griggs went over to him. "It's not much farther."

"What're we gonna do?"

Griggs pointed up the rise. "We'll head up that way, around back. I want to get behind the cabin so we can assess the situation inside. If there are any lights on, you can maybe hide in that shed while I make it to the car."

"Jesus, it's cold. My legs . . ."

"Come on," Griggs said tiredly.

They started up again and continued circling, the Perry cabin barely visible through the trees, climbing higher and higher until they were at the rear, the old shed and the garage below them. Near the front of the house, at the ridge, was the LTD, just where they'd left it. Good.

Griggs surveyed what he could see of the place—mostly the back of the cabin and part of the front. It was at least two o'clock in the morning. It had taken them a long time to drive down the mountain in the junk heap before finding a place to stop, and they had been climbing for what seemed like ages. All together, enough time had passed for the bastards in the cabin to fall sound asleep; so Griggs was a little more than irritated when he peered closer and saw what he thought was a single light burning somewhere downstairs. . . .

23

RACHEL TIPTOED quietly down the hall and into the first room on the right.

She had left Michael sprawled on the bed upstairs, sated. She tried to be as silent as possible getting up out of the bed, putting on her robe, and descending the stairs into the den. She hadn't wanted to disturb him; she didn't want him to know where she was going or for him to follow her. Not that she really cared. And she hadn't turned on any lights in the den because she didn't want to wake the Merediths.

She closed the door softly behind her and stumbled through the darkness until she felt the lamp on the bedside table, then found the knob under the shade, turned it once, on low.

The baby slept soundly in the crib, all snug and warm and beautiful. All she wanted to do was look. And allow herself to fantasize a series of emotions she had not felt in a long time. The overwhelming joy of an infant filled her; her heart beat a little faster as she placed her hands lightly on the rim of the crib and looked down at him. In sleep, the painful flushed face had calmed and been restored to its original fair complexion. The ampicillin was working, and she was glad; the poor thing had been burning up. And she was sure the lesions had begun to heal.

She was terribly lucky, Kate Meredith. Terribly, terribly lucky. Rachel still didn't understand everything that had happened with the two detectives. She hadn't paused to think about it objectively because the nature of Kate's love for this child precluded objectivity.

Rachel felt very much alone and very much afraid. Memories fought their way to the surface, and they were painful. She thought of her baby, so beautiful, as beautiful as the child before her now. Years had passed since the last time she had thought of him. So many, many years of reorienting her life and her soul. And guilt, too, there was always the guilt that haunted her, kept her awake at night: the guilt and the sorrow.

(*"My God, what have I done?"*)

She felt a spasm deep within her, a feeling moving steadily toward the surface. As Rachel looked at Brian her heart seemed to beat faster; this child made her relive experiences and feelings that had lain dormant for so long—that had lain dormant in the back of her mind where she had forced them fourteen years ago, and as the memories swept through her she realized what a mother would do to protect her own flesh and blood. And although Brian was not Kate Meredith's natural son, Rachel knew Kate would protect him as fiercely as she had protected her own son.

Rachel rubbed the back of her hand across one cheek. Blood rushing to her face had swollen her eyes, they felt hot. Enormous tears had welled up inside and began to trickle uncontrollably down her cheeks.

Staring at the tiny sleeping form, Rachel Perry quietly wept. And wept. . . .

Michael wasn't asleep when Rachel came back upstairs nor did he pretend to be. But he didn't say anything, just lay there in the darkness, the covers over him. His eyes were open and he watched the blackness. Then light tinged the blackness as Rachel emerged from the bathroom. Just as suddenly, it was gone. She was in bed now. In a few minutes she would be fast asleep.

Michael could not stop thinking about Kate. He knew from the luminous dial on the clock nearby that it was shortly after three A.M. He didn't have much time. Still, he had to wait until Rachel fell asleep; he didn't dare move now. So he folded his hands across his chest and lay quietly. There was no sound of wind outside. Calm had blanketed the night, and he thought for a moment of giving it up. Rachel had satisfied him tonight, and tomorrow they would be leaving. Provided, of course, he let them. But he couldn't give it up, not a chance like this. . . .

. . . what to do . . . he was starting to get drowsy . . . he imagined himself out under the pines now, tracking the magnificent buck . . . stalking her—him—stalking him and waiting patiently for that one good shot . . . yes . . . but he was drowsy, and—

—and then he heard a noise. Thought he did. Not even a noise, really, perhaps a sense, he sensed something. It could have been a sudden flurry of wind, a clump of falling snow.

After a while he wasn't sure he had heard or sensed anything at all.

But then he remembered the extent to which a person would go to get what he wanted. The extent to which he himself would go. And so he got up out of bed to make sure. . . .

24

THEY HAD continued circling around, closer down toward the back of the small shed. Griggs's feet ached severely now, it was all he could do to push them on.

No one could see them from the house, he was certain. When they finally reached the shed he noticed that the light inside the cabin had gone off—which could be either good or bad. It could be good if it had been a light in the john somewhere and whoever turned it off had finished doing whatever it was they had gone in there to do. It could be bad if someone had heard them and had turned it off so they could see outside. But he didn't think they'd been heard, although coming up through the rise at the rear of the cabin had proved more difficult than Griggs had anticipated. The climb was rough and steep, the snow messy, and they hadn't been able to maintain the restraint and silence they'd exhibited earlier: for one thing, they were extremely close; for another, they were exhausted.

But they were behind the shed now, hiding in the shadow it cast against the white ground. Griggs was wondering what Meredith's plan was. He was relatively certain he'd wait until morning to leave. He'd probably wait until his wife had rested up—and besides, Meredith had told Griggs that he would leave the LTD at some service station and he could pick it up *tomorrow.* But it didn't really matter what Meredith was going to do; Griggs knew that when it came time for Meredith to leave he would be leaving on foot—because he and Kavanaugh were leaving in the next half-hour with the kid, even if they had to eventually storm the place to get him.

Griggs was a big believer in the element of surprise. He knew where the kid was—back in the hallway just as you go in the front door, in one of those rooms. He would wait a little while longer for whoever it was that turned off the light to get back to bed, and then he'd make it around to the back of the LTD, get the spare .45 from the trunk, then he'd go to the cabin, pick the lock on the front door, and walk on in, flashlight guiding the way. And if he couldn't pick the lock? He'd just bust in the door and let the element of surprise work for him. And if someone were waiting for them? Well, he'd have the .45, and he'd do what he had to do to get the job done. But he felt it wouldn't come to that, because he believed no one would be waiting for them (after the kind of day that couple had had?—a distraught wife and a sick kid?), Griggs truly believed Meredith wasn't planning on leaving until morning, so there was no reason for anyone to get hurt. He and Kavanaugh, on the other hand, had to leave tonight. Because if he failed at this job (*Don't think that, you won't fail*), if he wasn't back in D.C. on Monday morning, that fucking fanatic Melchor would just hire somebody else and start all over again. Griggs smiled. When he thought about it actually, he had to admit that Melchor was a real lunatic, he should have left well enough alone—but no, the bastard wanted to keep alive the memory of that no-good junkie freak daughter of his, who hadn't really given a shit about the kid anyway. Jesus Christ, there just wasn't any fucking justice anymore. Just money, that was all.

Rachel stirred, felt for the edge of the blanket, and pulled it tightly up under chin. The dream had awakened her. The nightmare she had nearly forgotten existed in the recesses of her mind, but which had returned to her tonight—

—because of the child.

All I wanted to do was protect him, she thought. And she knew she wasn't thinking of Kate's child, but of her own child of many years ago.

He had needed protecting, she thought.

(*"No, don't touch him!"*

"Fuck you, I'm gonna kill him if you don't get out of the way"—)

—No . . .

And yet even though she was half-asleep, Rachel could not help shaking her head quickly back and forth, because she knew that the need to protect him was not the only thing that had cost her her child. There was also the selfish possessiveness: the need to possess that part of her which eventually *became* her, until she had destroyed it. . . .

Rachel thought she had cried herself out, but she reached up to wipe away a single tear that had begun trickling down her cheek. She brought her legs together under the sheet and squeezed them tightly together, her body tensing, curling slightly as if in a desperate effort to fit itself snugly into an imaginary womb. Instinctively, she reached out to the opposite side of the bed, touched the empty expanse, searched frantically. A sudden chill came over her. Michael. . . .

Rachel turned back in the bed; then tension constricted her entire body and she was afraid to move. She wanted more than anything to fall back to sleep, but she remembered Michael's face earlier in the evening as he performed his bloody ritual, and Rachel realized now, for the first time, that she could not sleep, because something different had happened earlier tonight during that secret ceremony. Something to change things. She remembered Michael kneeling on the bed, holding the arrow before her. But as she stared into his penetrating black eyes, a startling sensation overcame her: *she felt as if she were looking at him for the first time*. And that wasn't possible, she thought now, as she stirred and ran her hand nervously under her gown, across her scarred chest. Nevertheless it had surprised her when, as he hovered above her, a nausea overcame her with an intensity she had not experienced before; and the ritual that followed had seemed alien to her, and she knew she could no longer ignore the realization that when she had been staring at Michael's anxious face above her (*Where was he?*), she was not thinking of him, as she always had, or of the act he was about to perform, but of the people asleep downstairs, and that was when she thought: *This is happening for the first time.* A sickening feeling had begun spreading through her then—a feeling that even now had not dissipated—had in fact grown stronger. And because of this, Rachel knew she could not go back to sleep.

Suddenly she wondered if she could ever sleep again. . . .

Griggs was finally beginning to feel the cold. *Really* feel it. They had been standing in the shadow of the shed, not yet ready to move, Kavanaugh behind him shivering in his boots, clutching his injured arm. After a while, Griggs inched forward around the side of the shed, toward the door. He had to be careful now because the door faced the cabin. He edged around, indicated for Kavanaugh to remain where he was, entered into the moonlight and went straight for the door, pushed.

It didn't budge. At first he thought he'd have to work a lock, but then he saw that there wasn't a lock, just a rusted hinge with a flap, the flap secured to the eyelet with a thin coil of wire. Gloved fingers working rapidly, artfully almost, he undid the wire. Through the cold air, a whiff of something caught his nostrils. Smoke from the cabin chimney, he guessed. But it didn't really smell like smoke. He considered for a moment just forgetting the shed and going directly for the house, breaking in and getting the job done. But something held him back. Caution.

Within five seconds he had the wire loose, dropped it to the ground, opened the latch and signaled for Kavanaugh. The burly man sidled along the outer wall and followed

Griggs inside, bending his head under the low roof. Griggs shut the door, the hinges creaking, groaning quietly.

Inside, it was completely black; the boarded windows didn't allow them the advantage of the brilliant moonlight. They couldn't open the door all the way because someone might look out the window—although he still felt sure that the light he'd seen earlier was from a john somewhere in the cabin; the place looked quiet now.

And what *was* that smell?

No, they could only inch the door open to observe the cabin. But he could use the flashlight, because the windows were boarded up, and if they couldn't see out the windows it followed that no one could see *in*, didn't it? Right. Unless there were cracks in the wood, spaces between the boards which might let light escape. But there wouldn't be that much light. So he turned on the flashlight.

For a second he thought he was in Dodge City, or a comparable Hollywood set, right there in Matt Dillon's office. He wouldn't have been surprised to see Chester or Festus stepping out in front of those bars, calling in a hoarse voice, "Mist'r Dillon?" Because it was all there, the typical interior set for any movie Western—the desk with gun rack behind it, the table in the corner with the coffeepot, and the jail cell in the back.

But then he changed his mind; something was wrong. No Hollywood cowboy could fit behind that desk, it was too small; and that wasn't a gun rack behind it, but a bow rack. And although his eyes hadn't adjusted completely to the single circle of white light cast by the flashlight, that didn't look like a coffeepot sitting on the table in the corner. There wasn't any doubt, however, that it was a jail cell in front of them.

"What the fuck?" Kavanaugh whispered.

Griggs moved the light around. To their right, on the sawdust floor against the wall, lay stacks of firewood. Along the walls hung a large assortment of children's curios—small Indian tom-toms, rubber knives and hatchets, paper head-dresses, and a couple of cap guns. He brought the light back to the center of the room; his eyes were beginning to focus more clearly. As he looked carefully at the contents of the shed, it began to dawn on him that they weren't in any Hollywood sound stage at all, but in some little kid's playhouse. Some playhouse. Perry must have built it—but why?

"What *is* this?" Kavanaugh said.

"Hell if I know."

They stepped toward the cell. It ran a little more than halfway along the back wall, and was about four and a half feet wide. The door was ajar. Griggs pulled it open an inch and it grated loudly on its hinges. He couldn't see anything inside, except for some small red boxes in the corner, with white lettering on the outside. He didn't let the light stop long enough to read them. The steel bars looked sturdier than they probably were, and ran from the ground up through the roof, which wasn't very high; the shed itself was small, the ceiling low. But with the cell door shut and locked with the key on the ring hanging from the lock, it might very well hold someone for a while.

The tiny desk, its wood surface peeling and warped, sat in the left corner, a foot or two away from the angle of the two walls, and less than a foot from the left wall of the cell. In the dim circle of light, its flecked surface resembled that of tortuously gnarled oak. The rack holding a single bow and a number of arrows hung on the left wall behind the desk. The bow was small—like that which might belong to a child—and Griggs was puzzled by the sudden palpitation in his chest brought on by the curious mental image of a menacing child wielding that bow, about to kill a small animal. *A person?* Griggs shuddered, whirled the light around to their right, to the table on the other side of the cell, and walked over. What he'd thought was a coffeepot looked nothing at all like one; he had perceived it that way because of the association with the rest of the surroundings. Instead, it was a small aluminum electric heater with a set of three coils. Griggs moved the light around the decaying pine wall behind it and saw a crude electrical outlet near the floor. So the place had electricity. He pointed the light at the ceiling, saw a naked light bulb hanging in a brass socket from a dangling cord. The switch was on the wall near the door of the shed. He thought about turning it on, decided against it. The surroundings, in the dark, made Griggs tremble, as if he were intruding into the dead secrets of a sinister past—a past he didn't care to see illuminated. They had seen enough of the place, had felt the sickening atmosphere pervading it, and all they wanted to do now was keep an eye on the house through a crack in the door.

Kavanaugh was getting restless, stomping about on the sawdust floor, trying to keep warm. "Christ, it stinks in here."

"It's the damp sawdust," Griggs said, moving toward the door of the shed.

"What's that sonofabitch doing with a place like this? You see any kids in there tonight?"

"No—and there better not *be* any." Jesus, he hadn't considered that possibility, that Perry might have kids asleep in those back rooms, or upstairs. Oh, well . . .

"Let's get the hell outa here." Kavanaugh stomped delicately—as only he could do—to where Griggs stood by the door. His bushy salt-and-pepper hair stood out like a big mophead in the light bounced off the ceiling. "Why don't we just bust in now? You can take the kid while I cover you. It's too fuckin' cold in here."

"In a little while, Sam, in a very little while. I just don't want to blow this."

"We ain't gonna blow—"

"Shh." Griggs cracked open the door.

The Perry house lay still and quiet against the snow-covered pines. Nudging the door open a little farther, he took a quick step out and an even quicker look at the Ford parked just above the ridge. Nowhere was there any movement, just cold silence.

"Your keys," he told Kavanaugh.

The big man dug into his pocket, handed them over.

"You stay put, I'm going to go around and get the gun."

"Hurry, Jesus."

"I know, I know, it's too fuckin' cold in here. Hang on." And he slid through the cracked door, into the icy night.

Kavanaugh stood rigid—frigid, rather—for a few seconds, then started to pace, holding the flashlight with his wounded arm and rubbing the arm with his other hand because it throbbed like hell. He was going to pound that goddamned Robin Hood's ass, soon as he got the chance—and if by some chance, if by some rotten luck Griggs got to him first, Sam would pound *his* ass.

That was the way he'd *feel*, at least. Jesus, if something happened to Griggs, Kavanaugh would really be up the creek, he'd have to say goodbye not only to his job but to his slice of Melchor's fee. And that was about the worst thing he could think of right now. This was the first decent job he'd landed since getting kicked off the goddamn Encino police force for wasting a good-for-nothing wino who was so drunk he decided Kavanaugh needed a shave with the jagged end of a Muscatel bottle. The remembrance of the experience made Kavanaugh livid, but oddly it was of some benefit: it warmed him up a bit.

But not enough and not for long. So he began pacing faster, shining the light here and there, looking around at the desk and the cell, and wondering again why such a place existed, if not for a little kid to play in.

He walked over to the open cell door, shined the light around inside, over the sawdust floor and over some boxes stashed in the corner against the wall. The corner of one box read DANGER—KEEP AWAY FROM CHILDREN—BLASTING CAPS. Jesus-fucking-Christ, what was that kind of stuff doing in a kid's playhouse? Probably empty. Maybe they contained sawdust.

Kavanaugh inhaled deeply, still curious about the strange odor that filled the room. He moved the light around to the table in the corner, saw the small electric heater. If Griggs didn't get back here in a second he would plug the damn thing in, it was so fuckin' cold in here.

He brought the circle of light back to the interior of the cell.

The odor drew him inside.

It felt colder behind the bars, he thought. Colder and . . . musty? . . . The stench was sickening. He circled the inside of the cell with the beam of light, taking in the old pine wall at the back, the wall of bars to his left. He wrapped a hand around the cold steel, shook it. The structure rattled; it was falling apart. Kavanaugh could just see some guy running a tin cup across the inside of the bars. The beam from the flashlight drifted over the sawdust floor and stopped at a strange indented space at the left, far back. He went over, knelt, shined the light directly in front of him on the ground. There was a shallow impression in the sawdust, where the ground below had sunk down. He was pretty sure that the stench was coming from there—perhaps it was the stench of raw wet earth. But what was that beneath the sawdust? Was it earth?

What was keeping that sonofabitch Griggs?

Kavanaugh held the flashlight steady in his left hand, and with his right he began poking around in the ground. Jesus, it stank. He probed the damp earth below the dust and touched something that felt like cloth. He brushed away more of the sawdust, which by now was mixed indistinguishably with soil, and tugged on the strip of yellow cloth. The air was pretty foul now, and he started to move away, but he tugged a little more until the strip came away, and when he examined it in the light he saw that it *was* a piece of cloth, and that it had been ripped off a larger piece, possibly a . . . a . . . shirt? . . . Kavanaugh tossed it aside, began to paw at the shallow space, the air growing increasingly rank and his own heart starting to pound because the deeper into the earth he scratched and the more offensive the air became, the more certain he was about what he was going to find, but still he pawed the earth, flicking aside the rank debris until his hand touched something a little harder than cloth, and that was when Kavanaugh's stomach turned, and then he himself turned, jerking around toward the front door because Griggs had turned on the overhead bulb. Kavanaugh's eyes hadn't adjusted to the sudden brightness, but they didn't have to for him to see that the frame of the man who approached him now was too small and thin for it to be Griggs. Kavanaugh started to pull himself to his feet because he recognized that it definitely wasn't Griggs now, but whoever it was had his hands outstretched and the hands were holding something, and then he realized who it was, it was that fucking Robin Hood and his hands were holding that goddamn bow and it was drawn back—and realizing that, Kavanaugh started rising to his feet, but he didn't have enough time, he was halfway crouching and trying to stand, and that was when he saw Robin Hood's right hand let go, and that was the way the impact caught him, the force terrific, the sound of arrow cutting flesh and bone and cartilage a hollow thud, and suddenly he felt the warm wetness spreading over his chest and the light inside the shed wasn't so bright anymore, it was growing dimmer . . . and dimmer . . . not dimmer . . . black. . . .

Although he was certain Meredith wouldn't have gone probing about in the trunk, Griggs sighed with mild relief when his fingers touched the butt of the .45.

Hidden by the trees, he had crept silently down to the ridge, then, like an Indian, crawled stealthily to the rear of the car. He had the protection of the top of the car, which blocked his presence from view of the cabin. He opened the trunk, felt around, withdrew the gun, then clicked the trunk shut.

Kneeling by the car, he checked the weapon, found it loaded. Then he inched forward, peered around the car at the cabin and the surrounding area.

Christ! What was that idiot doing in the shed? From here, Griggs could see light seeping through cracks and spaces in the wood planks; he knew all that light couldn't be coming from Kavanaugh's flashlight, it wouldn't be that bright. That moron must've turned on the overhead bulb. Jesus, what a fool. . . .

Crouching, he doubled back through the trees, up around the hill toward the shed, his eyes darting every second to the cabin, to detect any movement from within.

He rounded the corner of the shed. The goddamn door was ajar and light spilled out onto the snowy ground. What the hell did that bastard think he was doing? He might just as well start shooting up the place, it would call as much attention. What a fool.

He rushed inside, closed the door behind him, and quickly reached up, about to turn off the light, when he noticed that Kavanaugh wasn't there. Damn him, where the hell was he—snooping around outside? But then his eyes caught something, he saw that Kavanaugh *was* there, on the other side of the room, behind the open cell door, slumped on the ground asleep.

Griggs hurried across the room, ready to kick that sorry bastard awake, but just as he reached the cell door he realized that a couple of things were very, very wrong. One was the way Kavanaugh's back was pressed against the wall and the way his head was hanging. The other was the long gold shaft protruding from his chest.

"Jesus Christ!" Griggs yelled. He stared down at Kavanaugh's body; at the same time he knew that he'd automatically put himself at a disadvantage: he was at the far end of the shed, and the person who nailed Kavanaugh had allowed him to get that far; also, his back was to the door. There wasn't a hell of a lot he could do about correcting the first predicament—he was standing there, that was it—but he could turn his back, and that was what he did, and at the same time his right hand reached into his coat, about to circle around the butt of the .45, but a voice from behind said, "No, don't move."

Goddamnit, that fucking creep *was* behind him.

"Turn around."

He did so, slowly, wishing his sense of caution would fail him so he could pull the gun out anyway and blow the bastard away. But he removed the hand, turned completely around.

Perry stood by the door, bow drawn. Jesus, Griggs thought for the second time today: staring into the gleaming point of a hunting arrow at full draw was terrifying—more so, he was learning, than staring into the barrel of a .45. Perhaps it was the tension and tautness of the string, the visibility of the potential force. A gun was scary, sure, but terrifying only when you saw the fingers holding it squeeze farther back on the trigger. Or perhaps it was remembering what Perry had said about the force. At 200 feet per second you just didn't take any chances, even if you thought you could get your gun out in time.

"I knew you'd be back," Perry said. "I told her so. I told her you'd be back."

What the hell was he talking about?

"Look—" Griggs began.

"I also told her you would never touch her."

"What?—"

"Step forward, please."

"Now, listen, this isn't even any of your business—"

Perry let out a short, chilling laugh. "On the contrary. I've made it very much my business. *You* could have stayed out of it. *Should* have stayed out of it. But I knew you wouldn't, and I told her so."

"Told who? What?—"

"You wanted to take her away."

"What the hell—"

"I said you wanted to take her away!" His hand drew back, and Griggs could see him shaking.

"I don't know what you're talking about—"

"*Yes, you do!*"

"Jesus, look—"

"Come." His tone was suddenly calm. "We haven't much time."

"What?"

"Come with me, we're running out of time."

"I don't—" Griggs saw the hand pull back even tighter on the string. He began walking toward the door. Perry stepped outside, holding the arrow on him, backing up.

Griggs stepped through the open door. He thought for a second that he might be able to overpower him with the cover of darkness, but the moon coming through the clouds and reflecting off the snow was too bright.

"Walk," Perry said, motioning up the hill beyond the shed. Toward the rising forest.

"Jesus," Griggs said, starting up. A number of things were running through his mind. He was thinking about the cold, the snow falling around him, and wondering what the hell this lunatic was talking about back in the shed. But what occupied most of his mind was the thought of failure. What had gone wrong? He was, after all, a man who detested risks and rarely took chances. Goddamnit, there just wasn't any fucking justice anymore. Just money. And pretty soon there wouldn't even be that, and then what? Why hadn't Kavanaugh been on his toes? *Why?* Jesus Christ, there just wasn't any fucking justice anymore. . . .

25

HE WANTED to return to the deep sleep he had been in, but Kate was nudging him.

David groaned, refused to open his eyes, because if he did he knew he would not be able to go back to sleep. And then, as his brain began to function, he realized that he was lying on his stomach, and that whoever was poking him was coming from his right, so it couldn't be Kate, she was on the other side of the bed. Someone else was in the room. Oh Christ, he thought—had he overslept?

Then he heard a voice. "Mr. Meredith? David?"

He blinked open sleep-filled eyes. The voice was Michael's.

David lifted his head, blinked faster because the lamp on the bedside table had been turned on and his eyes fought the glare. He managed to get out "Wha—?" Then he thought, *I didn't hear the alarm. Did it go off? What time is it? How much time have I lost?* He felt and heard Kate rousing behind him.

"Mr. Meredith," Michael said.

"What?" he said hoarsely, trying to wake up. He had to get going, start off down the mountain. "What time is it?"

"A little after three-thirty."

"Oh, Jesus . . ."

"Are you awake?"

"Uh-huh . . . yes. . . ."

"They're back."

David propped himself up in bed on one elbow, tried to focus on Perry's head. He was kneeling by the bed, holding something in his hand.

"What?" was all David could say.

"The two detectives. They're back."

Behind him, David heard Kate say quickly, "Oh, my God."

He turned to her. "Wait, easy now." He blinked at Michael. "Where—where are they?"

"One of them—Griggs, I think—is up the mountain." He smiled. "Unconscious. I saw him outside my window and sneaked out the back way. I made sure he went to sleep for a while."

"Jesus," David said. "And the other one?"

"I don't know where he is. I think in the garage, I saw a light out there."

David got up out of bed. "Let me get dressed, I'll meet you in the den."

"Right." Michael stood, left.

David began pulling on his pants.

"What're you going to do?" Kate said.

"I don't know. Maybe get rid of them once and for all."

"What do you mean?"

"*I don't know.*" He was buttoning his shirt, reaching for his coat.

Kate said, "I'd better check on Brian." She got up, sat for a second on the bed as David started for the door. David?"

He stopped, turned.

"Be careful."

He touched her cheek, left.

When he joined Michael in the den he saw that what Michael had been holding was a gun—the automatic they'd taken from Griggs.

"Here." He handed it to David. "You might want this."

David took it reluctantly. He felt numb, confused. He wondered if he could use the thing if he had to. And what were they going to do, anyway? This wasn't a film script, he and Michael couldn't battle it out with those two goons like cops and robbers.

"I have an idea," Michael said, rushing quietly to the front door of the cabin. David followed him. "You go up and find Griggs and I'll check out the garage." He picked up the bow and quiver from the hall table.

He opened the door, they went outside.

The air bit David's face; snow was falling and it was freezing outside. "What're we going to do then?"

"That's up to you."

"What? I don't understand. I mean, what do we do when we've cornered them, caught them?"

"Like I said, it's up to you. It's your child."

The implications of Michael's words hit him hard, but he didn't have time to think about them for long, because Michael was moving out toward the garage. David looked around them, then down the ridge toward the road.

"Wait!" he whispered.

Michael turned. "What is it?"

"The distributor cable." David rushed down the hill to where the Ford was parked, opened the hood, thinking there was a possibility Griggs or Kavanaugh had replaced the distributor before they made their move. But it was still missing.

Michael was coming up behind him now.

David said, "It's still gone. Shit, did you check Griggs's pockets, his coat?"

Michael shook his head guiltily.

"Jesus, I've got to get that distributor cable."

"I'll find the other guy, and you can check Griggs." He raised his bow, nocked an arrow.

"Where is he?"

Michael pointed up the mountain. "You'd better hurry before he wakes up."

"Christ," David said, and started up the mountain. He turned back once to see Michael darting toward the garage, where the light shone from within. If Kavanaugh was in there hiding, Michael could take him. Just looking at that deadly arrow, drawn back tight, would cause the burly man to reconsider whether or not he wanted his other arm punctured.

Clutching the cold grip of the gun in his hand, David ran up the mountain, gulping snow and icy air, soon leaving behind the relatively bare white ground and entering under the towering snow-covered pines. His eyes searched everywhere for a darkened patch of ground that might be Griggs lying unconscious in the snow, but so far he saw nothing.

The mountain rose steeply now; he was gasping, eyes still searching. He looked back and saw through clearings in the trees the faint outline of the distant shed and the garage, and wondered how Michael was making out with Kavanaugh. He also wondered, had Griggs actually climbed this high? It certainly was a good vantage point, but why the incredible distance? Or had David missed him somewhere along the way? Or, more frightening, had the detective come to and made his way down the mountain over another path? Was he back at the cabin this very moment, fending off Kate for the baby? David remembered Kavanaugh's revolver lying on the table in the den: he should have given it to Kate.

But just then he saw that Griggs *had* climbed this high.

He was lying on the frozen ground near a clump of trees right up ahead. David found his second wind and dug his feet into the snow, forcing the aching leg muscles on. If Griggs had the distributor on him, he and Kate could leave right away—or maybe Kavanaugh had it, since he was probably the one who'd taken it.

Then as he neared the supine form, David began to doubt his own eyes. At first all he registered was that something long and thin and glistening was rising out of the man's stomach. When he got closer he made out the fletching at the end of the arrow, and things began to click in his head. The sight was shocking; it brought with it the possibility of death, and death was not familiar to him, was not part of his reality—which was a silly notion because death is always present, always possible. But why now? Why here? And why was he mixed up in it all?

He slowed his pace, walking now over to the *body* of Laurence Griggs. He stared down at him—it—and prayed for a second that the man was still alive, that Michael had only wounded him, the way he'd wounded Kavanaugh—

—Kavanaugh—where was he?—

—but Griggs was dead, all right. His face was white, and not from the snow that was beginning to cover it. His eyes stared up at the sky, his mouth contorted in an awful grimace.

My God, David thought, did Michael realize what he'd done? What was going on, for Chrissakes?

He knelt by the body. He didn't want to touch it, but he wanted to search for the distributor cable.

He shivered, hesitated.

Why did he hesitate? Because he was afraid of touching the dead form? Yes, but there was something else. He reached into Griggs's right coat pocket, felt around. His brain was finally beginning to work, and as he was feeling around for the length of rubber cable, he wondered, *How did those two get back up here?* There was no way, no way at all they could have *walked* back up, not in this cold. And David had *seen* them going down. Surely the old Lincoln *couldn't* have made a return trip. So how did they get back up? Jesus, they must have another car. . . .

David reached around, felt in the other pocket. Nothing. He was about to reach over and try the left trouser pocket when the back of his neck exploded, caving in, and his vision went black. . . .

He wasn't as heavy as Griggs had been, but Michael had to drag Meredith a greater distance. As he pulled the man up through the trees, higher and higher up the mountain, he wondered why he hadn't just shot him the way he'd shot the two detectives. But he knew the reason; he didn't want Kate to think he was directly responsible for her husband's death. That Meredith would die there was no question. But he would die from exposure, because he'd gotten lost in the woods and it was freezing, and perhaps he'd stumbled, hit his head against a low-lying branch or something. But no arrow of Michael Perry's would be found in him. And if by some remote chance he *were* to survive, who was to say it wasn't Kavanaugh who bashed in his head with that sturdy branch? But there would be no need for explanations, because Meredith would die. He knew nothing of survival in the cold. That was why Michael was dragging him high into the woods—but not just high, he was circling far to the left, up around the outer rim. When Meredith came to he'd try to make it down, of course. But he wouldn't even get far enough to realize that he was practically on the other side of the mountain, and that there was no place where the incline leveled off, and there was no road, because the road wound in the other direction. Before he realized that, he would be stiff, his body would freeze. There was just no question.

Meredith was getting heavier and heavier the higher they went, but Michael kept tugging, harder and harder, spurred on by the renewed determination that came with imagining what was waiting for him back at the cabin. . . .

26

RACHEL WAS coming down the stairs when Michael entered the cabin. She stopped when he opened the door. A faded cotton robe was now wrapped around the pink nylon gown, and she stood there, her sleeping eyes squinted, watching him.

"Michael?"

He went quickly to her, took two steps up the stairs.

"What's going on?" she said.

"Shh. Nothing, go back to bed."

Her eyes opened wide now. She looked at him fearfully. "Michael?"

"It's nothing." He started up the stairs, urging her upward, back to the bedroom.

"What's going on, I want to know."

They stopped. "Those two detectives are back."

"Oh, no. Where?"

"Meredith's outside with them."

"What are you going to do?"

"We're handling it, you go on up to bed." He started her up again, they climbed to the second landing. His bow was strung over his shoulder; he took it off slowly when they'd entered the bedroom, then turned, about to return to the den. He was almost out of the room when Rachel said, "Outside?"

"What?"

"What are they doing outside?"

"I'm going to find out."

Perhaps it was something in his voice, maybe he faltered, but Rachel was looking at him now disbelievingly, her mouth open as if she were in shock. "No. . . ." Her voice was hollow, deep. She took a step toward him. "You're not telling me the truth." Her eyes widened. "My God, what are you going to do? Where's Mr. Meredith?"

"I told you."

"Where's Kate?" she said nervously.

"In her room."

"Something's happened, hasn't it? You've done something—or you're going to. Oh, my God, Jesus, you can't."

"Quiet."

A cry escaped her lips. She approached him; her arms went out and her shaking hands searched out over the front of his coat, then up over his shoulders. "You've got to stay here, Michael. With me. I need you. . . ." The terror in her voice reverberated throughout the room.

"No, I told you—"

"Michael . . ." Her hands moved frantically down over him; she reached around his waist and pulled him closer, tightening their bodies together. "You've got to stay here. . . ." Her whole body was shaking now. Michael could see the deepening horror reflected in her wide gray eyes. She was breathing faster, her eyes beseeching him, her face completely white, and Michael thought for a moment that she was mad. He pulled away from her.

"Michael!—"

"Be *quiet.*" He held the bow out in his right hand. "Don't leave here."

"No, stay here, I—"

"Shut up—"

"What are you going to do?"

He didn't answer her, but pointed the bow at her threateningly.

She said, "I know what you're going to do, and you *can't.*"

"*Shut up.* Get to bed. *Now.*"

She backed away fearfully, her mouth quivering, hands trembling. "You can't . . . you just can't . . . my God, Michael, you're . . . you're *crazy*—"

He lunged forward, slapped her hard, then grabbed her face and squeezed until the white skin turned bright red. "You're goddamned right. You're goddamned right! *And you know who made me this way!*"

She didn't hear him when he walked in.

"He wants you outside."

"What?"

"Your husband. David."

"Now?"

"Now."

"But—"

"We've got to hurry."

Kate looked at Brian asleep in the crib. Before Michael had walked in she had spoken a silent prayer, thankful because he looked so much better. He would be a healthy baby before long.

"He'll be all right," Michael said. "I've asked Rachel to look after him."

"But why?—"

"He'll explain. Hurry!"

She wondered why he was carrying the awesome-looking bow. "All . . . all right . . . let me get dressed."

"There's no time."

Kate could see the urgency in his face. *Had something happened to David?*

She hurried out of the room, dashed into the bedroom down the hall, grabbed her thermal coat and put it on over the flannel gown Rachel had lent her. She slipped quickly into her shoes and together they raced from the house.

Outside, Michael led the way to the small shed that was set on a rise above the cabin. "In here," he said, opening the door.

Kate went inside. "David?" she called, and heard the door close behind her.

The interior surprised her—all the toys on the walls, and the bars at the back. What was this? More important, where was David?—she didn't see him. She stopped halfway inside, turned around. "Where—where is he?"

Michael was bolting the door. "Who?"

"My *husband*," Kate said, certain now that something had gone wrong. And then she saw Michael Perry's eyes, and the muscles in her neck tightened as she realized that something was going wrong right now.

"David's outside looking for Mr. Griggs. He should be here shortly."

"Why—" Kate began, flustered "—then why did you tell me he was here?"

He was moving toward her, withdrawing one of the arrows from under the long green metal covering on the front of the bow. "Because I wanted to talk to you."

Kate found herself backing toward the strange row of bars behind her. Her heart quickened as she realized what was happening. My God, where was David?

"You don't *mind* if I talk to you?"

"Talk? What about those two men?"

"I told you that I wouldn't let them touch you. And they haven't."

"But where are they?" Her back touched something hard. Something behind her clanged—the bars. She was growing warm and thought it was because of the fear rising in her; but her eyes glanced down to her left and she saw behind the bars the glowing orange coils of a small electric heater. Her eyes didn't linger but looked back at Michael, who was moving to one side, placing the arrow on the string. "Mr. Griggs is outside. Don't worry; David will find him."

She looked expectantly at him, her back pressed against the rigid structure.

"The big one with the bushy hair?" he said. "He came in here just seconds ago, long after David had gone looking for his partner. But that's not important now. What's important is us. You *will* talk to me, won't you? And you'll listen to me?"

Kate's back pressed harder against what she knew must be steel. The skin on Michael's face was pulled taut over his high forehead and under his jaw, and his black eyes glistened in their sockets, giving him a chilling, skull-like appearance. "I—".

"Please say you will, Kate." He raised the bow, drew back, aimed the arrow at her.

"No, please, I—" She moved along the bars, her hands reaching, searching behind her, until finally they found an open space, probably the door, and, knowing she shouldn't keep backing up because she was running out of room and he was cornering her, she nevertheless could not stop herself, the action was instinctive, she was frightened to death, the sense of dread beginning to consume her, and her feet kept shuffling through some powdery substance covering the floor—and then her heart seemed to stop altogether because he had released the arrow; she heard the *twang* of the string and saw the pointed tip speeding through the air and she thought she'd faint, but the arrow came too fast and its course was too far to one side. She felt it whipping past her, and then she heard a hollow thud from behind, as the arrow hit what sounded like a bag of grain. Her whole body shook; a hysterical cry escaped her lips.

"He's right behind you, if you want to know," Michael said, and Kate wasn't sure what he meant. "Mr. Kavanaugh. See."

Her stomach began to sink; she turned around apprehensively.

He lay slumped against the wall, two arrows sticking from him.

The tiny shed filled with her screams. She collapsed against the back of the cell door, quavering, her breath coming in quick, spasmodic bursts. Out of the corner of her eye she saw Michael approaching.

"You see, Kate? He can't hurt you now."

She faced him, about to run, but he'd drawn another arrow and was aiming it at her. "No," she cried, looking panic-stricken at his flushed, demoniacal face.

"Move back, Kate. You know I mean business with this thing."

She couldn't move back, not inside with that . . . she just couldn't. Her stomach twisted; it was racked with spasms.

He drew farther back on the bow. "Do as I say, Kate. Please do as I say."

Slowly, she moved back, stepping far to her left, away from what lay in the corner. "What are you doing?" she said, beginning to cry. "What do you want?" She couldn't keep her eyes off the taut, determined face with its anxious expression.

"That should be obvious now. Shouldn't it?" He continued toward her.

She realized suddenly that she was behind the bars. Michael came forward, lowered the bow in his left hand and with his right reached out for the cell door and clanged it shut. A key ring jangled, the lock clicked. "I want you."

Kate froze. She stared unbelievingly into the intense black eyes, the terror and revulsion sweeping over her. It was the same look—the schoolroom years before. What he wanted. She rushed forward, threw herself against the door. "No! My God, *no*!"

The first sensation of which he was aware was the burning cold of his cheek. And at first David couldn't be certain if his skin throbbed from heat or from cold. The next sensation he felt was the excruciating pain at the back of his neck, and he wondered why it was there, what had happened, did he remember what might have caused such pain?

Then David remembered the cracking sound before his vision had gone completely black. He remembered searching in the pocket for the distributor cable—and that was when his neck had exploded.

Another sensation, and one that he only now began to be aware of, was the chill all around him.

His right hand clenched, relaxed; the fingers pressed downward, digging deep into snow. He rolled the burning cheek away from the ground and found there was no feeling. All the muscles and bones in his body ached.

With considerable effort David brought both arms toward his torso, crushed the snow with both hands and pushed his body up away from the ground.

His eyes could barely make out the snow, which appeared dark gray; everything else around him was black and indistinguishable. Soon, however, he recognized the dark trunks and lighter branches of the trees; then the view before him began to lighten and he saw patches of white sky.

Grunting, he pulled himself up. His entire head throbbed, the pain in his neck overwhelming, and he wondered for a second if something hadn't been severed—or if indeed his head itself hadn't been severed from his body. So intense were the racking throbs that he thought he might cry; and possibly he would have if two other emotions hadn't surfaced: fear and anger. David wasn't sure which outweighed the other in importance or urgency, but they were both there, and both drove him forward, forced him to his feet, upon which he could barely stand. He staggered over to a tree, propped himself against the trunk, looked around.

The surrounding terrain seemed unfamiliar. His eyes searched for the body lying in the snow, but he couldn't find it. Had he, upon falling, been turned around? He whirled his pounding head in every direction. Had Michael moved Griggs? Christ, had Michael moved *him*? . . .

He stumbled out over the snow, braced himself on another tree, and tried to find the path he'd come up. But it wasn't there. He was positive this wasn't the spot where he'd found Griggs.

He shivered, touched the cheek that had lain frozen in the snow, and thought that the feeling was slowly returning. He pulled the coat collar up tight around his neck. As he breathed the air his chest heaved, trembled. It was damned cold and he had to get moving or he would freeze.

Half-running, half-stumbling, he headed forward through the trees. Strange, but there was no sensation of heading downward; he was on level ground. Could that be?

It could if Michael had moved him when he was unconscious. . . .

But why would he do that? He'd killed Griggs, and the last time David saw him he was going to find Kavanaugh. Had he killed the burly man too? If so, why? It wasn't as if he were out stalking game, they weren't wild animals, there was no real need to kill them. Besides, if anyone should hate Laurence Griggs and want to see him dead, it was David. Griggs had wanted to take away his only son. But how had Griggs been a threat to Michael Perry? What had Griggs wanted of Michael, a perverse recluse who did nothing but hunt deer all day long? . . .

With this question still pounding in his head, David started off again through the trees, in a different direction, looking for the edge of the mountain, his heart quickening. The tops of the trees obscured the sky now, increasing the darkness. He stumbled through the white drifts, anxious, heart about to explode, eyes searching through gaps in the trees, searching for lights below, only there was nothing below, he wasn't descending at all, and he was still wondering what Michael Perry could *possibly* want of Griggs. But then, as he changed direction again, trying to get his bearing in the bitter night, the mental censor in his brain collapsed, and he suddenly visualized Michael's glowing face as he sat before the fire tonight, looking at Kate, and he realized that with the two detectives out of the way, it wasn't *what* Michael wanted, but *whom*. . . .

Rachel had not moved since Michael left her; she was still standing by the corner, at the foot of the bed. Still trembling. Her teeth tightened over the edge of her lower lip. She listened—for what she did not know, but it was all she could do, the only activity left her.

She had never seen him like that. They had argued in the past, certainly; but he had never lashed out at her like that, the unmistakable hate seething through his eyes, his entire being. *He could have killed her*. That was what terrified her. That and the fact that he might harm Kate and the child.

Shaking, she made herself move, sit down on the bed. She touched her lip with one finger and, taking it away, saw a speck of blood on the tip. Rubbing her arms through the pink nylon, she thought, *We have come this far and it is my fault; long ago I resigned myself to a life of never-ending penance*. And yet, she asked herself, *why must it involve innocent people?*

But asking herself *why* didn't change the reality that innocent people had already become involved. And so she thought, *Something should be done.*

Rachel was freezing and the room was not even cold. She continued rubbing her arms together. It has gone on this long, she thought. It has gone on too long. Something should be done.

But she knew there was nothing that could be done. He would kill her, there was no stopping him.

Memories began to surface, memories she had banished from her mind; but they rose and flooded into her head anyway, and she couldn't help herself, she knew she shouldn't do it, but she got up from the bed and walked over to the locked closet where the memories were stored. . . .

27

"KATE, YOU'RE not answering me. Why don't you answer me?"

She felt the heat on her ankles from the electric heater below, and took a step away, determined not to let her eyes wander to her right, to the still form in the corner. All she had been thinking about for the last minute was where David was, and why wasn't he here this very moment? She was frightened, for the first time since they'd left the Berensons' place late this morning, for herself. She had told David, in their room earlier, that she was afraid of what was happening to *them*, to his trust in her, but that was something they could work on together. She was frightened now for herself because there was no doubt in her mind that Michael Perry was insane.

"I asked you a question, Kate, yet you haven't answered me." He laughed. "That's funny, isn't it? I asked you why you aren't answering me and you won't answer to tell me. That's kind of funny, don't you think?"

He came forward, right up against the bars.

"Where's David?" Kate asked.

"Kate, you must not have heard me when I told you. He's out looking for Mr. Griggs."

"Then he'll be back soon. What do you think he'll do when he sees you've got me locked in here?"

"You don't have to be here when he gets back."

She looked at him curiously.

"You can be out by then, if we hurry."

"I . . . I don't understand."

"*I* can explain if you'll listen."

"I have no choice."

"*You do have a choice!*"

His outburst shocked her, she backed against the wall.

He calmed down and said, "If you think you have no choice, then you won't really listen. You won't *care* about what I'm saying, and then it won't make any difference. Do you understand?"

She nodded slowly, about to cry.

"Good." He stepped over to the desk, picked up the chair behind it, set it down in front of the door. He propped the bow against the bars, sat down, and encircled the bars with both hands as if *he* were the one on the inside, peering desperately out.

Kate just stood silently, afraid to move, aware now of the peculiar odor filling the cell.

"Why did you run out of the room tonight?"

"What?"

"When I was describing the mating of the deer. Why did you run from the room?"

"You know why."

"No, I don't, I really don't. Tell me."

She let out a whimper, brought a hand to her cheek. "It was cruel."

"Cruel? Oh no, I didn't mean it to be, to me it was exciting, and I'd hoped you might see it the same way."

"Please let me out, David'll be here soon."

His eyes went blank. "You said a little while ago that you'd listen. Are you reconsidering?"

"No, I just want to leave, I can listen out there, back at the cabin."

He shook his head. "It's got to be here, Kate. It just does, that's all. And besides—" He reached into his pocket, withdrew a length of black tubing with a cap at each end. "—no one's leaving here at all, not yet." He dangled the object before her. "Do you know what this is, Kate?"

Kate looked at the thing; she wasn't sure what it was, but she had an idea, and she nodded slowly.

"That's right, it's the distributor cable from the detectives' car." He smiled. "David thought they'd taken it, but I did, while I was out getting wood. So no one's leaving just yet, and you can't listen to me back at the cabin, it's got to be here. Do you understand that?"

She let out a cry, bent her head. "Talk, then."

He put the cable back in his pocket. "Good. You'll listen?"

She nodded again.

"Good. And you'll answer me when I ask you why you thought it was cruel?"

She raised her head, her eyes beginning to water. "Because you were staring at me, it was embarrassing, I felt like you were . . . were raping me. . . . Why'd you talk that way, in front of your wife, in front of my husband? It was embarrassing."

"Because I wanted you to know how I felt. I wanted you to know how I felt about you."

"*I knew that.*" She let out a sob. "Won't you please let me go?"

"NO!" He grabbed the bars, yanked them violently. "No . . . no, you've got to listen. You know, Kate, you're making me very angry, and I don't need that now. I *can't* get angry, do you understand? *Do you understand?*"

She trembled. "Yes. . . ."

"Now, then, I realize you thought it was embarrassing, and I'm sorry. And maybe it was cruel. But I couldn't help myself. Perhaps I was enjoying it—no, I *was* enjoying it, and perhaps I was angry with you, trying to get to you, but there are reasons. You see, I've never met anyone like you, Kate, never in my whole life. When I saw you out there stranded on the road, I told myself, 'I could get lost in her,' because that's the way I felt. You were so helpless, standing there holding that baby, wondering what was going to happen. You were *afraid*, and that made you *vulnerable*. And David, your *husband*, didn't seem to care about you, he was yelling at you, and all he wanted to do was get his car unstuck—"

"Because our son was sick, we had to get him to a doctor—"

"I'm talking about *you*. He was yelling at you. I could have killed him right then and there."

"You don't understand. We had to—"

"*You* don't understand, Kate, it's you who doesn't understand what I'm trying to say. When he has someone as beautiful as you, why would he be screaming—"

"David doesn't *have* me."

"I know." His eyes burned a deep black. "I do."

She cried. "No. . . ."

"Yes, Kate. I do for now. You're different, Kate, did you know that? You're so very, very different." He paused, rested his head against the bars, rolling it between the spaces, then pulled it back an inch, looked at her, although the eyes had become lifeless again, as if they were looking elsewhere. "You're a very loving person, Kate, I can tell. A caring person, and that's very important. You care for that baby, you probably care for David. But you care for the wrong people. It seems like such a waste, and that bothers me. Anyway, I have to tell you something. Something I've never discussed with anyone but Rachel, because she understands, she's learned to live with it, although it upsets her to be reminded of what happened to me, and she doesn't like to think about it. And because of that her understanding has become . . . passive; it's become simple acceptance, and I need more than that. So I want you to know."

"No, please, won't you just—"

"Look at me, Kate."

She saw the perspiration speckling his now feverish forehead; the hellish black eyes were fixed on her in a torturous stare.

"You've got to know," he said.

Fear paralyzed her, and her heart beat faster, she could hardly breathe.

"I grew up here, in that cabin, but mostly right here in this playhouse. My father was a builder and he built this place. I spent almost all my time here." His eyes traveled slowly around the room, looking at the objects on the walls. "Do you know why? Do you know why I stayed out here all the time, why I didn't live in the cabin with my mother and father? I mean, I actually slept right in there." He pointed to the floor of the cell. "Used to sleep on the sawdust, a blanket wrapped around me and the heater on. I stayed out here because of my father. He built this shed when I was very, very young, when he cared about me, about what happened to me. And then suddenly one day he didn't care anymore. He began to care more about liquor than he did about me or my mother. He used to hit her, my mother; he used to hit me, too, across the face—hit us when he thought one of us had hidden his bottle. When he . . . got that way, I'd come out here, because here it was always safe." He smiled. "Sometimes, even my mother would come out with me, when my father had gone off somewhere, and we'd talk about him, about what was going to happen. My father would go off at night a lot to his building sites, always drunk, or go into town and drink by himself. Always by himself. No one liked him, not even the people who worked for him, or the people at the real estate agency, they all hated him: Like I did, and my mother. And then sometimes he'd leave a bar, drunk, and haul supplies out to the site by himself for the next day's work—lumber, tools, dynamite, and stuff. Most of the time he'd forget where he left things, and people would laugh behind his back, but they were also afraid because some of that stuff was dangerous." Michael laughed. "Everybody thought one day he'd run off the road and blow himself up." The smile vanished. "But he never did."

He paused, pressed his face against the bars. "Anyway, he's gone now. The people in town think he ran away, abandoned us. But when he was here it was pure hell for us, my mother and me. She was all I had, and I was all she had. So she never let me leave this place—not that I wanted to. She even took me out of school early because all the kids would tease me about my father being drunk and all, and about me and my mother. And when he came home, I would stay out here in this play shed, and sometimes my mother would come out here too. She was very protective, you see, and she went insane whenever my father struck me; you can't imagine how she looked when that happened, because I was all she had—she certainly didn't have *him*—and he hated the fact that she loved me more than she loved him; she even quit her job so she could look out for me. And then pretty soon it was obvious that he didn't want either one of us, and he liked to hit me in front of her because he knew it made her insane, and he liked to make her think that one day he might even kill me, might even blow up this play shed with me in it."

He stopped suddenly, moved his face away from the bars, looked around questioningly. Kate's legs began to tire, but she didn't dare move. She thought it would be disastrous to make any disturbance now, he was so intense, so concentrated on what he was saying.

"You want to know why I'm telling you this, where it's all leading, don't you? It has to do with what's wrong with me, and it has to do with you, because you're part of it now, Kate."

The muscles in Kate's body constricted; she felt her entire frame tighten as he spoke those last words.

"Do you know how many girls I knew before Rachel? None. How could I, isolated up here, never seeing anyone? Oh, there were girls at school, but they were just that—girls—and they all knew about my father. But then one day something happened, right here, in this shed. It was after I had come in here to hide, after my father went on one of his rampages, hitting my mother, and I couldn't take it, and I didn't want to be hit, so I ran out here. And later my mother came in and held me. I was lying on the floor right there behind those bars, and she came to me and held me. She was crying hard and her face was bloody. We lay there a long while in the darkness with only the glow of that heater. And after a long time she touched me—"

Kate stepped forward. "Please—" She knew the minute she'd broken the silence and the stillness that she shouldn't have, that he would lash out at her again. But he didn't. He was too deeply into his own remembrance, and Kate wished he weren't, she wished he really would scream at her, because she didn't want to listen anymore, afraid of what she might hear—

"—she touched me," he continued, "and she let me know what I never thought I would ever know with a woman." He stopped again, for what seemed like an eternity. His mouth was slightly parted, and there was a curious expression on his face. "It was the ultimate possession, you see," he said at last. "And that's what my father couldn't understand. *Because he found us in here*. That's right, he busted in here and found us, and he couldn't understand, he went crazy, and he would have killed me—both of us—with his shotgun that he was carrying, if he hadn't been drunk. My mother got it away from him, the shotgun, and just as he was about to beat me I heard it go off. He fell to the floor and at first I thought maybe he had suddenly just passed out, but then I saw the blood."

He smiled, pressed his lips together, and looked over to where the detective lay slumped against the wall.

"Ever since then, Kate," he continued, "things have been different; I've been different. Rachel understands, but that's not enough. I want *you* to understand, Kate. And I think you will because you're a caring person. No one else cares. There *was* a girl, once, in town, but she didn't care, she laughed and screamed and I got angry." He stood up, leaned forward. "You won't make me angry, will you, Kate? Will you?"

Kate looked, horrified, at the crimson face, the skin stretched taut against the shining cheekbones, the onyx eyes staring at her beseechingly, never blinking, and yet behind them she detected the ever-present burning glow of expectation. She took a step back.

"You refuse to answer me again. I said, 'You won't make—' "

"I heard you." Her voice broke. "I heard you."

"Then answer."

"I . . . I don't—"

"I want you to care about me, Kate. I care about you. You see, the trouble here is that you care for the wrong people."

"No." She began to cry again. "No, I don't. Please—"

"I've just never met anyone like you before, and I probably never will, so I can't let this opportunity escape."

"Please, *please*, let me out. David will be back soon—"

"He's not important, how can he be?"

"Please—"

"I asked you a question, Kate, and again you don't answer—"

"He's my husband, he'll be back—"

"You mean just for that reason he's important, you care about him? I think he wanted to slap you when you were arguing there on the road—"

"Don't you understand? We were trying to get our baby to a doctor, he was sick, still is, we had to—"

"*Our* baby? You're right, I don't understand. That's not your baby. Otherwise those two detectives wouldn't have come all the way from Washington to take him back—"

"He's our baby!"

"David couldn't give you a baby."

Kate was about to explode. My God, what was happening? Where was David?

"Did you hear me, Kate? I said David couldn't—"

"*He gave me a baby, he did!*" She screamed as loud as she could, and the tears flooded down her cheeks. She sobbed violently.

"Then why isn't that your child back there at the cabin?"

She could barely get it out. ". . . because . . . we . . . adopted . . . oh, please, *please* . . ."

"Yes, but *why*, if David could—"

"Because . . . I . . . couldn't . . ."

He didn't respond right away. The shed was silent except for her constant cries. Then he said, "I just can't believe that, Kate; I'm sorry, but I just can't."

"Oh, please, won't you let me go, we've got to leave, my baby is—"

"You know, Kate, either way, I can't understand why that kid is so important to you. I've tried to understand, but I can't. I want you to try not to think about him anymore, at least not for now—"

"He's sick, we need to get him—"

"I said I didn't want you thinking about him anymore—"

"I can't, he's my baby, I want—"

"You *want* him?"

"Yes!"

His eyes seemed to be protruding farther from their sockets as he stared menacingly at her. The tiny vein near his hairline began to throb. "You want to leave here and you *want him?*"

"*Yes*! Let me—"

"Let you go? I can't. That baby that isn't even yours is more important to you right now than I am, isn't he?"

"Please—"

"He's keeping you from thinking about me, listening to me; why, I'll bet he's more important to you than David is right now, isn't he?"

"No. . . ."

"And you want him now, is that it?" His eyes flickered then glowed with a frightful determination. "Well, fine, Kate, you just sit down right there and I'll bring him to you—"

"*NO*! Don't touch him, goddamn you, don't you lay a hand on him, you hear me, don't—"

"You just sit down there and I'll go get him, since he's so important to you, maybe you should have him right now—"

"DON'T TOUCH HIM!"

"Oh," Michael said, turning around and heading for the door, "I'll touch him, all right. . . ."

28

HE THOUGHT he'd made it to the edge. He could feel the force pulling him down, he was reasonably sure he was heading down the mountain and that just a few more yards would reveal the tiny outline of the Perry cabin. But after stumbling over brush and trudging through snow for what seemed like a hell of a long time, David gave up hope of seeing anything but more trees, more terrain. His lungs felt about to burst; he didn't know how much longer they could continue to breathe in the frigid air. He was panting heavily, his face flushed and burning. But all the running he'd been doing deceived him as to his ability to interpret his own body temperature. He knew he must be literally freezing to death and that frostbite was a reality he couldn't ignore, and although earlier he'd kidded himself with an exaggeration of old Doc Bristol ready to saw off his frozen purple toes, it was no longer a joke or an exaggeration.

It was anger now that drove him on now. Without that he would no doubt collapse in the snow, his quick death a certainty, so why put it off? The anger wouldn't let him stop, however, the anger and the fear. He had no idea where Kate was at this moment, or *how* she was, but he had to get to her because he knew Michael was up to something. David thought he would never, ever stop cursing himself for not bashing that sonofabitch's face right there in the den before the fire. The man was crazy. And right now David was a little bit crazy too. Because he was out to get blood.

Moments later David realized just how far Michael had dragged him. And he realized where he was heading. He wasn't getting closer to the cabin because he was near the other side of the mountain. The way he knew this—aside from the obvious fact that the terrain itself seemed unfamiliar—was because of one factor that the maniac Perry had not considered when planning this mad scheme.

It was getting light.

David wasn't positive at first, he wasn't sure that was what was really happening, because it could have been the moon emerging into a clear patch of sky.

But after a while there was no doubt. The forest was beginning to lighten. David thought he could make out the branches of the snow-covered trees a little more clearly, and when he looked up at the sky he knew it wasn't the moon at all, the sky was getting lighter and it was because dawn was nearing.

He looked about him in every direction, searching for a clearing in the trees, anything to help him make up his mind which way to head.

He started up the hill he was on, climbed as far as he could, trying to get back to the spot where he was when he'd regained consciousness. He'd take his bearings from there, no use trying to go about it blindly without a starting point.

But in the meantime his movements were becoming sluggish; he felt as though he were watching himself in slow motion. His legs would surely have to be sawed off now, and perhaps his hands as well, although he tried to keep them in his pockets as much as possible.

He trudged onward, faster now even though his lungs ached like crazy, because his body needed the circulation, and he kept on up the hill, legs about to fall off, higher and higher, pausing every now and then for just a split second in hopes of hearing some kind of sound—

—screams?—

—Jesus, no, just some kind of sound to lead him in the right direction. And then he quit lying to himself, because he was in the middle of nowhere, there weren't any houses around and so there wouldn't be any sounds—the only possible sounds he might pick up would be those coming from the Perry cabin, and there wouldn't be any of those if they weren't screams, so goddamnit, he forced himself on, knowing he would kill Michael when he got there, and this thought was slightly disconcerting to him, it took him by surprise because David had never before promised himself he was going to kill someone, except perhaps in jest, as a figure of speech, but this was no figure of speech, this was a promise he was making to himself.

A promise he planned to keep. . . .

Kate was looking at the big man slumped over in the corner. She found she could no longer keep her eyes away. After Michael had left she tried forcing the door open, but it was locked tight, and no amount of pushing or pulling made any difference.

She had screamed for a long time after he left. Screamed and cried, hoping David would hear her. Where *was* he? Where was Rachel? Why didn't she put a stop to this madness, stop him before he went too far? Perhaps she was asleep, unaware of what was going on. . . .

Kate tried not to think for very long, because when she did all she could envision was Michael Perry reaching down and picking Brian up—roughly, not caring, he didn't know how to handle him. Oh, God, please don't let him touch my baby, *please*. . . .

She leaned against the wooden wall, exhausted from the crying, nauseated from the sickening odor in the cell. . . . Oh . . . please—

"Here we are, Kate," Michael said, kicking open the door, coming toward her. The bow was strung over one shoulder; in his hands he carried a blue bundle—

—God, no—Brian—

"I told you not to touch him!" she screamed. "Take him back, it's cold out here, he'll *freeze*!"

He clutched Brian in one hand, took off the bow with the other, propped it against the bars, then began fumbling with the keys on the ring hanging from his belt.

"Kate wants to have her baby boy with her." The tone of his voice scared her; it was thick, threatening, sarcastic.

"Please, take him back, what are you doing?—"

"What does it look like I'm doing, Kate? You can't seem to think of anything else but this kid who isn't even yours, don't you want him now?"

"No, please—"

The door creaked open. "Let's see, now, how can I give him to you? One must be very gentle with babies, there's a proper way to hold them, isn't there? Step back, Kate, you're getting too near."

"Oh, Jesus, please—"

"*Step back, Kate, you're getting too near, I want you back against the wall.*"

Sobbing, she took a step back, her eyes riveted to the blanket in Michael's arms.

"How can I best give him to you, Kate? I don't dare come too close with only one hand free, without my bow, so you'd better hold out your hands so you can catch him—"

"NO! I'll come for him, please, I'll come for him, just let me—"

And then she screamed because the tiny form went up out of his arms, into the air straight at her, and she was petrified she wouldn't catch him. "*NO-O!*" And the bundle hit her on the chest, she scooped her arms up to hold it, and as she looked down to cradle her baby, the blanket fell open and she screamed again as the bloodied body of the gray cat slithered down over her breasts, over the coat and the flannel gown, dropping to the floor, a broken arrow through its throat. Kate jerked away, hit the back wall. Frozen with terror, she was unable to speak or scream.

She slumped down to the floor.

Michael stepped back, reached for the bow, removed one of the arrows, put the bow back and stared at her for a long time. Then he said, "I hated him. Hated him almost as much as I hated that baby. You see, cats show absolutely no affection whatsoever. They're useless animals. I hated that cat almost as much as I hated that baby."

Hated? It took a second before Kate registered what he'd said. She could barely hear him through her crying. "What?" she sobbed.

"Nothing." he said.

She tried to control herself, tried to fathom why he'd said *hated* instead of hate. Her bleary eyes opened wide, looking at him disbelievingly. "Where's Brian? What did you do?"

"Nothing, Kate, he's fine."

"I don't believe you—"

"You must believe me, he's sound asleep, didn't even stir when I took his blanket—"

"Then let me go see him, let me—"

He held the arrow up high. "Shut up and listen to me, Kate—"

"Let me *go*—"

"*I said shut up and listen to me!*" He pointed the tip of the arrow at her face. He indicated the dead cat, its blood beginning to soak into the sawdust. "That—what I just did—that was cruel. What happened earlier tonight was not cruel. Do you see the difference?"

She said nothing.

"I said, *Do you see the difference?*"

She could only shake her head.

"That's too bad, because there's a world of difference." He paused. "But we're running out of time now and I want you to listen good to what I say and, more important, *accept* what I say."

"What did you do?—"

"*Nothing!* The kid is fine."

"*Then let me go!*" She pulled herself up, lunged for him, teeth grinding, hands clawing outward, but just as she reached him he hit her hard against the face and she stumbled backward against the wall. He went to her, stuck the arrow under her chin, held it there, pressing lightly.

"Now listen good, Kate. They're gone—those two detectives are dead. I killed them for you. Not because they were going to take the baby away, but because they would have hurt you in the end, maybe even have killed you. But they're gone now. It's you and me, Kate, just you and me now."

He drew back the arrow. She breathed easier, looking at him through watery eyes.

His own black eyes stared through her. "And you don't want to make me angry, do you? Because remember I told you there was a girl once, in town? Well, she made me angry, and we were in this motel room, and I thought maybe she would care at first, but she didn't, she didn't care at all, and she started calling me all these names I didn't understand; I had to keep pushing her back down and she kept screaming, her hands beating on me just like my father's had, and I couldn't take that anymore, so all I could do was reach out for this lamp by the bed and I hit her with it until finally she wasn't screaming at me or beating me anymore, and so you don't want to make me angry, do you, Kate?"

She looked at him in disbelief.

Michael began to smile. "And you know what, Kate?" He looked over to where the detective lay. "Mr. Kavanaugh almost found her—the girl, that is."

Kate's stomach began to turn.

"That's right," he said. "And if he'd dug a little deeper he would have found my father as well."

Kate forced her eyes away from the other side of the cell; she was about to be sick. Oh . . . God . . . no. . . . Shaking, weeping, and thinking she would never, ever stop, she said, "You can't do this. . . ."

He cocked his head. "Can't do what? I haven't told you what I'm going to do, not exactly, not in detail."

"Whatever it is—"

"But I will now." He brought the arrow tip under her chin, pressed. "I'm going to take you, Kate. You're going to take off your coat and Rachel's old gown and lie right here in the sawdust, and I'm going to do what I've never been able to do with anyone but Rachel, and you're going to help, because you're a caring person, and you're gentle, and so that's what I'm going to do, now you know for sure, and if I can't, and if you don't help, then I'm going to kill you. . . ."

SHE STOOD there in the open closet, mesmerized by the face in the photograph before her. It was the most beautiful face she had ever seen—quite possibly the most innocent and angelic face that had ever been conceived. She looked around, savoring the memories, burying herself in them.

She stood there for a long time, and she was standing there when she heard the front door open, close, footsteps pounding over the oak floor, stopping, starting again down the hall. She didn't think about them, really, just registered them, then returned to the glories of her private closet, to the mementos she and she alone would ever possess.

And then she thought about Michael. His face, presently called to mind, jarred her for a moment and she stepped away from her memories and very slowly and methodically shut the closet door.

The footsteps . . . Were they Michael's? Mr. Meredith's? Kate's? No, not hers. And surely they couldn't belong to either of the two detectives, could they?

Rachel listened carefully. The cabin was still and the quiet was deafening. Then she thought she heard a noise downstairs, the sound of someone or something moving. And then silence.

A minute later the footsteps sounded again over the oak floor, running, and then she heard the sound of the door opening, slamming shut.

Rachel's heart beat furiously, but still she did not move.

She did not move because she was terrified.

Straining her ears to hear the slightest movement from down below, she detected nothing. Then she walked slowly over to the mirror above the dresser, stopped directly before it, looked at herself. She stared at herself for a long time before finally removing the cotton robe, then reaching up and slipping the left sleeve of the nylon gown over her shoulder and pulling the top of the gown halfway down her chest. And then she stared for an even longer time at the patchwork of threadlike scars over her skin, her breasts. Strange, she thought—strange what she'd been willing to do, to have done. What was it in her? She shook her head, her thoughts drifting. . . .

Then suddenly she remembered that whoever had come in a little while ago had left, and she wondered if anyone was in the cabin now.

The child. She remembered the beautiful tiny boy asleep

downstairs. Was anyone looking after him? It was awfully quiet.

She thought of the look on Michael's face when he left, and she knew he was going to Kate, so she doubted Kate was down there with the child.

She trembled. Michael's going to her meant two things. First, that he would not be able to consummate his desires with her; it was a fact that he could not and would not ever be able to accept. Only with Rachel could he carry out his secret acts. Because Rachel understood. The second was that the child had been left alone. Perhaps it needed caring, and caring was something Rachel also understood, something she could do.

She found herself pulling up the sleeve of the gown and moving toward the bedroom door, heading out, because she needed to see about the child. It wasn't until she was out the door and on the landing that she recalled the absolute hatred in Michael's eyes before he left, and as she remembered that, something occurred to her that filled her with a mixture of revulsion and dread, and suddenly she was running, stumbling down the stairs, dashing across the den and tearing down the hallway, plunging into the baby's room.

It was only then that she heard the tiny cries, and then the cries became painful wails which seemed to stretch forever. The room was filled with the deafening squeals by the time Rachel reached the crib. When she looked down apprehensively at the tiny form, a knot gripped her throat, and then a terrified scream escaped her lips. . . .

Standing against the frozen trunk of an enormous pine, David wished he were with Berenson in the renovated courtyard behind the office, sweating in the scorching sun of a broiling August afternoon. It didn't even have to be August, David thought; in El Paso now the temperature must be, as Griggs had said, around seventy or eighty, even in November. Yes, that was where he wished he were now, in back of the Berenson office, sweat pouring down his back, tinkering with the units he and Berenson had designed together and had been working on for months. And he could see Berenson eventually looking up at the sun, saying, "Jesus Christ, it's hot; I can't wait to get up to the mountains—did you know it's snowing up in Ruidoso, for Chrissakes, I can't wait, why don't you and the wife come on up with us this weekend?" And then David imagined himself looking Nick right in the face, saying, "Gee, Nick, that's a great offer, we sure appreciate it and all, but the truth of the matter is *I hate the goddamn snow and I hate your goddamn cabin and I never want to see either one of them again!*"

At least, that was the way he'd *feel* the next time Berenson brought up the subject.

The next time . . . but could there be a next time? . . .

He pushed himself away from the trunk and forced his feet onward. Up ahead the trees were thick, the brush dense. He wasn't sure how high he'd climbed until he cut through the pines and he came to a clearing, where he saw below him another thick cluster of pines and an acute descent over the edge of the hill he was on.

He started down.

His frozen feet refused to bend, they just covered ground like stiff poles, as if he were traveling with crutches, so it was inevitable that he'd have trouble making the descent, and he did; his body lurched forward and he tried to compensate by throwing his weight back, but it was too late, he stumbled forward, fell against a scraggly white bush, crushing it beneath him as he dropped onto the icy ground. Pulling himself up, he believed for the first time that he really couldn't make it any farther. There was just no way. He knew he'd traveled far enough around the mountain, that he'd probably made it to the side facing the Perry cabin; but he didn't know how high up he was, the trees blocked the view, and for all he knew the cabin might be half a mile farther down, and he couldn't make that, just couldn't.

He slumped against the tree, let himself slide down, and sat there, the snow falling heavily around him. What would happen to him if he just stayed right there? How long would it be before he actually froze to death? He seemed to remember hearing somewhere that the advice to keep moving in cold weather was a fallacy because moving used up all the strength a person needed to stay warm, and the perspiration formed by running about only compounded the problem because the sweat froze and defeated the protection of your clothing. David thought of this because he would like more than anything now to believe it, to use it as rationalization for staying right where he was. But he remembered Kate.

Shoving his hands deep into his pockets, he wondered if any extremity had already frozen. He clenched his hands, tried to get them warm, they had remained outside his pockets too long. Then he took them out when he was sure they hadn't frozen and that they could move, and cupped them over his ears, left them there awhile. There was nothing he could do about his feet. He doubted they had succumbed to frostbite yet. What worried him more was his lungs. He'd been breathing heavily, and his chest burned; all he needed now was to start coughing up blood.

The thought of blood brought him staggering to his feet, and he started down the mountainside again. It wasn't long, however, before the exhaustion became too much and he was ready to collapse against the trunk of another tree—and he was about to do just that when he began blinking very quickly and anxiously because up ahead through a group of closely spaced pines he thought he saw something, and he wasn't entirely certain at first, but after straining a little while longer he had no doubt at all.

There was a body lying in the snow. . . .

Lying on the sawdust floor, clad only in her gown, her torso propped up with her right arm, Kate backed farther into the corner until there was nowhere to go: her back touched a small box that lay in the corner.

Michael Perry stood before her, still clutching the arrow in his hand. He set the arrow on the ground next to him and slowly he began removing the white thermal coat. He tossed it on the sawdust beside him, then unbuttoned the red-and-navy Pendleton, took it off, and dropped it on top of the coat.

Kate's stomach tightened. "Please . . ."

But Michael continued, pulling the blue turtleneck shirt over his head, dropping it to the ground. Beneath the shirt he wore a layer of thermal underwear. Then he loosened the belt on the beige woolen trousers and slipped them down over the lower half of the underwear. When he had discarded them he began removing the underwear.

"No-o-o . . ." Kate said, a sickening feeling spreading rapidly throughout her body.

But Michael continued, until the thermal underwear lay piled in a heap with the rest of his clothes. He was naked except for a pair of white shorts. Then his thumbs gripped the ribbed top of the shorts and pulled them down until finally he stood before her, completely naked.

"Now Kate," he said, coming nearer, "Rachel's gown."

Kate said nothing. Did nothing. She thought she might begin vomiting.

"The gown, Kate."

She didn't move.

He picked up the arrow and gripped it near the fletching, pointing it at her.

"You're about to make me angry, Kate. I can't get angry, I told you that."

Her back dug into the corner of the box.

"Kate? . . . The gown . . ."

"Please, won't you let me go, just let me see about my baby—"

"I don't want to hear another word about that baby."

"O-okay, all right, but please let me go, I just want to go back—"

"The gown, Kate."

"David will be here soon—"

"I don't think so."

"What? What do you mean? Where is he? What have you done?"

"He's fine, Kate, maybe a little cold out there looking for Mr. Griggs, but I'm sure he's fine—you see, I don't want you to think I did anything to David or to your baby. You don't think that, do you?"

"I don't know—"

"I didn't do anything, Kate."

"All right, but then why isn't he here?"

"It's just taking longer than he expected. But time is passing and we're wasting it. The gown, Kate."

"No. . . ." She backed farther against the box, heard the cardboard crushing in.

He was right above her now, his legs spread over her ankles. He bent down, bringing the tip of the arrow up under her chin. Kate didn't dare move, but her eyes flashed down to her chest as he took the gleaming tip and used it to spread apart the edges of the gown around her neck, pulling apart the buttons. "You do it, Kate. You undo the rest."

". . . please, no . . ."

He raised the point to her breastbone, pressed. "Look, Kate."

She lowered her eyes and watched as the razor-sharp point pressed deeper into her white skin until a hairlike streak of blood appeared. Kate caught her breath; she wanted to cry. ". . . oh . . . please . . ."

"Your skin is beautiful, Kate. I don't want to scar it. Not yet . . ."

". . . God . . . in . . . heaven . . ."

"The gown, Kate."

Terrified, she brought up her hand, undid the first button that he hadn't ripped apart.

"Much better, Kate. I knew you'd help. This is going to be gentle, because you're gentle."

Tears spilled down over her cheeks.

Her hand stopped.

The razor-point pressed again.

She undid the second button.

Straddling her legs, he bent his knees, lowered himself upon her.

Rachel stood before the crib, unable to move for a second, so horrified was she at the sight before her.

Brian's flannel pajamas had been ripped apart in the middle, exposing his soft, tender chest. A patchwork of tiny, hairlike cuts, about three inches in length, had been etched across his chest, barely breaking the surface of the skin and leaving an almost imperceptible trickle of blood.

A paralysis consumed Rachel as she stared, sickened at the lines—the calculating and methodical crisscrosses in a frightening mirror pattern.

"Oh . . . Jesus . . ." She could barely hear her words above the agonizing cries of a baby unaware of the violation that had been taken against him—aware only that somewhere there was an overwhelming pain. . . .

Rachel began retching uncontrollably, and she was afraid she would vomit.

He can't take this away from her, he just can't—why, he's no better than Amos Perry himself, he just can't—

Frantically, she reached for the remaining blanket and began pressing it over the tender skin, blotting up the blood, the muscles in her throat constricting, suffocating her as she began to comprehend what he had done, what he was capable of doing—

—oh, sweet Jesus, he's gone too far—

And then hatred—self-destructive hatred—engulfed her, as she realized that she could no longer say to herself *something should be done*, the way she had all these years, but *something must be done*, and so as she continued frantically pressing the blanket into the tender skin, she could think of only one thing, and that was Amos Perry's old shotgun hanging on the wall in the den, below an antlered head. . . .

"I'm getting angry, Kate."

". . . I . . . don't . . . care. . . ."

"You *will* care. You don't know what happens when I get angry. I already told you what happened to one girl." He pulled away her arms, tore open the front of the gown.

"No-o," she cried.

"Just a little way to go now, Kate."

He started for the buttons, yanking savagely at the splitting flannel.

Kate raised her hands, began striking outward. "No. . . ."

"God*damn* you!" He slapped her hard across the face and she collapsed onto the edge of the box, screaming hysterically. "I told you not to do this, I told you not to make me mad, *goddamn you, Kate!*"

He continued tearing at the gown until it ripped open. Then he inched back on his knees, grabbed her ankles, and pulled her away from the corner, until she lay flat on the sawdust. He stuck the razor-tip under her chin. "It doesn't take much pressure until this will rip a hole in your throat. You don't want that, I don't think you want me to do that."

She knew she shouldn't, but she couldn't at that moment stop herself—she reached and grabbed at the shaft of the arrow and began yanking it away, knowing that any moment he might puncture her throat, but also knowing she had to do something because she figured he was going to kill her anyway, and she screamed, *"You're crazy!"*

Then he jerked back the hand holding the arrow, jerked it away from her feeble grip; he drew back his other hand and swung the fist into her jaw. The impact sent her flying back, her jaw throbbing from the shock and pain. "Why do you make me angry, if I'm crazy, why do you dare to make me lose my temper, *why*!"

His naked body shook violently.

Kate tried to get up, but his thighs pressed against her hips, locking her down painfully in his vise.

"Lie still!" he shouted, hatred in his voice, and Kate wondered what was wrong with her, why didn't she do as he ordered, because her life was at stake?—but she couldn't, she brought her arms up and again struck at him, but he fended off the blows and began beating her across the face repeatedly, his fists pounding, crunching into her cheeks, her jaw, until she felt the wetness of blood trickling from her nose over her lips and she could taste the liquid, could feel the swelling under her eyes, yet all she could see was his hands striking forward, closing in again and again, and then he brought himself down upon her, tearing away what remained of the gown, forcing her legs apart, pressing himself over every inch of her body, and she felt her face burning and heard her own cries and screams, and still she raised her arms in defense, tried to push him off, but his weight was overpowering, he was on her, and she then felt all strength and determination forsake her; she thought all she could do now was give herself up to him, so her body went limp, all resistance gone; but then she felt her head being raised, she was looking into his eyes, and he was suddenly cursing her because of his own impotence, screaming at her and again striking her swollen face, his rage building and building, and she knew he would eventually beat her until she was dead—

—and he might have done so if suddenly he hadn't stopped—something diverted his attention and the blows ceased, his head turned and he looked out through the bars to the door, and now he was off her, standing up, reaching for the bow propped against the cell door, placing the arrow on the string, drawing back—

"Goddamn you!"

It was David's voice.

Kate saw him rushing into the shed, heading for the cell.

"David!" Kate's scream reverberated through the tiny shed.

But Michael was already aiming, had already released, and Kate saw the arrow disappear and then saw David ducking, falling backward against the stack of firewood, the arrow barely missing him, and she screamed, pulled herself to her feet, tried to run past Michael, out the door to David, but Michael spun around just as he was loading a second arrow and struck out at her with his arm, the blow knocking the wind away as it made contact with the middle of her neck, and she fell back—but also rebounded, determined to get out of there, so she threw all her weight against the naked figure struggling with the bow, knocking him aside, her bare feet kicking over sawdust until she reached her husband, who was up now, rushing toward the cell and to the waiting arrow—

"You goddamned sonofabitch," David screamed, "you goddamned sonofabitch!—"

—and just as he was about to lunge into the naked figure a voice from behind screamed, "*Stop!*"

Rachel Perry stood in the front doorway, a shotgun in her hands, raising it, pointing it at David and saying, "Move aside, goddamnit, *move aside now*!"—and David stepped back just as Rachel aimed the barrel at Michael, who had dropped the bow now and was gasping in disbelief at what he saw before him.

"Goddamn you," Rachel cried. "You're no better than he was, and to think that all these years I went along—goddamn you, you're no better—don't you understand—it's all she has, *you can't take that away*—"

"What happened?" Kate screamed. "My baby! . . ." She cried uncontrollably, stepping forward, choking between her sobs. "Oh, God . . . my baby . . . what's happened—"

And then she stopped. She found herself the object of Rachel's beseeching stare. Their eyes locked for just an instant. Rachel's luminous gray ovals, only a second ago filled with raging hate, flickered briefly, knowingly, in the dim light of the overhead bulb, silently answering Kate's question. In the fleeting second their eyes were locked on each other, Kate detected a subtle look in Rachel's face: a look that seemed to bring the two women together in a union of mutual mercy and understanding. And on Rachel's face, an expression of sorrow and pity, mixed with compassion and envy . . .

But then the eyes flickered again and Kate once again saw the consuming hatred fill Rachel's face. "Get out," she said. "Go on!—"

—Then Rachel turned to Michael. "Goddamn you, you're no better than your father, you can't take that away—and you never will, *because I stopped him and I'll stop you!*"—

—and then she aimed the gun at what looked like

Michael's abdomen, then brought it lower . . . lower . . . and Kate couldn't believe her ears when Michael dropped the bow and held his hands up high, lurching forward, screaming, "No . . . no . . . *Mother, no!*—"

—and then the room exploded, the blast deafening, and that was when Kate turned away and grabbed David.

"Get out of here!" Rachel cried again. *"Get out of here now, this is over!"* Kate saw her point the barrel toward the back of the shed, and then she turned, saw that Michael had been thrown by the blast far to the back of the cell but was now stumbling forward, clutching himself, blood everywhere—but before he got through the door, Rachel turned to David again and shouted, "Goddamnit, go *on*, get out now!" and then she aimed the barrel at the small box in the corner, the box Kate had lain against, and that was when David gripped Kate's arm tightly and pulled her with him as they fled from the tiny room out into the freezing cold.

They had just made it to the cabin when the shed really did explode, ripping apart with a noise that rocked the ground—the pine walls splintering apart, debris flying into the lightening winter sky, and Kate screamed, collapsed against David, his arms encircling her as she started sliding down to her knees, beginning to weep for what would be infinity, weeping not for Rachel, or for the woman's son, but for the eternal penance of the mother who had sacrificed her own son so that another might survive. . . .

EPILOGUE

August 1979

THE HEAT from the sun made a rippling mirage of water across the :sphalt in the distance as the car covered the miles down the endless highway.

David glanced at his watch. They would reach Phoenix soon, where they would fill up with gas before going on to San Bernardino, another seven-hour stretch. They planned to stay in San Bernardino a day before continuing on to San Jose.

Kate rested her head lazily against the window, eyes closed, but not sleeping. Between them, Brian sat in his car seat, tugging curiously on a string of large plastic blocks, smiling with satisfaction each time he managed to pull one of them off and toss it to the floor, or onto the seat next to him.

David looked at Kate. "Asleep?"

Kate opened her eyes, smiled wryly. "I'm trying." She looked at Brian, shook her head in mock disgust, and leaned down to collect the fallen plastic block. She held up one end of the string Brian was clutching and carefully threaded the block onto it, and as she did so, Brian squealed with delight at the prospect of pulling it off again and tossing it to the floor.

"Give up," David said cheerfully. "He's never going to get tired."

Kate smiled again. "Tell me something I don't know."

She was silent for a while, her large brown eyes watching him, her mouth turned up in a satisfied smile, and then the smile faded and she said nervously, "Do you think you'll like it? California, I mean?"

David thought a moment, then shrugged. "I don't know."

He had given up his job at Berenson Engineering a month ago for an offer he could not turn down: Chief Engineer of West SolarCon laboratories in San Jose. It was an opportunity he had dreamed of, but that he had never thought would present itself; and he had left his former job with Nick Berenson's personal blessing.

"You'll like it," Kate said, as if to reassure him. Because she wanted to make the move. Wanted it desperately.

David smiled. "I think so," he said, and watched as Brian threw the plastic block onto Kate's lap.

Fifteen minutes later they arrived in Phoenix, where David pulled into a filling station that was attached to a combination gift shop and café. He asked the attendant to fill up the car with gas, and then he told Kate, "Be right back."

He got out and walked over to the gift shop, went in, and bought a copy of the *Arizona Republic*. He took the paper back to the car—a 1978 cream-colored Chevelle station wagon. It could never replace the old Malibu, not in a million years; and when, eventually, David had taken a truck up to haul the wrecked automobile back to town to sell it for scrap, he had almost wept.

He got into the car and began flipping through the pages.

"Anything?" Kate said.

"Don't know yet."

They had both heard the news on the radio an hour ago, and now David wanted to read about it. In December, he had read in the El Paso paper that Senator Richard Melchor had suffered a stroke—succumbing, most people thought at the time, to the shock over his daughter's death. He had been partially paralyzed ever since.

"Here it is," David said. He read the article slowly.

"Does it say anything else?"

David put down the paper, shook his head. "Just that it was due to complications from the stroke he had last year; it was simply a matter of time. He died in his sleep."

As David looked at Kate, he saw her eyes beginning to glisten, and for a moment he thought she would cry. But then she blinked a couple of times, turned to Brian, and began toying with the string in his hand. She smoothed back a strand of the child's light brown hair and stroked his chin. Below the red jump suit that Brian was wearing, the scars were healing; and now, after nine months, all that was left was a series of barely detectable intersecting white lines. David looked at Kate. Her face had picked up its color, and her eyes glowed with a vibrancy he was not used to seeing. On her, the scars were not visible.

The attendant came over and David handed him the money. When the attendant had left, David said perfunctorily, "Ready?"

At that, Kate leaned down, placed a kiss on Brian's head. "Yes," she said with an air of certainty. "We're ready."

David pulled out of the station. Brian said something completely indecipherable and threw another plastic block onto Kate's lap. "Oh!" she said, pretending to be upset. Brian was delighted. She picked up the block, threaded it back onto the string, then rested her head once again gently on the window of the car, eyes closed, but not sleeping.

David glanced at his watch. They had a long way to go.

Also in Hamlyn Paperbacks

James Patterson

THE JERICHO COMMANDMENT

A ghastly secret born in the Nazi extermination camps now rises again to corrupt the living. And the innocent as well as the guilty are sucked into its horrendous vortex.

– A mysterious terror group so hungry for vengeance that justice is distorted into madness.

– An 80-year-old millionairess whose defection from 'the Cause' provokes a series of murders that panic America.

– Successful young doctor, David Strauss, driven by the massacre of his family into desperately following the 35-year-old trail of phantom Nazis.

– Beautiful Alix Rothschild, survivor of Dachau, now America's leading fashion model yet somehow part of the deadly scheme.

– The FBI gradually hunting down the killers and discovering a plot more horrible than even they could have fantasized . . .

With an ultimatum delivered at the 1980 Olympic Games in Moscow this heritage of malignant passions is finally brought to a gruelling climax.

'The Jericho Commandment is a stick-to-your-chair thriller that will give a large body of readers galloping nightmares' – Thomas N. Scortia, author of *The Glass Inferno*

UK £1.00 0 600 35273 0

FICTION

HISTORICAL ROMANCE/ROMANCE/SAGA

☐ Flowers of Fire	Stephanie Blake	£1.00
☐ So Wicked My Desire	Stephanie Blake	£1.50
☐ Morgana	Marie Buchanan	£1.35
☐ The Enchanted Land	Jude Deveraux	£1.50
☐ Mystic Rose	Patricia Gallagher	£1.25
☐ Alinor	Roberta Gellis	£1.20
☐ Gilliane	Roberta Gellis	£1.00
☐ Joanna	Roberta Gellis	£1.25
☐ Roselynde	Roberta Gellis	£1.20
☐ Love's Scarlet Banner	Fiona Harrowe	£1.00
☐ Lily of the Sun	Sandra Heath	95p
☐ Daneclere	Pamela Hill	£1.25
☐ Strangers' Forest	Pamela Hill	£1.00
☐ Royal Mistress	Patricia Campbell Horton	£1.50
☐ The Tall One	Barbara Jefferis	£1.00
☐ Captive Bride	Johanna Lindsey	£1.00
☐ The Flight of the Dove	Catherine MacArthur	95p
☐ The Far Side of Destiny	Dore Mullen	£1.50
☐ The Southern Moon	Jane Parkhurst	£1.25
☐ Summerblood	Anne Rudeen	£1.25
☐ The Year Growing Ancient	Irene Hunter Steiner	£1.10

HORROR/OCCULT/NASTY

☐ The Howling	Gary Brandner	85p
☐ Return of the Howling	Gary Brandner	95p
☐ Dying Light	Evan Chandler	85p
☐ Curse	Daniel Farson	95p
☐ Trance	Joy Fielding	90p
☐ The Janissary	Alan Lloyd Gelb	95p
☐ Rattlers	Joseph L. Gilmore	85p
☐ Slither	John Halkin	95p
☐ Devil's Coach-Horse	Richard Lewis	85p
☐ Spiders	Richard Lewis	80p
☐ Poe Must Die	Marc Olden	£1.00
☐ The Spirit	Thomas Page	£1.00
☐ The Force	Alan Radnor	90p
☐ Bloodthirst	Mark Ronson	90p
☐ Ghoul	Mark Ronson	95p
☐ Ogre	Mark Ronson	95p
☐ Return of the Living Dead	John Russo	80p
☐ The Scourge	Nick Sharman	£1.00
☐ Deathbell	Guy N. Smith	95p
☐ The Specialist	Jasper Smith	85p

WESTERN BLADE SERIES

☐ No. 1 The Indian Incident	Matt Chisholm	75p
☐ No. 2 The Tucson Conspiracy	Matt Chisholm	75p
☐ No. 3 The Laredo Assignment	Matt Chisholm	75p
☐ No. 4 The Pecos Manhunt	Matt Chisholm	75p
☐ No. 5 The Colorado Virgins	Matt Chisholm	85p
☐ No. 6 The Mexican Proposition	Matt Chisholm	75p
☐ No. 7 The Arizona Climax	Matt Chisholm	85p
☐ No. 8 The Nevada Mustang	Matt Chisholm	85p

WAR

☐ Jenny's War	Jack Stoneley	£1.25
☐ The Killing-Ground	Elleston Trevor	£1.10

FILM/TV TIE-IN

☐ American Gigolo	Timothy Harris	95p
☐ Meteor	E. H. North and F. Coen	95p
☐ Driver	Clyde B. Phillips	80p

FICTION

GENERAL

☐ Stand on It	Stroker Ace	95p
☐ Chains	Justin Adams	£1.25
☐ The Master Mechanic	I. G. Broat	£1.50
☐ Wyndward Passion	Norman Daniels	£1.35
☐ Abingdon's	Michael French	£1.25
☐ The Moviola Man	Bill and Colleen Mahan	£1.25
☐ Running Scared	Gregory Mcdonald	85p
☐ Gossip	Marc Olden	£1.25
☐ The Sounds of Silence	Judith Richards	£1.00
☐ Summer Lightning	Judith Richards	£1.00
☐ The Hamptons	Charles Rigdon	£1.35
☐ The Affair of Nina B.	Simmel	95p
☐ The Berlin Connection	Simmel	£1.50
☐ The Cain Conspiracy	Simmel	£1.20
☐ Double Agent—Triple Cross	Simmel	£1.35
☐ Celestial Navigation	Anne Tyler	£1.00
☐ Earthly Possessions	Anne Tyler	95p
☐ Searching for Caleb	Anne Tyler	£1.00

WESTERN BLADE SERIES

☐ No. 1 The Indian Incident	Matt Chisholm	75p
☐ No. 2 The Tucson Conspiracy	Matt Chisholm	75p
☐ No. 3 The Laredo Assignment	Matt Chisholm	75p
☐ No. 4 The Pecos Manhunt	Matt Chisholm	75p
☐ No. 5 The Colorado Virgins	Matt Chisholm	85p
☐ No. 6 The Mexican Proposition	Matt Chisholm	75p
☐ No. 7 The Arizona Climax	Matt Chisholm	85p
☐ No. 8 The Nevada Mustang	Matt Chisholm	85p

WAR

☐ Jenny's War	Jack Stoneley	£1.25
☐ The Killing-Ground	Elleston Trevor	£1.10

NAVAL HISTORICAL

☐ The Sea of the Dragon	R. T. Aundrews	95p
☐ Ty-Shan Bay	R. T. Aundrews	95p
☐ HMS Bounty	John Maxwell	£1.00
☐ The Baltic Convoy	Showell Styles	95p
☐ Mr. Fitton's Commission	Showell Styles	85p

FILM/TV TIE-IN

☐ American Gigolo	Timothy Harris	95p
☐ Meteor	E. H. North and F. Coen	95p
☐ Driver	Clyde B. Phillips	80p

SCIENCE FICTION

☐ The Mind Thing	Fredric Brown	90p
☐ Strangers	Gardner Dozois	95p
☐ Project Barrier	Daniel F. Galouye	80p
☐ Beyond the Barrier	Damon Knight	80p
☐ Clash by Night	Henry Kuttner	95p
☐ Fury	Henry Kuttner	80p
☐ Mutant	Henry Kuttner	90p
☐ Drinking Sapphire Wine	Tanith Lee	£1.25
☐ Journey	Marta Randall	£1.00
☐ The Lion Game	James H. Schmitz	70p
☐ The Seed of Earth	Robert Silverberg	80p
☐ The Silent Invaders	Robert Silverberg	80p
☐ City of the Sun	Brian M. Stableford	85p
☐ Critical Threshold	Brian M. Stableford	75p
☐ The Florians	Brian M. Stableford	80p
☐ Wildeblood's Empire	Brian M. Stableford	80p
☐ A Touch of Strange	Theodore Sturgeon	85p

FICTION

CRIME/ADVENTURE/SUSPENSE

☐	**The Organization**	David Anthony	90p
☐	**Stud Game**	David Anthony	95p
☐	**Five Pieces of Jade**	John Ball	85p
☐	**Siege**	Peter Cave	£1.15
☐	**The Execution**	Oliver Crawford	90p
☐	**The Ransom Commando**	James Grant	95p
☐	**The Rose Medallion**	James Grant	90p
☐	**Barracuda**	Irving A. Greenfield	95p
☐	**The Halo Jump**	Alistair Hamilton	£1.00
☐	**The Desperate Hours**	Joseph Hayes	95p
☐	**A Game for the Living**	Patricia Highsmith	95p
☐	**The Blunderer**	Patricia Highsmith	95p
☐	**Those Who Walk Away**	Patricia Highsmith	95p
☐	**The Tremor of Forgery**	Patricia Highsmith	80p
☐	**The Two Faces of January**	Patricia Highsmith	95p
☐	**The Heir**	Christopher Keane	£1.00
☐	**Cranmer**	Steve Knickmeyer	90p
☐	**The Golden Grin**	Colin Lewis	£1.00
☐	**Confess, Fletch**	Gregory Mcdonald	90p
☐	**Fletch**	Gregory Mcdonald	90p
☐	**Flynn**	Gregory Mcdonald	95p
☐	**To Kill a Jogger**	Jon Messmann	95p
☐	**Pandora Man**	Kerry Newcomb and Frank Schaefer	£1.25
☐	**Sigmet Active**	Thomas Page	£1.10
☐	**The Jericho Commandment**	James Patterson	£1.00
☐	**Games**	Bill Pronzini	85p
☐	**Crash Landing**	Mark Regan	95p
☐	**The Mole**	Dan Sherman	95p
☐	**Swann**	Dan Sherman	£1.00
☐	**The Peking Pay-Off**	Ian Stewart	90p
☐	**The Seizing of Singapore**	Ian Stewart	£1.00
☐	**Place of the Dawn**	Gordon Taylor	90p
☐	**Judas Cross**	Jeffrey M. Wallmann	90p
☐	**Rough Deal**	Walter Winward	85p
☐	**The Ten-Tola Bars**	Burton Wohl	90p

HISTORICAL ROMANCE/ROMANCE/SAGA

☐	**Flowers of Fire**	Stephanie Blake	£1.00
☐	**So Wicked My Desire**	Stephanie Blake	£1.50
☐	**Morgana**	Marie Buchanan	£1.35
☐	**The Enchanted Land**	Jude Deveraux	£1.50
☐	**Mystic Rose**	Patricia Gallagher	£1.25
☐	**Alinor**	Roberta Gellis	£1.20
☐	**Gilliane**	Roberta Gellis	£1.00
☐	**Joanna**	Roberta Gellis	£1.25
☐	**Roselynde**	Roberta Gellis	£1.20
☐	**Love's Scarlet Banner**	Fiona Harrowe	£1.00
☐	**Lily of the Sun**	Sandra Heath	95p
☐	**Daneclere**	Pamela Hill	£1.25
☐	**Strangers' Forest**	Pamela Hill	£1.00
☐	**Royal Mistress**	Patricia Campbell Horton	£1.50
☐	**The Tall One**	Barbara Jefferis	£1.00

NAME ....

ADDRESS ....

....

Write to Hamlyn Paperbacks Cash Sales, PO Box 11, Falmouth, Cornwall TR10 9EN.

Please indicate order and enclose remittance to the value of the cover price plus:

U.K.: 30p for the first book, 15p for the second book and 12p for each additional book ordered to a maximum charge of £1.29.

B.F.P.O. & EIRE: 30p for the first book, 15p for the second book plus 12p per copy for the next 7 books, thereafter 6p per book.

OVERSEAS: 50p for the first book plus 15p per copy for each additional book.

Whilst every effort is made to keep prices low it is sometimes necessary to increase cover prices and also postage and packing rates at short notice. Hamlyn Paperbacks reserve the right to show new retail prices on covers which may differ from those previously advertised in the text or elsewhere.